Candace Evans . . . A reigning queen of the fashion industry, she had everything it took to become a success—looks, drive, connections. Her name means high fashion to millions, and millions in profits for her company. But having it all is not enough.

Because nothing she has will last forever.

This is the fashion world as it really is . . .
The scandal, the greed, the glamour.

These are the fashion people as they really are . . .
The schemers, the lovers, the liars.

Threads

High fashion. High stakes.

THREADS

B. A. HIRSCH

DIAMOND BOOKS, NEW YORK

This book is a Diamond original edition,
and has never been previously published.

THREADS

A Diamond Book / published by arrangement with
the author

PRINTING HISTORY
Diamond edition/March 1993

All rights reserved.
Copyright © 1993 by B. A. Hirsch.
This book may not be reproduced in whole or in part,
by mimeograph or any other means, without permission.
For information address: The Berkley Publishing Group,
200 Madison Avenue, New York, NY 10016.

ISBN: 1-55773-868-8

Diamond Books are published by The Berkley Publishing Group,
200 Madison Avenue, New York, NY 10016.
The name "DIAMOND" and its logo
are trademarks belonging to Charter Communications, Inc.

PRINTED IN THE UNITED STATES OF AMERICA

10 9 8 7 6 5 4 3 2 1

To Marc,
whose love, patience and encouragement
made this dream as well as
our others all come true.

—BAH

THREADS

One

WRAPPED IN A man's black wool car coat she had picked up at Andy's Chee-Pees, Liz Browne emerged from the subway entrance onto Seventh Avenue. The wind whipped so hard against her that she had to walk head down. It was a typically miserable March day, but this would be a quick walk to 550 Seventh, a garment center building known only by its address.

She was the last to squeeze into the crowded elevator before the doors closed.

"Ten, please," she said.

She had planned to get to the office before anyone else to arrange all of the clothes for the models' fittings this morning, but last night she had stayed out partying until after 4:00 A.M.

She glanced at her watch and shifted her weight from foot to foot. The elevator man stopped the car at almost every floor—at Bill Blass on two, Ralph Lauren on three—until, finally, Candace Evans on ten.

Liz zoomed through the doors and headed straight for the pattern room. Now she'd have to dash around, grab the samples from the sewers' workbenches, hang them up, and hope everything would be in order. And there was precious little time left before the models would start to arrive.

While Liz searched frantically for the key samples she needed, New York's top runway model was stepping off the elevator. Stephanie, swathed in her black cashmere muffler and oversized gray wool reefer coat, lugged her battered leather duffel bag over her shoulder. The bag contained several pairs of shoes, a makeup kit, and clothing changes.

She started down the long hallway with its recessed

lights and caught her reflection in the floor-to-ceiling mirrors.

Nothing there to make people stop on the street and stare at her—they always did, though, and Stephanie was always surprised. She was really just average-looking. Well, maybe not average, but not far enough above average to explain the stares or her status as a top runway model.

She stopped in front of the reception desk and its striking receptionist.

"Maxie Siegel, please."

"Stephanie, right?"

Stephanie nodded. "Tell her I'm here for my fitting."

Moments later Maxie appeared.

"It's only nine, Maxie," Stephanie said. "Why are you looking so crazy already?"

"Believe me, you don't want to know. Candace is doing her last-minute 'change-the-entire-line' routine. I'm trying to appease her and still get the job done. But this time I really don't think we'll make it. I won't be able to relax until after the show. Till then I'll be a basket case."

Stephanie smiled. She'd lived through line openings with Maxie before.

They made their way through the maze of offices to the pattern and fitting room area—a large, very bright space with windows covering one entire wall. There was the steady hum of industrial sewing machines, the underlying Spanish and Cantonese chatter of the sample hands. The pattern makers, all six of them, were talking Italian in the center of the room. It was like the United Nations.

"Stephanie's here," Maxie said. "Let's get her into her outfits." She looked around for her design assistant and spotted her in the middle of the room with an armful of garments. "Liz . . . where the hell are Stephanie's out-fits and why aren't they pulled so we don't waste her time? You know the damned fitting schedule—why isn't everything organized?"

"I was just pulling them." Liz started toward them, grabbing errant sleeves and pant legs as they slipped through her hands. "They're on the rack over there by the mirrors."

"Oh, yes, I see them now. Sorry—I'm really on edge today. Why the hell Candace called this emergency design meeting is beyond me! I've been here since dawn trying to pull it all together, so please bear with me and—hey, I *am* sorry."

"That's okay, I understand. I wanted to get here early myself to get all this organized but I partied too late last night and then just couldn't get out of bed this morning. So I'm sorry, too."

"Now that we're both sorry, let's get on with this fitting."

"Great. Oh, one thing—Luigi told me the four-button blazer, the new high-waisted pants, and the jersey chemise still haven't come through yet. So we won't be able to fit Stephanie's first three ensembles today, she'll have to come back next week."

"Luigi!" Maxie said. "We're ready for Stephanie's fitting—why isn't everything finished? Surely it doesn't take an entire week for a workroom of ten ladies to sew three lousy things, does it?"

Luigi Ferraro, Candace Evans's head pattern maker since the beginning, was used to Maxie's hysteria as each season's show date drew near.

"Look here, Maxie. You give me ten new sketches just last week. I'm to do them first, you say. So that's what I do."

"Oh, right, I forgot. Okay then, let's get this fitting going with what we do have."

Maxie hurried Liz and Stephanie over to the tiny cubicle they used for a fitting room. "Candace was having her usual second thoughts about the collection, so I promised her I'd add some fashion pieces. You know she always says go commercial, commercial, commercial—till we get near show time, then she panics. She's afraid the press will think she's sold out to the stores and not been innovative enough—Liz, help Stephanie get her clothes off—then we have to stop all sewing midstream so we can add some fun things. What she doesn't realize is that it throws the entire schedule off and then suddenly we're late. Why she won't let me be different to begin with is beyond me!"

Stephanie and Liz exchanged looks. They had heard this speech before.

Just then, Luigi entered. Stephanie—undressed except for her tiny bra and panties—might have been a mannequin for all he cared. As soon as she put on the single-breasted wool gabardine blazer and matching skirt, he started calling out corrections to his assistant while repinning the garment and chalking all over it. To the uneducated eye the outfit was perfect; to Luigi, it still required hours of work. Maxie, silent for once, allowed Luigi full license to do his thing. Everyone in the room knew he was as much a factor in the continuing success of Candace Evans as either Candace or Maxie.

An hour later the fitting was over. Before Stephanie zoomed off to her next fitting, she had Liz sign her invoice: $500 for the hour, half the price she charged for runway work. At this time of year, right before the collections, fittings were nonstop.

Maxie and Liz went back to the design area, a well-lit open space that contrasted with the cubicles that made up the Candace Evans back rooms. Both Candace and Maxie had partitioned offices. The rest of the huge space was taken up by the design bull pen where Liz and the two assistant designers responsible for fabric development and knitwear had their desks. Candace's office, done by Jose Alvarez in the high-tech black, white, and gray that was his signature, was a sharp contrast to Maxie's soft pastels and neutrals. But the striking difference between the two offices wasn't a matter of size or style—it was the prominent display on Candace's clean black lacquered desk of her Coty statuette, the fashion industry's most coveted award.

"Have the other wool gab colors arrived yet?" Maxie asked.

"The gab's in, but we've got a problem," Liz said. "It looks like shit."

"Oh, Christ! Just what we didn't need!"

"Judy's already called Shoji. He's coming over by noon to see what we're talking about. The colors are all much dirtier than we approved, and there's a streakiness in the cloth, too."

"What the hell's with them these days? Everything they ship is a problem. What about the wool and silk houndstooth from Italy?"

"According to Paolo, it's en route. He supposedly has all the shipping information on them, but frankly I don't trust him either. With him it's always on the way, on the way, then somehow we never get it till the last minute. Anyway, that's his story. I've already screamed at him to push, and he says he will, but I just don't know—"

"Okay. Bring me the swatches of the gab so I can see how bad it is so I can decide whether to jump out the window now or wait for the next disaster. The way things are going, that shouldn't take too long."

"I know what you mean. We check and double-check and somehow it still gets messed up. But I don't think it's worth jumping out a window yet. Wait and see what else happens."

"All right. In the meantime, I'll be in my office reworking some sketches. If anything else happens, let me know—but I think we've had enough for one morning, don't you?"

Maxie caught a glance of the brightly polished Coty award as she headed to her office. Here she was, working her ass off, and Candace was getting all the glory. Something was going to have to change, and soon.

Ten floors below, Jason Gold was stepping out of his navy stretch limousine. The chairman of Candace Evans and Candace's husband negotiated his way from the sidewalk to the building, Hermes attache case in hand, sidestepping the wares of the booksellers and jewelry peddlers who lined the block from one end to the other.

On the elevator, Jason thought about the latest counter-offer he had received from the company's third partner, Andrew Lewis. After fifteen years of a pleasant business association, they were all trying to dissolve the partner-ship amicably. Andrew, an accounting genius who had talked the banks into giving them the money to first open the doors of Candace Evans, seemed to be having cold feet about Jason's plans for expanding into other ventures. In a way, Jason couldn't blame him. Andrew's dreams didn't include producing Broadway plays and possibly movies. And Andrew, who was going through his third divorce, needed to be liquidating assets rather than tying them up.

The counteroffer wasn't unreasonable, but Jason just didn't want to deal with it until after the opening of the fall collection. For now, the rest of his life could be put on hold.

Retail sales in general were down, and Candace Evans was feeling the pinch. After all of the mergers and lever-aged buyouts, the major department stores were heavily in debt. They were monitoring their money much more closely, leaving buyers on the line to make sure their merchandise performed to expected growth levels. If not, they were out.

Numbers men—not merchants—now controlled the retail business. The stores had all told Jason that the Candace Evans lines had done poorly for the last year, and if the coming fall line didn't perform on target drastic action would have to be taken. That might mean dropping the line altogether, or, at the very least, cutting back on the number of stores in which the line would be sold.

Either alternative was unacceptable to Jason. His over-head had grown by leaps and bounds over the past few years, his personal expenses even faster. The Fifth Avenue apartment, the houses in the Hamptons and Vail, the suite at the Mayfair Regent for secret trysts—none of them were things he wanted to give up. He had discussed the situation with Candace, who knew she had to get things back on track.

He emerged from the elevator, caught a glimpse of himself in the mirrors, and sucked in his stomach. The weight he lost on these crash diets kept creeping back, marring the stylish silhouette tailored into his $2500 Bijan suits.

When he was nervous, he ate—and Christ, he had a lot on his mind right now. How the hell could he be expected to diet? Candace's nagging only made it worse. His diet, too, would have to wait until after the line opened.

He had just returned from a long weekend of skiing in Vail. Overall his appearance—with the tan and the full head of wavy black hair, graying at the temples only— was still impressive enough to ensure that women were never in short supply. In fact, at the moment, he had almost too many social obligations.

By the time he reached the end of the corridor, he was walking tall. He was used to having the world by the balls—and would do whatever it took to keep it that way.

Eleven o'clock came and went and so did the scheduled design meeting Candace had so urgently ordered. Maxie wondered what unreasonable changes Candace wanted this time—they wouldn't be able to handle many more in time for the show. She had seen the gabardine fabric, and the colors really looked awful. This fabric, the most important in the entire fall line, would never make the desired impact on the runway. How could they get it redone in time for the show?

Candace was delayed. Jason, refusing to wait until she could finally pull herself together that morning, had taken their limo to the office. Now she refused to take a taxi, leaving Sarah, Jason's secretary, to deal once again with the "Candace problem." Sarah reached Charles, their

chauffeur, on the car phone, and told him to head back
uptown to get Candace and bring her to the office.

The car crawled through midtown traffic. Charles,
who had anticipated Candace's wicked mood, figured
he had best pull over and do a couple of quick lines of
white magic. That was the only way he'd be able to deal
with "Miss Candace" today.

He was on Fifth Avenue, nearing the building, when
he spied Candace pacing at the front entrance.

*Just look at her. I can feel those laser-beam eyes from
behind those sunglasses. Yup, this is definitely gonna be
one of those rides. Oh well . . .*

He stopped the car in front of the building and jumped
out.

"Morning, Miss Candace. Ready to go downtown?"

He took her Fendi case and assisted her into the car.
No need to further annoy her by not helping.

Candace settled into her seat, grabbed the phone, and
punched in the office number. After nine rings it was
finally picked up.

"Good morning, Candace Evans."

"Mona, why does it take twenty rings to pick up the
phone? What if I were a buyer? I'd have hung up by
now and bought someone else's line. Put me through to
Jason."

When Sarah answered, Candace told her she would be
there within fifteen minutes. "And Sarah, have everyone
ready—I've got a busy day ahead of me, I don't want to
waste any more time."

Charles eased the car to a stop in front of 550 Seventh
Avenue. He jumped out of the car and ran around to
the curb in time to help Candace, who stalked into the
building and then the elevator.

Upstairs, she worked her way through the showroom,
flashing a warm smile at the few buyers who were
there. When she blew into the design room, everyone
looked busy.

"Hello, everyone," Candace said.

"Hello, Candace." They all responded with that same note of false cheer.

"We're ready for the design meeting as soon as you are," Maxie said from across the room.

"I'll meet you all in the conference room in five minutes. Call Jason for me and tell him, too."

In the conference room designed by Jose Alvarez everyone took his or her usual seat around the black granite table. Although there had never been a formal seating chart, no one ever deviated from these places. Candace was at one end and Jason at the other, with Maxie next to Jason.

This arrangement had been uncomfortable at first. Jason's roving eye had once alighted on Maxie, right in front of Candace—a misdemeanor that ignited a verbal war between them, embarrassing everyone caught in the cross fire. Jason had learned his lesson, but the incident had permanently altered the relationship between Candace and Maxie.

Candace got everyone's attention and began the meeting.

"For the past few seasons I haven't been happy with the direction the line has been going in," she said. "It's entirely too conservative, too safe. I've always been known for giving a humorous twist to tailored clothing that keeps it young, young, young. But for the past few seasons, I've made the mistake of allowing others here to take a more important role in the designing, and it now appears that the customer is rejecting the conservative direction. And so I've decided to take a more active role again in the actual designing of Candace Evans and give my customer the look she wants."

Maxie, along with everybody else in the room, was stunned into silence.

That bitch! She's been involved in and has approved everything! She was the one who pushed for the conservative direction in spite of my best efforts to liven it up. She's the one who's out of touch with her customer, not me.

Jason looked from person to person. "I guess what Candace is trying to say is that the stores are warning us this fall collection had better be right on or Candace Evans will be out of business. I don't intend for that to happen, so I've asked Candace to get more involved."

Maxie was fuming.

This is obviously the result of Candace's pillow talk crap. She probably tells him all night long that she can save the line, that I'm the one who's going in the wrong direction. No wonder Jason's been so cool to me recently—she's been turning him against me.

Maxie didn't say anything. Nor did anyone else.

After a long pause, Jason said, "Well, with that said, let's look at the fall concept boards and anything else you've got ready."

"Sure, Jason." Maxie pulled out her concept boards, color story, fabrics, sketches. Jason reviewed each of them slowly, occasionally asking questions about a particular sketch or fabric.

Finally, he leaned back in his chair, nodding his head. "This all looks fabulous! The colors and fabrics are great, the sketches look new and on target. I'm very pleased. Candace, you've really pulled it together."

"Thanks. I had Maxie add these sketches last week because everything was looking so old. The fabrics, we've worked long and hard on. I'm pleased they came out as well as they did."

Maxie had wanted to do these styles from the beginning, but Candace wouldn't have anything to do with them. Finally, last week she had relented and let Maxie try her ideas. As for the fabrics, Candace had nothing to do with them—Judy had researched every one of them herself.

"Well, not everything is as perfect as we would like," Maxie said. "Both of you should know we have a problem with the gab duplicate yardage. It's arrived and the colors are muddier than we approved. I'm afraid it's not going to show up well on the runway at all. Of course, we can correct it for production, but let's face it—this is our major base fabric. If it's not perfect, we're dead. We're already seeing what they can do to correct it."

Jason slammed his fist on the table. Everyone jumped. "Goddamn it—just what I need! That company is screwing me over."

"Don't worry, Jason," Candace said. "I'll take care of it. Any other problems, Maxie?"

"No, the sweaters and the balance of the fabrics are all en route. I just hope they're all okay, but we won't know that till they show up."

"Okay, Maxie, just keep me informed," Jason said. "Now you have Candace here to help you get it all done." He rose from his chair and moved out the door.

Candace glanced at her solid gold Cartier Panther watch. "Oh, got to run," she said. "Sorry—lunch at the Four Seasons with Bill and Oscar. You take care of that gab problem for me, okay?"

"I already am, Candace. Judy has arranged for Shoji to come in at noon to discuss it. I'll let you know what happens."

"Thanks. See you all later." And she breezed out of the room.

"So much for that," Liz said.

Maxie sighed. "Liz, you know I just love the way Candace is *personally* going to take care of all our problems and do the entire line herself. It's going to be a little tough with all those lunch dates and shopping expeditions getting in the way, don't you think? But what really kills me is that she makes Jason think she's actually doing it."

"I hear you, but you've got to relax, Maxie. There's nothing anybody can do about it."

"I know, but sometimes it really gets to me."

"Let's get a move on. Shoji's due any second. Let's just hope he can replace the gab in time."

Two

JASON, FEELING NEWLY confident because of the progress being made on fall, passed through the showroom on the way back to his office. The sales people were standing around schmoozing.

"Get Taylor into my office right away," he told Sarah.

Five minutes later, the president of Candace Evans walked in. Larry Taylor was a rather soft-looking man with thinning white hair. He had married his secretary several years ago, causing quite a stir in the company. Jason still couldn't believe it. *He* had been seeing her, too, and Larry knew it. Jason thought that made Larry seem weak.

"Larry, do you know what your sales staff is doing right now?"

"Well—"

"Well, nothing, I'll *tell* you. They're hanging around gabbing, not working."

"I don't think so—"

"You don't? I know so. Meanwhile my design team is breaking their asses to turn out a beautiful fall line so we'll still be around this time next year. No wonder we're in trouble. Why aren't they on the phones making appointments for market week or out landing new accounts?"

"They know what they have to do. But I'll check up on them anyway."

"You do that. Because I'm telling you, if they don't shape up they're all outa here. The days of an easy ride at Candace Evans are over. We're trying to survive now. I don't need a bunch of salesmen putting out less than a hundred percent. Do I make myself clear?"

"Totally. Now, do you have a minute to discuss another problem that's just cropped up?"

"Sure, what's one more?"

"We just got the markdown money requests from Saks, Bloomie's, and Macy's. We've got a serious problem there. Last fall was a bomb, what with the short skirt fiasco, and now spring is looking bad too. We're talking major money we'll have to give them just to stay in for next fall."

"What's major?"

"Almost a million all together."

"A million! Are they kidding?"

Larry shook his head. "We'll never get them to agree to much less."

"Well, right now, we have no choice. You buy however much of that business you have to. The new fall collection is looking fantastic and I want us in those stores."

"That's great news. We'll need something terrific to really turn us around."

"This could be it. So you do what you have to, but keep us in. We've really got nothing to lose—we'll either make it or break it with this season. Now go light a fire under some of those sales people you've got out there."

When Larry left, Jason called Andrew to hear about his meeting with the banks. Candace Evans was behind in payments on the ten million dollars in loans. Taking back so much merchandise from the stores last fall had left them with too much inventory, and they had been murdered by the industry "undertakers" who bought overstocked merchandise at cutthroat prices. They hadn't even recovered their costs, let alone made a profit.

Andrew said he had held them off yet again, but only for one more month. "After that, they'll want a revised business plan, and if that isn't satisfactory they're likely to pull the plug."

"I'm not worried," Jason said. "The fall line will open by then, and the reactions will be in."

What *did* worry Jason was what he would do when Andrew left. Andrew was the one with the banking relationships, not Jason. All he'd have left would be Maurice, Candace's brother. Maurice could crunch numbers, but that was it. He didn't know the bankers, didn't have the finesse to play them. Jason couldn't afford to let Andrew leave until he had everything under control.

Sarah buzzed. "Pamela would like to know if you have a few moments to see her."

Pamela St. Clair, director of public relations, provided the pure blonde WASPishness that was everything Jason was not. She closed the door behind her.

"Oh good, Pamela. I was just going to have Sarah get you. Sit down and tell me how arrangements are going for the show."

"All the press has RSVP'd—looks like we'll be getting great coverage."

"Good, good. What else?"

"Larry says the buyer response is on target as well, so I expect about three hundred in the audience. The Plaza is being terrific. Even Ivana is helping with the arrangements."

"I thought she would—she and Candace are old friends."

"Well, I just wish I was getting as much cooperation from Candace. I haven't met with her on anything. We still have to go over shoes, makeup, accessories."

"Why haven't you set up an appointment?"

"I've been trying to for days. Now we're supposed to do it tomorrow—if she doesn't cancel on me again. All eighteen models are booked and confirmed—at least for now—and I understand fittings have already started. Luigi knows the schedule. I'll give him a list of how many of each outfit is needed after my meeting with Candace and Maxie tomorrow. I just hope it all gets done—we have only ten days."

"Sounds like you've got everything pretty much under control, as usual."

"It's always crazy right up to the end. But somehow I'll pull it off and make it look easy for Candace."

"Last time I checked, that's what you're paid to do."

"I know that, Jason. And I love it. But a little praise from you every now and then would go a long way. I need you to be proud of me."

"Okay, okay, I'm proud of you. Is that it?"

"Don't brush me off, Jason—"

"Look, I have a business to run here. Entertaining Pamela St. Clair just isn't my only priority at this moment—I'm sure you can understand that."

"I can remember when entertaining me *was* your only priority. And you seemed to love it." Pamela got up from her chair and leaned over Jason's desk. "I can make you feel that way again. Please, Jason, it's been too long. I want to see you again. I need to see you again."

"Not now, Pamela. I thought I'd made myself clear to you—you can continue working here because you do a terrific job, but that's it. We're finished. Over. Finito."

Pamela stalked out, slamming the door behind her.

Jason stared at the closed door for several moments. He had to keep Pamela calm until the show—then he'd get rid of her. She was coming unglued, and he didn't need that kind of trouble. And besides, she was starting to look like shit.

Judy, Candace Evans's fabric designer, ushered Shoji into Maxie's office. He readily agreed that the fabric looked bad and promised he would do whatever was necessary to get the yardage replaced in time. He said he'd call Osaka right away, even though it was long past midnight there, to see what could be done.

Maxie felt hopeful after the meeting with Shoji. She had two more fittings that day, both of which went smoothly. Finally convinced everything would get done in time, she began to relax.

In her good mood, she shared her ideas for the next season, resort, with her other designers. Creativity began to flow from one to the other.

Judy showed some swatches she had recently found. After seeing one of these newer spandex-blended fabrics, Liz sketched an outrageously shaped dress. Maxie laughed at some of their silly suggestions but pulled together a very exciting story.

And then Candace returned from lunch. It had been three hours since she had left.

"Well, Maxie, what's going on here?"

"We met with Shoji—"

"Who?"

"Shoji, the gab salesman. Remember?"

"Of course I remember. Well, what happened?"

"He seems to feel he can get the mill to replace the goods by the end of the week. With any kind of luck, we'll have yardage by Monday or Tuesday."

"Good."

"We also had some fittings. Are you planning to go to any or do you just want Luigi and me to handle it?"

"Why don't you handle it. I'll do any corrections I find necessary in the production fittings. Anything else?"

"No, that's all for now."

"Good."

Candace glanced down at the concept board the designers were working on. "I don't like this yellow. And this other color story is too weird for the American market—too European. Pastels with navy would be right for resort." And walked out.

Maxie looked at the other designers, then began removing the color balls from the boards.

"Talk about old colors," Liz said. "Pastel and navy are as old as the hills. I'm so glad she's keeping the line 'young, young, young.'"

"Yeah, that's a joke," Judy said. "Now we're back to the old-lady stuff."

"Look, you guys, Candace is the boss," Maxie said. "So we've got to do what she says. I'm not thrilled about it either, but we don't have a whole lot of choice."

*   *   *

Candace gave Jason an update on the gab situation—taking full credit, of course—then left the office. She had to be home in time for her personal trainer's appointment, then get dressed for a dinner at Le Cirque with Jose and his friend Tony. Jason said he would be working late that evening.

Actually, Jason would be at his suite at the Mayfair Regent with his new girl friend, Tina Carruthers, an assistant editor at *Elle*. Like Pamela, Tina was a statuesque blond WASP, but in her early twenties. Like most fashion editors, she led an exhausting social life. Unfortunately, their salaries kept them in a class apart from the designers and socialites with whom they associated.

Tina and Jason had met at one of those less-than-intimate gatherings. Jason was immediately attracted to Tina's freshness and exuberance, Tina to Jason's apparent wealth and power. They began seeing each other, Tina thoroughly enjoying the attention and the little extras Jason began to supply. The secrecy of their relationship made it even more exhilarating. Their relationship was a casual one—just what Jason was looking for.

Tina wasn't interested in settling down with anyone yet. She had too much to experience first. She learned quickly that Jason wasn't interested in sex, at least not in the usual sense. He liked Tina to be attentive . . . affectionate when they went out in public, and occasionally to fulfill certain sexual needs in private—but never intercourse.

Tonight, during the quick hour they spent together, Tina offered Jason warmth and solace, trying to relax him after his rough day. They took a shower together, giggling like teenagers, then got dressed to go off to their separate evening appointments—Tina to the Oak Bar with her friends, Jason to a meeting with some potential business associates.

As they walked out of the Mayfair Regent lobby, Candace, Jose, and Tony were entering Le Cirque right

next door. Jason and Candace never even noticed each
other.

Maxie grabbed a quick dinner at Bill's—a garment
center hangout—with the other Candace Evans designers, then called the company car service and headed
for home. Home was a 2000-square-foot loft on Duane
Street, in TriBeCa.

The loft was wonderfully light and airy, the few pieces
of furniture done in soft colors just like her office. The
space was large and sparingly but warmly decorated.
Maxie lived there with Buddy, a beagle who had come
with her from Columbus as a puppy and was now very
old. He still greeted Maxie every night with jubilation,
barking and yelping for joy. Tonight was no different.
And Maxie really needed his show of love and affection
after the day she had spent at the office.

In her twenties Maxie had partied long and hard. At
an East Village night spot, she had met Martin Cohen,
an up-and-coming artist who moved in with her almost
immediately and married her two years later.

And then it all seemed to fall apart. Martin wanted to
spend more and more time partying; Maxie, hating the
drugs that increasingly went with the partying, wanted
to spend more time at home. Drugs made Martin increasingly paranoid when high, melancholy whenever he came
down. One night, in a rage, he struck out at Maxie.

That was it. She left the house, spent the evening at
her best friend Susanna's place, and initiated divorce
proceedings the next day.

Now in her mid-thirties, Maxie either went out for
dinner with friends in the garment business or spent a
quiet evening in front of the tube. Weekends she ran
errands and caught up on the personal needs and chores
she had no time for during the week. Summer weekends,
she and three friends rented a house in Bucks County.

Of course, she had dated since Martin, but none of
the men had made a deep impression. Her mother was
always pushing Maxie to meet men who had moved to

New York from her hometown, Columbus. Her latest find was a guy named Steve Levine, a lawyer from Columbus specializing in mergers and acquisitions, now relocated to a big Wall Street law firm. Their mothers, who knew each other, thought it would be perfect if their children got together.

Maxie, tired of her mother's badgering and the state of her social life, decided to give Steve a call to welcome him to New York. Maybe he'd actually be nice.

She gathered her courage and dialed the number her mother had thoughtfully provided. No answer! She hung up quickly when his machine started, then regretted not listening long enough to hear his voice. Oh, well. She'd try him again.

Three

JASON AND CANDACE both returned home about the same time. Their apartment, a spacious prewar classic overlooking Central Park, was anything but cozy. Here, too, Jose Alvarez had left his mark of stark modern coldness on every room. There was no dog or cat to greet them; the foyer was spacious and silent. The apartment had not one but two master bedroom suites, a library/den, a small guest bedroom, a living room, formal dining room, and a large kitchen with separate laundry room and maid's quarters.

One of the best-kept secrets in the garment industry was that Jason and Candace, married for more than twenty-five years, had never made love. During their early years together they had tried every treatment and every therapist available, none of which had enabled Candace to escape the demons she carried with her from Hungary.

It was the autumn of 1956. Stalin had been gone for more than 3 years. A hunger had been set off in Soviet satellite nations—especially Poland and Hungary—for greater intellectual freedom and closer ties with the West. Hungary protested against communist rule and the tides of change swept through the country.

Katrinka Szabo, a fifteen-year-old student in Budapest at the time, became caught up in this wave of desire for freedom, as did thousands of others. On a crisp October afternoon, Katrinka and her schoolmates went to Parliament Square to be a part of the demonstrations.

The night before, her parents had tried to convince her to stay home.

"But, Mama, everyone should go," she said when they objected. "You, too. They need *all* our support. You and Papa are teachers—you should want this even more than I do."

"I do, I do. We all want the Soviet troops to leave our country. And to be able to think and speak freely— I talk of this to my students all the time. But Parliament Square?" She looked over to her husband. "You tell her, Papa."

"Katrinka," he said, "it's going to be a mob there. Already people have been hurt. I don't want you to go."

"But I've already promised Anna and Nadia I'd go with them. I want to help make Hungary all that it should be—free."

Her parents were so exhausted from trying to dissuade her that when her brother, Miklos, said he'd be going as well, they gave their permission.

Now, here she was with her two best friends as well as thousands of others, marching toward the Radio Budapest building to issue their demands to the government.

It was there that the demonstration became violent. The security police—armed with rifles, which they eventually used—turned the peaceful demonstration into a scene of terror.

Katrinka, Nadia, and Anna raced away from the square, holding hands so as not to be separated in the crowd of some two hundred thousand. At this point the Hungarian government called for Soviet reinforcements. Tanks, armored cars, artillery, and a whole division of troops were unleashed on the crowd.

They set up barricades, blocked the bridges and squares. Suddenly the three girls were unable to get home—a terrifying prospect for fifteen-year-olds, even idealistic ones. The city they loved was being shelled, buildings either destroyed or their walls pocked from mortars. Fires broke out everywhere—cars were burning, buses were overturned. Stray bullets came from all directions.

They hid in a doorway on a narrow side street. Katrinka, her face tear- and smoke-stained, was crying. Anna held her in her arms.

"It looks as if every square is being blocked with tanks," Nadia said. "They don't care if you're innocent or not, they're shooting anyone that walks by. So we've got to avoid the squares."

"Then how do we go?" Anna said.

"We can split up, and each one head down a different side street until we get home," Nadia said. "That way, we're less likely to be stopped."

Katrinka wiped her tears with the back of her hand. "I don't think we should split up. Couldn't we just stay right here until it's over?"

"I think we should wait," Anna said.

And they waited. Night finally came. The city was smoldering; still the pitched battles raged on. The girls were cold, tired, and hungry. Eventually they decided they had no choice but to split up and try to get home.

They held each other tight for a long moment, then fanned out in three directions. To the staccato sounds of shellfire, Katrinka took off down the street and headed toward the river. Keeping to the side streets and away from the public squares, she moved on very cautiously until she was almost home.

And then, directly in her path, she saw a group of Soviet soldiers, vodka bottles and rifles in hand.

One of them called out in Russian, "Hey, pretty girl, come here." They swung their rifles around in the air and moved toward Katrinka, who looked behind her. The street was deserted. Katrinka stopped dead in her tracks. Her face turned white with fear and, in spite of the cold, she could feel herself begin to perspire.

In seconds, they were upon her—four of them. They made a circle around her and started nudging her with their guns. She felt herself begin to sway but held herself ramrod straight, not moving an inch.

When she didn't give them the reaction they sought, the nudges became jabs. But the soldiers were young, practically boys—maybe they were as scared as she was.

"Look, I don't mean you any harm," she said. "Please let me pass. My home is nearby and I'm sure my parents are worried to death about me."

One soldier said, "Hey, she says she means us no harm—"

"Good," another said. "Then she'll do what we say."

"What do you mean?" another said.

"I mean, guys, this girl is gorgeous."

One soldier ran his hands through her long hair. Katrinka moved her head from side to side, trying to free it from his grip. He wouldn't let go. Instead, he pulled handfuls of silky auburn hair.

"You're hurting me. Let me go!"

For an answer, he pushed her to the ground. "Come on, guys, help me get her down on the ground so we can have a go at her."

"I don't think we should," the youngest one said. He looked up and down the street.

"Oh, come on."

"Yeah, come over here and help."

"No, no—please, let me go!" Katrinka struggled with all her strength.

"Georgi, get up there and hold her arms down—this is a wild one. I only hope she's as wild inside."

He tore off her coat, then ripped her blouse and skirt down the front. Another one yanked at her wool stockings; and yet another beat her until she stopped struggling.

They entered her brutally, one after the other. Katrinka lost all sense of time, all feeling. The soldiers finished, left her in a heap, then beat a hasty retreat.

Katrinka didn't move for a very long time. She heard unearthly sounds—half sobs, half screams—and looked around to see where they could be coming from. There was no one. *She* was making those sounds. They grew louder and louder with each replay of those moments in her mind.

At last she gathered her torn clothing around her and managed to stand up. She stumbled the few short blocks home, then fell against her front door, still making the sounds. Her parents heard them and opened the door.

"Oh, my God!" her mother said. "Papa, help me—take her to the bedroom."

For a week, Katrinka slipped in and out of delirium, ranting from the depths of her mind about what she had suffered at the hands of the soldiers. Her mother would put washcloths on her forehead, ice water on her body, soothing salves on her wounds. In the rare moments when she actually left Katrinka's side, she made soups and broths.

The neighbors and Katrinka's schoolmates were told of the savage beatings she had received. No one was told about the rapes—that was a secret only her mother knew, and she would not speak of it.

The physical wounds healed within a few weeks.

The Soviets still had a stranglehold around Budapest. Force alone wasn't working, so they started to starve the people into surrendering. Fuel supplies dwindled as winter approached. There was little coal left to heat the homes.

Katrinka's parents urged their children to escape through Austria and Switzerland to France, where they had relatives. Thousands were escaping across the border every week, but Red Army patrols shot at fleeing refugees on the Austrian frontier.

But as unsafe as leaving Hungary might be, the alternative—remaining in this prison—was worse. Katrinka's parents, indoctrinated with the belief in a utopia under communist rule, had seen their ideals shattered. They wanted that utopia for their children and knew that it could be realized only in the West.

And so, late one December night, Katrinka and Miklos bundled up against the cold and kissed their parents goodbye. They made their way to the Danube, avoiding the patrols that roamed the streets, got ferried across, and headed for the Austrian border. They learned to look and listen, always ready to jump for cover at the least unexpected sight or sound. Partisans hid them each night. Finally they reached Austria and freedom. From there, they were sent to the refugee center and, after several more weeks, on to Paris.

They found out through the underground press that their parents had been rounded up with thousands of others and sent east to Russia.

Katrinka had learned a lot about herself in these few brief weeks. She knew she could survive, whatever came her way. She knew also that she would do whatever was necessary to get what she wanted.

In Paris, Katrinka and Miklos were welcomed by their aunt and uncle. Katrinka completed high school and went on to study at the Sorbonne. Her life compartmentalized, the horrible memories shoved to the farthest recesses of her mind, she embraced the lifestyle of the young Parisians—the coffee shops and jazz clubs that were filled to capacity all day and night.

In this open atmosphere in which all classes of society mingled, Katrinka befriended some of the next generation of the European aristocracy. Their easygoing attitude toward life and money was foreign to her, but she quickly adopted it as her own. The easiest place to break into society, she decided, would be a free country where no one had a lengthy family tree and money was what counted—the United States.

When her aunt and uncle received word that her parents had died in Russia, Katrinka decided it was time to make the move. To Miklos she said, "There's nothing to keep us in Paris any longer. You can learn English and finish your accounting studies as easily in the States as here. Mama and Papa wanted us to be free, and in America we would be the most free. We should go in their memory."

"I know what they say about America. But who do we know there? No one."

"We'll have each other, Miklos—always. And that's the most important thing. In America, whatever we want can be ours."

"At least here we have our aunt and uncle."

"We can't stay with them forever. It's time we were on our own—and besides, what kind of future can they offer us here? They're struggling just to make a living. I want more than that, and I just know it will be easier for us in America."

Four

KATRINKA QUIT SCHOOL and started working full-time in a ladies' clothing store to save the money for their passage to America and for living expenses in New York until she got a job there. She wouldn't let Miklos drop out of school to help raise the money—his education was too important for their future.

Within the year they landed in New York. Katrinka was so taken by American life that she took speech lessons to rid herself of her foreign accent.

By now she had become a true beauty, tall and slim with a sense of style that made her a natural for modeling. She took assignments as often as she could to support herself and Miklos while he finished his studies. When the modeling agency suggested that she Americanize her name, she became Candace Evans. Her bookings increased.

Miklos wasn't as anxious as Candace to abandon his Hungarian roots, but she persuaded him to change his name to Maurice. He insisted on keeping their last name, Szabo, and he found them a one-bedroom apartment in the Hungarian section of Manhattan, the east eighties. But as soon as Maurice finished school and had a steady income, Candace found an apartment of her own in the Village.

To save money, Candace sewed all of her own clothes. In Hungary everyone made their clothes, and Candace had always made hers. It was much easier to indulge her flair for style and color with the wide choice of fabrics available in America. People kept complimenting her on her clothes and asking the name of the designer—no one could believe everything was handmade.

While she was modeling, she learned what she could about the garment business from snatches of conversation overheard in the fitting rooms and the showrooms. Perhaps she should try to design clothes for the American woman—being a designer would surely give her the opportunity she needed to move into a more glamorous world.

Her first attempts to find a job in the industry were unsuccessful. Candace, undaunted, kept looking until a small house took her on despite her inexperience and made her an assistant. She worked hard and quickly established herself as an up-and-coming designer.

For the next five or six years, she threw herself into refining her craft and moving ahead. She was expressing herself creatively in a way she had never dreamed possible. People in the business began to notice her, and eventually other manufacturers began to woo her.

One coat and suit house in particular captured her imagination. Actually, it wasn't so much the company as the president. Jason Gold cut a rather dashing figure with his olive skin, thick wavy black hair, and seemingly inexhaustible supply of energy. There was a sexiness about him that attracted as well as frightened Candace.

She had never been romantically involved with anyone. She had plenty of male friends, and that was all they ever were—friends. But Jason, for no reason she understood, was exciting her. And she was scared.

He pursued her relentlessly until finally she agreed to join his firm. They worked closely together—she the designer, he the merchandiser. In a few months they were not only working harmoniously together on the collection but finishing each other's thoughts about the direction of the line.

Candace was even beginning to relax around Jason. She had learned to hide her excitement around him.

Then, late one night, after an exhausting three-hour design meeting, Jason said, "I've been working you much too hard. How about joining me for a quick dinner?"

"Thanks, but you really don't have to. I'm sure you have something else you'd rather be doing."

"I have no other plans—please come."

"All right, then, just give me a few minutes to clean up my desk."

Candace raced back to her office and pushed a few sketches around on her desk, stalling for time. What should she do now? He must know she liked him—he could probably see it in her eyes. But what if he tried to make a move? She didn't think she'd be able to let him, and that could ruin everything. And she did love her job. She'd heard so much about him and his friends and how they ran with all those models and salesgirls. What if he thought she'd be like that, too?

She rummaged through her desk until she found a hand mirror in which she saw the fatigue she always felt after a long day. She checked that her false eyelashes were in place, then refreshed her heavily caked eyeliner, blush, and lipstick. Her hair was au courant, a Sassoon cut, and she knew her legs—her best asset—were shown to maximum advantage in her very mini minidress with its striking paisley pattern. She knew she looked good.

Which might make matters worse.

But Jason didn't make a move. In fact, Candace found herself thoroughly enjoying this warm, charming, comfortable man.

They went to a local garment center restaurant. They were hungry, it was late. Jason steered her toward a corner booth in the rear.

"You don't have to hide yourself way back there," Candace said. "Out near the bar would be fine with me. That way you'll see your friends when they come in."

"I don't want to see my friends. I'm here with you."

By then they had reached the booth, all soft padded black leather and wood. Candace looked up at Jason.

"Don't worry, I'm not going to fire you. I just thought after all the time we've been spending together, we should get to know each other a little better. Slide in."

Candace took one side of the booth, Jason the other. *That* was a relief. Jason signaled for the waitress and they ordered drinks and dinner, since it was so late.

When the drinks arrived, Jason sank back into his corner of the booth and took a long pull on his scotch.

"So tell me about yourself. Even with all the time we spend together, I really know nothing about you."

"I could say the same thing about you, you know."

Jason laughed. "But ever since I suggested dinner, you've been jumpy about something. Are you afraid I have some deep, dark secret? Or maybe you do?"

Candace laughed. "Me? I have nothing to hide. I was just thinking about the reputation you have at the office for being quite the womanizer."

"I do? I have that kind of reputation? How fabulous!"

"What?"

"I mean it's such a joke."

"Why? You're a powerful man in this business, you know a lot of people, and you're wealthy. Naturally girls are all over you."

"But I'm not like that at all. In fact, it's only for the past few years that I've even been on my own."

"What do you mean?"

"Before then, I lived with my mother. I took care of her until she passed away. My dad died years ago, right after I graduated from high school. I had to go out and work to support my mother and younger brother so he could finish school—Dad left us with nothing when he died."

"How awful."

"It was. And without my dad, my mom was at loose ends, never having been on her own. She refused to move from the apartment in the Bronx near Jerome Avenue where we'd grown up. All of her brothers and sisters still lived there. But the neighborhood had changed, and she was afraid to stay by herself—especially since she'd never spent a night alone in her life. So I had to stay there with her. There was nothing else I could do."

"I'm so sorry, Jason. I had no idea."

"I'd even gotten a scholarship to college, which I had to give up. Believe it or not, I was planning to major in theatre."

"Theatre? I can't imagine you as an actor."

"I can't either, anymore. But I still love the theatre and see plays every chance I get, both on and off Broadway." Jason stared into his empty glass. "I guess those dreams are *just* dreams now."

The food arrived. They stopped talking long enough to start eating.

"This is delicious," Candace said. "So how did you get into the garment business of all businesses?"

"My dad had been a cutter all his life, and his old boss got me a job as a production assistant. From there, I just worked hard and started moving up. I really loved the merchandising end of the business more than sales, so I concentrated in that area. And from there . . . it's, as they say, history."

"I never would have suspected you got so far on your own. That's quite a story—it's terrific, Jason."

"But I've been doing all the talking—what about you? It's your turn."

"Oh, there's not much to tell." Candace pushed her food around with her fork. "Let's see, I was born in Hungary—but you already knew that. I escaped to Paris with my brother in '56 and started modeling when I came to this country. I've worked hard to get where I am. And that's really all there is to it."

"No boyfriends? Husbands? Children?"

Candace shook her head.

"I can't believe that. You're too beautiful to be unattached."

"Well, I am. And I think that's about enough on that subject."

They finished their meals in silence. Then Jason said, "I hope I haven't made a total ass of myself. Would you consider seeing me again?"

"I don't know, Jason. It's probably not a good idea for us to mix business and pleasure."

"But we work so well together—that can't be by accident. I think we should understand each other better."

"I think we understand each other just fine now."

"Please think about it. You'll have nothing to worry about with me, really. I respect you too much to push myself on you. Besides, you're the best designer I've got."

"I'm the *only* designer you've got."

"I mean it, Candace. Promise me you'll think about it?"

"All right. I'll think."

The more she thought about it, the more attractive he seemed—and the more dangerous. But Jason was persistent over the next few weeks, and Candace gave in.

They started seeing each other regularly. Candace could tell that Jason was smitten, and she didn't know what to do. More alarming than his feelings were hers—she was crazy about him too, and didn't want to risk losing him.

She was afraid, and she was in love. Their work together had never been more inspired. They introduced coordinated sportswear before anyone else, which changed the entire coat and suit concept for the American woman. The business grew, and along with it their reputations.

Jason told Candace he loved her; she finally admitted—at least to herself—that she loved him, too. She loved his solidity, and that survivor's strength in him. She wanted that, she needed that. Here was a man who could fulfill all her dreams.

But how could she possibly fulfill his? Sooner or later, she would have to tell him her story. It would be risky, but it was a risk she had to take.

One night, she did.

He was the first and the only person with whom she had ever shared the whole horror. Even her mother had been spared any details. Jason was shocked, not so much by her secret but by her success in keeping it hidden. But he loved her deeply, and if anything, her suffering made his love even stronger. She had endured so much and

had never crumbled—she was independent and strong,
everything his mother had never been.

"I want to help you get over your past," he said. "Then
we'll have real happiness, both of us for the first time."

He insisted they marry immediately, convinced that
the security of marriage would help Candace lose her
fear. He was extremely patient and considerate of her,
touching her gently, never once pushing himself on her,
despite his intense desires. Several times he even sensed
her longing but when he attempted to take them to the
final stages of lovemaking, her eyes lit up in hidden
alarm and her body became rigid. Nothing Jason tried
could penetrate that barrier. This disappointed him greatly. They sought psychiatric help, to no avail. But Jason
never gave up hope that one day he would break through
all of Candace's walls and wipe away that primal fear
from her eyes forever.

They finally accepted the fact that Candace could not
even share the same bed with Jason, and that hurt him,
too. They settled into a platonic relationship, but Jason
never gave up the hope that one day their marriage would
be complete.

After several years of continued business success,
Jason met Andrew Lewis and the three of them opened
Candace Evans together. Candace's sense of style, a
good-looking rich husband working at her side, and a
mysterious Eastern European background, all contributed to the image. It was an image that New York
society in general and the fashion world in particular
couldn't seem to get enough of.

And so Candace achieved her dream of acceptance
into New York society. She became one of the best
known and most highly regarded designers in the fashion world, designing striking, well-made clothes for a
confident, classy, well-tailored clientele.

But for Jason, the pleasures of sharing their work
were not enough. Feeling guilty about his mounting
frustration, Candace agreed to an open marriage. After
all, what choice did she have?

But Jason, for all of his running around, never actually made love with any of these women. So thoroughly had Candace invaded his mind that even when he was about to penetrate the body of the first woman he'd ever been with since his marriage to Candace, he only saw Candace's eyes, the look full of fear and agony. He went limp. It could only be with Candace—if that day would ever come.

So the tensions built up, and the fights began. Jason was seeing more women lately and while Candace understood, she couldn't stand to have it flaunted in front of her. From his point of view, Candace's inability even to touch and hold him was making him crazy— particularly now when he was feeling frightened and vulnerable over the business. It wasn't just a matter of sex. He needed support from her and he was getting nothing.

Jason arrived home a bit drunk after his evening out. His business meeting had not gone well.

"You know," he said, "you're what's made us hit rock bottom."

"Me? What have I done?"

"For one thing, you designed a line that doesn't sell. You're so out of touch you don't even know what women want. If you can't please a man—and we know you can't do that—then at least please women."

"How dare you blame me! You were the one who wanted me to slow down. You said, 'Live a little, Candace. You deserve it.' Remember that speech?"

"All I can tell you is you'd better start working on this upcoming line, and it had better sell—or it's all over for us. All your dinners, your vacations, your shopping sprees—*finito!*"

"Don't you dare lay all the pressure on me. You run the company, if you didn't like the lines you could have done something about it. But you didn't. So don't blame me."

Candace stormed off to her room. She slammed the door behind her, threw herself on the bed, and lay there for several minutes.

What she knew—but didn't want to admit—was that she *was* responsible for the previous lines that had bombed. Maybe she really was washed up. That would mean Candace Evans, the designer house, would come tumbling down. And then what would she and Jason have?

Five

IT WAS NOT even eight o'clock in the morning, and already all of the machines in the workroom were running. Spring was in the air, the day was bright and sunny, and the sewers were humming over the drone of the machines. They, at least, seemed to like the clothes coming through. It was always a good sign.

Many of these women had been with Candace Evans for years. They were good judges of when the line was looking good and when it wasn't, and there hadn't been such an upbeat mood in the workroom for several seasons. Quite a few completed garments hung on the racks, which made Maxie feel a little better.

She caught Luigi's attention and motioned him over to the rack of clothes. She thumbed through the samples.

"Nine days left till show time, Luigi. How are we ever going to get everything fitted and sewn in time?"

"Maxie, we go through this every time. I have the ladies come in this Saturday and Sunday, they're going to work late every night. Should be okay. But who knows, right? So no more changes if you want it all done."

"I know, I know. I'm not planning any changes, but I'm meeting with Candace today and God knows what *she'll* want."

"Maxie, I tell you now. If it's major changes like you did to me last week, I'm gonna go right to Jason and say forget the show."

"I hear you, and I'll do my best to hold the changes to a minimum. Keep your fingers crossed." Maxie turned to leave, then said over her shoulder, "I'll be back soon with Laurie for her fitting. She's coming in early today so we could squeeze everyone in."

"We'll be ready."

Maxie returned a few minutes later, Laurie and Liz in tow. Laurie undressed and put on the first suit.

"How this jacket feel?" Luigi said.

Laurie moved around in the clothes for a moment. "It's tight across the armhole, and I'm having trouble buttoning it through the hip."

"I see, I see. Turn left to me a bit. That's right . . . Good, good."

Laurie stood perfectly still while Luigi chalked and ripped seams.

"So Laurie, what's been going on with you?" Maxie said.

"The usual hysteria that happens every year at this time. I've been running around to fittings like crazy. All these shows, you know."

"Believe me, I know. We had trouble with your booker finding any free time for you at all."

"Maxie, you know whenever that happens, just call me and I'll squeeze you in."

"Thanks."

Luigi finished with the suit and Liz handed Laurie her next one.

She slipped it on. "Oh, this skirt is fabulous! I love the lines."

Maxie said, "Does the length seem right to you?"

"You know, everyone's asking me that."

"Well, with last year's fiasco no one is sure which way to go. But I still think short is right. What's everyone else doing?"

"You know that's not fair, asking me that," Laurie said.

"Well, you can't blame me for trying."

"All right, I'll tell you—even though I shouldn't."

"Come on, Laurie, you love having the inside track on everything."

"Well . . . everyone I've fitted for is doing som and some long. Playing it safe right down the l

"That's their problem, then. It'll be boring. They won't make any fashion statement whatsoever."

Laurie was turning this way and that so Luigi could get on with his job. Then she put on the last outfit.

She zipped up the pants. "Now *these* are different."

"Good different or bad different?" Maxie said.

Laurie laughed. "Good different. This leg line makes my ass look great!"

"Luigi, you've done it again. I tell you, you do magic with my sketches."

"If only talk could get this line done."

She patted him affectionately on his back. "Come on, lighten up. This looks great—you did a beautiful job interpreting it!"

"You know, these clothes really are special," Laurie said. "So different from the stuff you've been putting out the last few seasons. I get a charge out of wearing them."

"Thanks. Candace has finally let me add some less commercial looks."

"Well, they're fabulous. And it's a relief this fitting has been so calm. Everywhere else I've been in the middle of tantrums or else the tension in the room has been so thick—"

"Where, where?"

"You know I can't tell you that. Just believe me when I say I have seen nothing remotely like these samples anywhere on the street."

Luigi finished his note-taking while Laurie dressed in her street clothes. She slung her heavy duffel bag over her shoulder.

"I can't wait for the show to see what else you have here—because this line is going to make news. I mean it."

"Thanks."

Maxie and Liz exchanged an excited look. Maxie was feeling a *lot* better. Her design decisions seemed to be right on target.

*   *   *

Andrew was always in the office early going over the daily shipping numbers from the night before. Today he noticed a sealed blank envelope underneath the computer printout.

Inside, he found a typed memo:

How long are you going to let Jason Gold steal you blind?

Jason got to the office relatively early, about 9:30. He went directly into a meeting with the sales team to get a general idea of fall projections for each store and also an update on the spring selling.

Spring was not going well. The line had been shipped in the latter rather than the earlier part of the season, and the cold snap in March hadn't helped move the merchandise. Once again, the sales department was anticipating large markdown requests from the stores.

After such a dismal spring, their fall projections weren't going to be particularly aggressive. After all, the team could expect to get only the same dollars the stores had for them last fall. And even that level could be achieved only if Candace Evans once again came up with the markdown money the stores requested.

Jason suggested alternatives to a straight cash deal with the stores, such as promotional goods; the sales force nixed even that. The stores didn't want any extra Candace Evans clothes, on any terms, until the product was better. For now, the house would be lucky to maintain the same volume as before and not be cut back.

Jason buzzed Sarah to bring him in a box of chocolate chip cookies from the stash he kept in a cupboard outside his office. He munched a half dozen or so, then met with the warehouse manager, who had more bad news to report. They were behind their projections of dollars and units to ship for the month of March. Everything was delayed because they were experiencing manufacturing problems.

Jason buzzed Sarah. "Get Vince for me, will you?"

Vincent DiPasquale had been vice-president of production at Candace Evans for just over a year, having come to them from another major house with an excellent reputation which he lived up to.

He had been an old-time Italian tailor until his first job as production head some years back. While he didn't understand all of the new procedures computerization had brought to the industry in the past decade, he did know everyone in the business and could accomplish miracles no army of programmers could imagine. Jason knew that any problems in manufacturing were unlikely to be Vince's fault.

Several minutes later he was ushered into Jason's office.

Jason motioned Vince into a seat. "What the hell's going on with summer?"

"What do you mean?"

"I mean why am I just finding out today that we're going to be late?"

"I was hoping I could somehow get it all done without having to tell you about the problems," Vince said. "We've been pushing the factories like crazy, but they can only do what they can do. I won't let them jeopardize quality. I think you'd agree with that, right?"

"Of course I would. You know how I feel about quality. But how the hell did we get so far behind? I'm in the dark here."

Vince looked down at his tie and smoothed out some imaginary creases, then looked up at Jason.

"Well . . . the patterns were approved late. That's the bottom line."

"What do you mean the patterns were okayed late?" Jason slammed his fist onto the hard wood surface of his desk top. "I'm going to kill Luigi. I pay that fucker a goddamned fortune to run a professional pattern department. And that means not just well done but on time. Get his ass in here now!"

"Hold it—in his defense, his patterns were ready on time. Candace wasn't here to sign off on them though.

Remember when she went to Vail for the whole month of February? She refused to either fly back and approve them or let Maxie look at them. You know how Candace is about keeping control of production patterns. I hate to be the one to tell you—"

"Christ! Why didn't someone let me know before? I'd have gotten her ass on the next plane . . ." Jason grabbed a cookie and stuffed it into his mouth. "Okay, okay. How quickly till the stuff is in?"

"We can get it all in here complete by the first week of April, so the warehouse should be able to ship it all complete by mid-April. Even though that puts us two weeks behind on our March shipping, at least it makes us two weeks ahead on our April dollars. And that'll give us all April billings to the stores—no May ones."

"Hmmm. That just might make this whole disaster workable. I'll have to make up some story for the banks, but I think they'll go for it." Jason stared down at his hands for a moment. "How's everything else going?"

"Transition's on the way and fall's looking real good."

"Yeah, I'm getting pretty excited over what I've seen so far."

"Don't blow up when you see the fall cost sheets. Labor costs are going sky high, and these new numbers they've designed are pretty complicated."

"Look, I've always said that if the stuff looks like a million, I can get a million for it. Lately it hasn't even looked like a buck and we've been charging a fortune for it anyway. So you make sure that everything looks great and we'll be just fine. And in the future let me know when we've got a problem, don't try and solve it all by yourself. Maybe I can help, you know—I've learned a few things in my day."

"Will do. I just thought this time I could put the squeeze to my friends and get the job done. Sorry."

Jason shrugged off Vince's apology and smiled. "Just don't let it happen again."

Vince shook his head and walked out of the office.

Jason looked down at the pile of work yet to be done,

then lifted his head again and leaned his chin on his hands.

When did this place get so out of control? He'd better start lighting some fires or there wouldn't be anything left for Andrew, Candace, and him to split.

The intercom lit up.

"Christ, don't I ever get a break." He punched the button. "What is it, Sarah?"

"Joe from *Women's Wear,* line one."

"Okay." Jason paused a moment to shift gears. With a broad smile on his face, he lifted the receiver. "Hey, Joe, how's the news business these days?"

"Pretty good. Listen—a disturbing rumor just crossed my desk, so to speak, and I thought I'd run it by you."

"What ya got?"

"I heard Candace Evans is about to file Chapter 11. Any truth to it?"

Jason sat upright in his chair and hunched over the phone. "What, are you nuts? Who told you that?"

"You know I can't say, Jason."

"Well, you can listen to me now. There's *no* truth to that, absolutely none."

"Okay guy, calm down. I had to ask. This seemed like an inside tip."

"Look, we may be going through lean times right now, but so's everyone else these days. We'll be just fine. In fact, our fall line is going to be an absolute show-stopper."

"Okay, Jason. Just doing my job."

Jason hung up the phone and watched his hand shake as he reached for another cookie.

In Maxie's office down the hall, Shoji was telling her that he'd been on the phone with his people in Osaka for half the night and had even called the mill direct. The mill had admitted that the fabric wasn't right, and had agreed to pull out all the stops to replace it.

"The problem now," Shoji said, "is it can't possibly clear customs in New York until next Wednesday."

That, Maxie knew, would give them only one night to
sew all the gab outfits, and one night just wasn't enough
time. She and Shoji eventually came up with the idea
of sending someone to pick the fabric up in Japan and
hand carry it back. The fabric would actually be ready by
Friday; customs clearance was what took so long. Hand
carrying the cloth would avoid the bottleneck. One of
the design assistants could fly over tomorrow, get the
fabric, and fly back by Sunday afternoon, latest.

Shoji would arrange for a special customs team to
be on hand at JFK to clear the goods in person. All
the paperwork, he promised, would be in order. If all
went well, they'd have four working days to sew the
gab. While that wasn't a lot of time, at least it was
workable. And Shoji's company would pick up the tab
for the designer's airfare and hotel.

All the assistants wanted to go. These sudden trips
were the kind of perks that made assistant designers
happy for a while. Their salaries, for all the long hours
and hard work, were fairly low. First-class travel to
Europe and the Orient was one way to make up for it.

Maxie decided that Judy should make the trip. She,
more than anyone else, knew what the fabric should look
and feel like.

Judy wanted to do some last-minute shopping even
for this one day trip (which would amount to almost
three days in the air), so Maxie let her leave work early.
Maxie figured she'd spend most of the night celebrating
her good fortune. She'd have plenty of time to sleep on
the long plane ride. At least, that was the way Maxie
had operated when she was younger.

Maxie's phone rang. She reached for it and knocked
several sketches to the floor.

"Oh shit."

The man at the other end of the phone laughed. "Well,
hello to you, too. May I please speak to Maxie Siegel."

"Speaking."

"Hi, Maxie, this is Steve Levine. I guess I've caught
you at a bad time—"

"No, no, not at all. You must have been reading my mind. I tried to call you last night, but there was no answer."

"That's because I've been working late almost every night. Since I've gotten to New York I've barely seen anything of the city but these four walls."

"That sounds so dull! Working in New York can be that way at times, but you can't let it get to you. Right now I'm in a crunch myself. We've got a fashion show in about a week, so we're pretty crazy here."

"Oh, that's right. My mother mentioned you were a fashion designer—or something like that."

Maxie leaned back in her chair and laughed. "'Something like that' is an apt description. Right now I don't know what I am—traffic manager, sewer—but fashion designer is definitely the least of it. Where are you living? East Side, West Side?"

"Upper East Side. My firm found me my apartment and everything. I guess they didn't want me wasting even one second of their precious time looking around, so they just took care of it all. And for now, it'll do."

"Well, you must have *some* free time."

"You're right, that's why I called. I was hoping you could join me for dinner some night soon. Frankly, talking about anything besides a new leveraged buyout or a merger would be a welcome relief—even good ole Bexley High."

"Bexley? I haven't thought about that place in ages." She grinned. "Did you go there?"

"Actually I went to the Academy."

"Oh ho, an academy boy!"

"Hardly that anymore, believe me. Well, can I twist your arm for that dinner?"

"Sure. Why not? When's good for you?"

"How about Sunday?"

Maxie dug her datebook out of her purse, just to double check. "That'll be great. Where and when?"

"Why don't you pick the place, since I really don't know my way around town yet."

"What kind of food do you like?"

"Oh, I don't care. But I'd prefer someplace relaxed. I'm already tired of big-deal midtown places."

"Okay, let me think about it and I'll make the reservations. Maybe someplace downtown. Now what time is good for you?"

"I don't know, seven o'clock?"

"Fine."

"I know. Why don't I pick you up at seven and we'll go from there?"

"Sounds perfect." She gave him her address.

Steve was busy writing for a moment. "Now, before we meet, I just wanted to let you know I'm not in the habit of going out on dates that my mother suggests."

Maxie laughed again. "Me neither."

"Well . . . I guess I'll let you get back to whatever it was I was interrupting. From the sound of it, it couldn't have been too good."

"Oh, that. I was just reorganizing the mess on my desk and now it's all on the floor."

"Sorry about that."

"Don't be sorry, that's probably where it all belongs. See you Sunday."

"'Bye."

Maxie hung up the phone, the grin still on her face. She resolved that nothing would spoil her mood—for at least half an hour.

Tina was opening her office mail when a small white envelope slipped out of the stack. She picked it up. Very strange, very strange indeed. It had no address or stamp, just her name typed across it.

Inside, she found a memo-sized white piece of paper with these words typed on it:

Check it out—JG and CE have separate bedrooms. Seventh Avenue's longest surviving marriage is no marriage at all! Think about AIDS!

*   *   *

Tina's hands shook as she reread it. JG—that had to be Jason. Could it be true? And who sent this note? Maybe *that's* why Jason never wanted to have sex with her. He must be gay!

Oh God, why did this have to happen to her?

Six

CANDACE ARRIVED AT the office a little after noon. Before she and Maxie began their meeting, she ordered lunch for them from the deli downstairs.

Then they started reviewing each style for every fabric. Candace made a few changes here and there. Some Maxie agreed with and some she didn't, but today she had decided to stay cool and not work herself up to the state she was in yesterday. Luigi would be relieved to learn that the changes would not really affect his work flow.

Then they prepared for the two o'clock meeting with Pamela in which the makeup, shoes, accessories, and hairstyles that would complement this line would be selected. Not wanting Pamela to see the design team disagreeing, they made sure they settled on everything beforehand.

Pamela looked at her watch—time for her meeting with Candace and Maxie. She pulled out the hand mirror in her top desk drawer, applied fresh blush, powder, and lip gloss. One last look in the mirror and she was off to the design room.

She found Maxie first and pulled her aside.

"How's the witch today?"

"Behaving herself. Willing to compromise to get things done."

"Glad to hear it," Pamela said. "But she always makes me so damn unsure of myself."

"Just be honest about what you can and can't get done and it'll all work out. You'll see."

"Hope you're right."

They walked into Candace's office. Candace, on the phone, waved them into seats in front of her desk. Pamela twisted the rings on her fingers while she waited.

Finally Candace hung up. "Well, let's get this over with."

Maxie pulled out the notes and sketches for each group, then turned to Pamela.

"We have some specific ideas of the overall look, but we need your help to pull it together."

"Great. That's my job."

Maxie began her review of the sketches and attitude for each group. Pamela took extensive notes; Candace drummed her pen on the desk.

"Sorry this is taking so long," Pamela said. "But I like to be real clear on the attitude you want for each group so I pick just the right accessories."

Candace waved her hand. "Do what you have to, but get what we want."

"Don't I always? It's just that Jason has really got me controlling the budget for this show. And with eighteen models each needing three changes of shoes as well as all the other stuff, that's not going to be easy—I bet the only shoes that'll look right will be one-fifty to three hundred a pair. I hope I can persuade my contacts to lend them to us. But don't worry, I'll get what we need without going over budget."

"Have you confirmed Michael for everyone's hair and Linda for the makeup?"

"Yes, and they'll need to meet with you tomorrow or the next day."

"That's fine, just let me know when."

"Okay."

She looked at Candace, tried to read her expression. Then the phone rang. Candace picked it up, listened, then started out of the office.

"I've got to see Jason," she said over her shoulder. "Don't wait for me—you go on."

"I wonder what *that* was all about." Pamela was twisting her rings again. "Well, I think I've got everything I

need, so I'll get going. I've got a lot of running around
to do in the next few days."

"You'll do fine. And remember, if you have any
doubts about a certain shoe or bracelet or anything,
I'm here."

"Thanks. I get this way before every show. She makes
me so nervous—and I'd hate for her to tell Jason I'd
done anything wrong."

They walked out of Candace's office together.

"I really wonder what made her run out of here so
fast anyway," Pamela said. "Did you see her face?"

Jason was still meeting with Andrew. They had discussed the shipping delays and their strategy in dealing
with the banks. Andrew suggested that it would be better
for Candace Evans if they gave out the news now about
the summer delays rather than waiting for the banks to
ask for their quarterly statement which would let the cat
out of the bag anyhow. This way, the principals would
seem to be on top of the situation. Also, this way they
could explain how all summer dollars would show up in
April instead of some being billed in May.

Andrew would tell them this was a new marketing
plan developed by the company for coordinated sportswear. The concept would be to ship the entire country
a complete line rather than letting the clothes straggle
into the stores—thus making the strongest possible presentation on the floor. Such an approach might well help
sales; more importantly, the banks might be placated by
this scenario.

Candace appeared at the door less than a minute after
Jason's call to her. A brilliant smile lit her face, yet her
left eye was twitching slightly.

"What is it?" she said. "What's the problem?"

"I understand the production patterns for summer were
all held up waiting for your approval. And you were off
in Colorado and wouldn't give the okay for Maxie to do
it instead. We're almost a month behind in production.
Do you remember any of this?"

"I knew they were ready right before I came back from Vail. Believe me, no one mentioned a critical time problem or of course I'd have let Maxie look at them. Someone really should have explained things better to me."

"Well, that's not the way I heard it—"

"But that's the way it was, Jason."

"In any case, I don't ever want to hear that you've delayed production because you're too busy with your social calendar. I don't need to remind you that without this company you'd *have* no social calendar. So you better get with it. Do I make myself clear?"

"Believe me, I had no idea. There should really be better communication from the production department on these things. Is that all, Jason? You caught me right in the middle of a design meeting."

"That's all, see you later."

Candace nodded to both of them and left.

Andrew said, "This was not the time for her to have pulled one of her prima donna numbers. What with the lines she's been giving us, we're lucky we're still in business."

"To be fair, she says she hasn't been very involved with the designs of the past few seasons. Maxie has."

"I'm not so sure that's true."

"Well, that's what Candace says, and I've got to believe her. Anyway, now she's promised to get real involved. All I can say is, I've seen fall and it's looking terrific."

"Well . . . you can believe what you want. But let's face it, for years now she hasn't worked that hard, and I'm not sure she'll pull it off for us now when it counts. Better keep a real tight rein on her."

"Don't you worry, I'll be on top of not just her, but everyone. There's been too much shit going on here for too long."

"Glad to hear you say that. But remember, my friend, Candace has never understood that there's more to running a company than simply designing the clothes."

"That doesn't matter, *I* know there is. And in the end, she'll do what I say."

"Good. I'll see what I can do with the banks and get back to you. Oh, one more thing—"

Jason looked up.

"I'm having my accountants go over the books again."

"What for?"

"Just want to be absolutely sure everything's in order, that's all. With all these bank people snooping around, I don't want any surprises."

"Good idea."

Andrew rose to leave. All he knew was that he wanted out of Candace Evans as soon as possible. Jason would never be able to pull the company through—there were too many holes to plug up. And Candace might have worked hard when she was young, but she wasn't young anymore.

That note had been unsettling. Jason skimming from him for months now? Impossible! But all the same, he had to make sure.

Maxie stayed late at the office to check over details with Luigi. With so many fittings, some alterations could easily be overlooked. Luigi had told her often that he appreciated these quiet moments without other people's interruptions. The rapport they had always had was especially evident at these times. Today Maxie could see he had everything under control. The garments, coming out quickly now, looked fresh and exciting. Maxie left the office at eight o'clock and went downtown to meet some girl friends for a quiet, gossipy dinner. It had been a long day but a good one, not nearly as draining as the day before.

Liz had set her alarm for nine P.M. A quick nap was all she needed to keep going until morning. Charles had left her a gram of coke. Two good hits would send her dancing.

She grabbed a cab and headed downtown to Kitamasushi to meet Judy. The place was small and quiet and impossible to find if you weren't in the know.

The real difference between this sushi bar and others was the help. Here, hairstyles were not simple, straight bobs. Some had their hair sculpted—haircut as a work of art. Others had it painted various shades of a neon rainbow. White T-shirts and black shorts, artfully torn and ravelled, were de rigueur.

When you walked in, you knew something different was in the air. The food, too, was slightly more inventive than the typical uptown bars. A touch nouvelle. Liz loved eating here. She and Judy sat down at a small table, away from the bar. They ordered saki, which came nicely warmed.

"Could you believe Candace yesterday in that design meeting?" Judy said. "Like she's really going to give up her manicures, luncheons, exercise classes, and shopping sprees to work full-time on the line—what a joke!"

"I almost fell off my chair when she said that," Liz said. "And for her to blame Maxie for the failure of the recent lines . . . I mean, who does she think she's kidding? Did you see Maxie's face?"

Judy nodded. "If looks could kill . . ."

"She was really upset. I talked with her afterward. And I can't believe Jason is so gullible that he can't see through Candace."

"Maybe he does, maybe he doesn't. Who knows? All that matters is that when he's dealing with us, she's the one who counts. Not us. He'll back her every time."

"I know. And she's really going to change the atmosphere around the place. I love working with Maxie— I learn a lot from her; she's so willing to involve us in everything. But with Candace, it's all going to go downhill. I'm not sure I'll be able to take all the bullshit that'll be flying." Liz signaled for a waitress, and they ordered.

"What are you saying?" Judy said.

"What I'm saying, my dear, is that it's time to start looking for a new job. The tension between Candace and

Maxie is going to be a real drag. And frankly, I want out before Candace really screws up the line. Candace Evans work experience will look good on my resume—as long as I get out in time."

"Well, I don't know. I love the fabrics I get to work with and develop here. Someplace else, I might have to work with polyester—"

"Polyester? Yikes!"

"You know what I mean, Liz. I don't think I'm ready to make any changes yet."

"Listen to your friend, will you? Get yourself ready. Remember, it's easier to get a job while you still have one than when you don't."

"I hear you, but right now I'm staying put. I love what I'm doing—you can do whatever you want."

"Look at the direction she wants for resort. That's young and humorous? I think not. Your problem is you're scared to move on. Believe me, when I change, I'm going to be moving up as well."

Just then their sushi arrived, and they gratefully ended the volatile discussion to eat.

At about midnight they met up with some friends at one of the newer bars in Soho. From there they moved on to a night spot that was never at the same location for long. In spite of the long line in front, they got in.

Inside, the music was blasting, the lights were turning, and there was no room to move on the dance floor. Swarms of people surged on and off the floor. One crowd would move in as the last faded out.

Girls danced with girls, guys with guys, and girls with guys. Their clothes ranged from preppy to bizarre, but the prevailing color was black.

The party continued until after four in the morning. Judy, Liz, and three other friends—all of them class-mates from Parsons—wound up at a dingy all-night coffee shop for breakfast. Over greasy eggs, toast, and coffee, their conversation, as usual, reverted back to the business.

Liz grabbed a slice of bacon from Paul's plate. He jabbed at her hand to retaliate.

"Judy's willing to stay even with Candace back in the picture," she said. "Not me, guys. I tell you, I'm outa there."

"Well, you've always been pushy, Liz," Paul said, "even in school. Judy has reason to be satisfied with her lot right now. Let's face it, she gets to work with the most exquisite fabrics and everything. And she has this fabulous jet-set existence. I mean really, going to Japan for the weekend. Don't you just love it?"

Seven

THE CLIMATE WITHIN the walls of Candace Evans was as dark and forbidding as the gray sky outside. Winter would exert itself one last time before it surrendered itself completely. The scheduled resort design meeting with Jason and Candace loomed over Maxie's head all day. Nothing new and exciting had popped into her head overnight to change the essential dullness of the way resort was looking—particularly after the strong fall line.

She decided to take a lunch break. Most days, they all ordered in sandwiches or salads from the deli downstairs and ate at their desks—there never seemed to be enough time for a real lunch. But some days lunch was necessary, and today was one of them. Maxie and the other designers ended up at Bellevue on Ninth Avenue, a newly opened French bistro and a welcome mecca for garmentos able to actually go out and grab a quick lunch.

They ordered a bottle of white wine, hearty soups, and salads. With each bite, Maxie relaxed a little more. The meal became more raucous as they drank more wine, and soon her dismay over the next season faded into the background.

On the East Side, Jason and Candace were lunching with Jose Alvarez. Candace had chosen a spot with good food and quick service. She knew Jason, who didn't like long lunches, hadn't been pleased when she begged him to attend this one with Jose.

He never seemed to have time to discuss things with her anymore—business *or* personal. But she had her own agenda for this meeting and had Jose for moral support.

Candace grabbed a bread stick and nibbled the end
of it. Jason was already buttering his second piece of
bread. Candace almost caught herself about to glare
at him, then shook her head for a second, as though
clearing her mind. Now was not the time to nag him
about his weight.

Instead she gave him a big smile. "I have an unbelievable idea for something, and before you say a word
I want you to promise to hear me out."

"Go on."

"Well . . ." She looked over at Jose, who gave her a
slight nod. "I found this absolutely incredible space on
Madison that's available right now. It would be ideal for
our first boutique."

"Our first what?"

"Our first boutique."

"How can you be thinking about boutiques when we
may not be here next season?"

"Jason, please—keep your voice down. People can
hear you."

"I really don't care. Sometimes I don't know what
goes on in your head. You must know how tight we are
right now—how can you be thinking of spending money
we don't have?"

"Because in my gut I know the fall line is going to
turn us around and I want us to be on Madison Avenue
to exploit it. Listen to me, Jason. I truly believe one of
the biggest reasons we haven't been retailing—"

"You mean besides the fact that the lines haven't cut
it?"

"Hear me out, please." Jason nodded. "One of the
biggest reasons is the simple fact that the stores just
don't know how to buy our clothes, display them, or sell
them. You and I both know that coordinated sportswear
needs strong displays to promote the proper look. Our
own store could be a sensation. Jose would give it the
atmosphere I've always wanted for our clothes—that
could make all the difference." She sat back.

"I'm sure you're not wrong, but now just isn't the time

for it. We have to worry about fall coming out."

"Promise me you won't rule the idea out? I know what I'm talking about, Jason. Fall will be our comeback and we have to be ready for it."

"Look, once fall is a success, then we'll talk boutique. In the meantime, where's my lunch?" He glanced around for the waiter, signaled him to hurry with the food, then looked at his watch.

"Relax, Jason. The food's coming—in fact, here it is."

Jason put away a full plate of pasta while Candace and Jose mostly talked.

"I have so many fabulous ideas for the space Candace found," Jose said. "Finally you'd have a place that would represent the Candace Evans taste level rather than settling for the way those department stores handle you."

"Jason, couldn't we just stop by there on the way back to the office? It's right on the way."

Jason turned his palms up. "Okay, okay, you win. I'll look at it, but that's all. Nothing else until we see how fall does."

"Thank you. It means a lot to me."

Back at the office, Jason met with the design team in the conference room. The team spent ten minutes showing the resort boards to Jason.

"This is shit!" he said. "How can you guys show me this after the fall you've just done? It's back to the old stuff—if I see navy for one more resort season, I'm gonna throw all of you out the fuckin' window. I don't pay this design team a fortune for you to come up with last year's leftovers." Jason grabbed the boards and threw them off the table. "Get this shit out of here. Now!"

They all sat without moving a muscle for a few seconds.

Then Maxie jumped up. "Wait a second, be right back. We have one more storyboard we forgot to bring in that might be more what you had in mind. I'll go get it."

She ran to the design room to get the original storyboards and colors Candace had nixed, rushed back in, and handed them to Jason.

"Now *that's* more like it," he said. "Really different from the usual resort colors and fabrics. I like it, I really do. But I don't appreciate having my time wasted while you guys play games with me. Next time show me what I want first thing. Develop this new board some more— I think we're on to something."

Candace jumped in before Maxie could say anything. "Definitely much fresher looking. I saw this board in passing and thought it looked a bit off, but now I see what you mean. This is the way to go."

No one said anything. Candace glared at Maxie, who kept her silence. And what could she say that wouldn't make her look like a bad sport?

Exhausted by her roller-coaster day, Maxie took off early. It was becoming painfully clear to her that she really had no choice but to leave Candace Evans. She knew that right before a show was no time to think about that kind of change. But she also knew she had to hold on to some hope or she wouldn't be able to pull through.

Why should she do all the work, bring innovation to the line in spite of Candace, and get none of the credit? Her own line was definitely the way to go. It was time.

The snow that had been threatening all day finally arrived that night and dumped a foot of white over the city. Children with the day off from school were already heading to Central Park, sleds in tow. Their parents had no such excuse. For them it was business as usual. New York City, except for its traffic, doesn't even slow down for a few inches of snow.

Maxie and Luigi and their crews made their way to the office only a little late. Both the design and pattern rooms were littered with boots—rubber and fur-lined— and wet coats.

Judy telephoned Maxie from Osaka late that morning. It was already Friday night there, and she had
just seen large swatches of the redone gabardine. The
fabric, she told Maxie, would be more than workable.
At least something was going right! Maxie gave Judy
a quick rundown on the resort situation and ended the
conversation.

Judy stared at the receiver for a few seconds, then put
it back on its cradle. She was astounded at Candace's
behavior.

Here Judy was flying halfway around the world for
a day to pick up some lousy fabric to save Candace's
company, and Candace couldn't even admit her own
mistakes. It seemed monstrous that the designers should
have to put up with Jason's attack for something that
was Candace's fault, only to have her grab the credit
for someone else's solution.

Still Judy had only two nights in Osaka, and she was
planning on having fun.

The Royal, where Shoji's company had booked her,
was a Western-style hotel, huge and ornate, a complete
contrast to the traditional simplicity of Japanese art and
architecture. The lobby held both a waterfall and a foot-
bridge. There was an alcove where you could sit quietly
and drink tea, and a noisy, glitzy shopping arcade.

Since she had gotten hardly any sleep in the past few
days, Judy decided to put off the fun until tomorrow and
stay in her room and rest up for the next day's trip to
the mills. She couldn't really do the nightlife in Osaka
anyhow. Western women did not go out unescorted—it
was considered inappropriate.

But Judy was unable to sleep. Her body clock said it
was still the middle of the afternoon, even though the
stars were out. If she was going to be at all coherent
tomorrow, she needed to get a few hours sleep. Finally
she dialed up for a massage.

The masseuse was a slight Japanese woman wearing
a kimono and obi. Using not only her hands but also her

elbows and her feet, she worked miracles on Judy's muscles and joints. After being kneaded, pulled, punched, and stepped on, Judy was finally able to fall asleep.

Saturday, two members of Shoji's Osaka bureau, Hiro and Tomio, drove her out to three of their textile mills. They had opened the plants especially for her, and it was worth the trip. She saw a number of treatments she felt could be developed for resort. She agreed to meet Hiro and Tomio for dinner that evening.

A few minutes before they were to meet, she came down to the lobby dressed in a pair of black leggings and an oversized men's cotton shirt cinched with a wide black leather belt. Some of the Japanese businessmen bustling about the lobby stopped to stare at her.

"We want to take you to a special place tonight," Hiro said, as they joined her. "We hope you like Japanese food."

"I don't like it, I *love* it. I eat it all the time in New York."

"Well, this isn't quite what you get in New York. This is more traditional Japanese food."

"I'm sure I'll love it. Let's go."

They made their way to the tiny side streets behind the Sheraton Hotel. Halfway down one little alley, they ducked into a small room with a U-shaped eating bar. Not only were there no foreigners in the crowded room, there were also no women.

The mama-san greeted them at the door and led them to seats at the bar. She was a lovely, petite woman of indeterminate age. She wore a richly colored kimono and obi and glided along the floor in her sandals. It was obvious Hiro had been here many times before— the mama-san treated him like an old friend.

Hiro introduced Judy to the head chef, who handled the food as delicately as if it were spun sugar. The two men started a lengthy discussion in Japanese while Judy stared off into space.

Hiro turned to Judy. "Let me explain, if I may."

"Please."

"This restaurant is a very special place. The chef here has cooked for the Emperor three times. Not once, but three times, which means he really liked it. Since you say you like Japanese food, we wanted to take you to one of the best, most authentic restaurants in town. We hope you will like it."

Warm bottles of saki were brought over to them. They had time for one toast before the food started coming— course after course after course.

The meal began with an order of drunken live shrimps. The chef, Hiro, and Tomio all watched Judy pick one up with her chopsticks and swallow, then broke out into wide smiles. Apparently she had passed the Gaijin Food Test—the one given to foreigners. Just to prove the point, she took another shrimp and smiled. Inside, her stomach was turning over, but she smiled.

The sushi and tempura dishes were wonderfully delicate and fresh tasting. And there was more saki and beer as the evening progressed. But Judy didn't drink very much. She couldn't afford to lose face.

Both the chef and the mama-san gave Judy a farewell gift; a sure sign of respect. Judy knew enough from her trips with Maxie to return the honor; she gave them some small things from her handbag.

She finally collapsed on her bed just after midnight. This having fun was hard work!

Eight

MOST OF THE Candace Evans design and production staff worked through the weekend. Pamela brought in accessories for Maxie's approval. The sample hands were sewing frantically; the designers were all available to help oversee the samples and run out for last-minute trimmings.

Jason had finally received all of the costings and was pricing the line. Vince was right about what they'd have to charge—the fabrics were all more expensive, and labor rates were up ten percent. And the one thing Jason could not afford to do this year was cut into his markup.

In the good old days, when Candace Evans was a smaller concern, the partners could take down a profit of thirty to forty percent. But now, with overhead, advertising, cost of financing, and markdown money to the stores much higher, Jason knew he'd be lucky to see ten percent. Even though he was so conservative with the company's sales projections that there would be little or no excess inventory, he still had to protect himself against disaster. And that meant high prices.

Jason grabbed Maxie in the hall.

"What do you think of wool jackets retailing for eight hundred dollars and pants for four hundred?" he said. "Don't those prices scare you a little?"

"They seem high, yes, but no higher than anyone else's are going to be. After all, everybody's buying the same type of fabrics we are, at about the same prices. We won't be out of line."

Jason ran his hands through his hair. "I know, I know. We may not be out of line, but I'm not so sure people are going to pay these prices—"

"They won't if the clothes are ordinary. But this season, ours are anything but ordinary. From what the models are saying, everyone else is playing it safe and it's going to be boring, boring, boring. We're really going to stand out."

"But these prices . . ."

"The line looks *great*! If you don't sacrifice on the quality, we'll get these prices."

"I've already told Vince quality has to be up there, and he'll get it for us."

"Then charge what you have to charge."

"I just don't know." Jason went to the cookie cupboard, grabbed a box, and took it back to his office.

Maxie woke up very late Sunday morning. Her bedroom was bright and cheerful—the sun reflected off the patches of snow still clinging to the rooftops long after the snow at ground level had disappeared.

She got up slowly, savoring the one day of the week she was able to relax. She sprawled out on her bed with a cup of hot chocolate and the Sunday *Times,* and called her parents in Columbus.

She had planned to keep her date with Steve Levine a secret until it was over—what if she hated him?—but she told her mother anyhow.

"Oh, that's terrific! Be nice to him. His mother swore to me that he's a wonderful guy."

"Actually, he seemed pretty nice on the phone. Who knows, maybe you've pushed a decent guy at me this time. Stranger things have happened!"

"Well, I hope so."

"What else is going on?"

"Your sisters were over yesterday with their children. Four kids running around all day—I was exhausted."

Maxie laughed. "Oh, Ma, you know you loved every minute of it. What are you complaining about?"

"You're right, I really do love it when we have them over. And we've slowed down so much since your Dad's heart attack that the kids are just about our only excitement."

"Slowed down? You? With all your political meetings and club events? And isn't Dad back playing golf at the club every weekend? I mean, I know he isn't going to the health club anymore, but I thought he'd be back to his golf." Maxie stretched the phone cord to its full length and maneuvered herself around to the kitchen for another cup of cocoa.

"No, he's not back to doing anything yet. The doctors say to give him time, but I think he needs to see someone about this."

"You mean a shrink?"

"Uh-huh. But he won't even discuss it."

"How long do the doctors say it could take him to recover?"

"Anywhere from six months to two or even three years."

"Jeez, that long?"

"Well, I hope not. But your father's acting like an old man. Do you know we've given up almost all the entertaining we used to do? I've even cut back on my committees. He wants me with him all the time."

"I can't believe that. When I was out there, right after the heart attack, you couldn't even tell he'd had one." She buttered a bagel, the phone tight between her shoulder and her ear.

"Well, he's changed. Why don't you come out again and see for yourself?"

"I really can't right now. We're getting ready for the fall show next week so it's pretty hectic. I can't even think past that for now. But I'll definitely try to afterward."

"That would be nice for him."

"I'll try, Ma, really. Listen, give my love to Dad and everyone else."

"Let me know how it goes with Steve."

"I will, I will. Take care. 'Bye."

Maxie hung up the phone wishing she hadn't called home.

*   *   *

Judy was at the airport with the customs broker, and they were about to meet with a customs officer. These guys always gave her problems. Even though she had nothing to hide—she'd even declared the gag gifts she had brought back for the other designers—her hands shook slightly and her mouth twitched. The men in the room always made her feel like a criminal, even though she had done nothing wrong.

By the end of an hour-long search of every single one of her cartons and bags, Judy was close to tears. Fortunately, one of the company drivers was there to take her home. She practically crawled up her apartment steps, threw her belongings on the floor and fell, fully clothed, onto her bed. So much for the romance of international travel.

At seven o'clock, Maxie's apartment buzzer sounded. She sprinted through the apartment and buzzed down to Steve.

"I'll be right down."

She ran back to her bedroom to double-check her outfit and makeup in the mirror. God, if only she were taller. She hated being petite. And her mop of blond curls—would it *ever* behave? At least she knew how to make the most of what she had. Her makeup drew attention to her big blue eyes, and the black wool jumpsuit showed off her trim yet curvy body. She had to admit, the overall effect was appealing.

She grabbed her coat and ran out the door. When the elevator let her out in the lobby, there was only one person standing there—it had to be Steve.

She held her breath as he turned to face her. A nice, strong face with an olive complexion and lots of curly black hair. And his eyes—they were gorgeous!

Maxie crossed the lobby. She could tell he wasn't exactly disappointed either by the eagerness with which he took her outstretched hand in both of his and shook it.

"Nice to meet you, Maxie."

"It's really Maxine. Way back in my tomboy days, in Bexley, I was furious at not being a boy so I had everyone call me Maxie. It stuck."

"Well, you're hardly a tomboy now."

They headed out onto the street. "Oh, I don't know," she said. "There are times when tomboy toughness comes in mighty handy even now. If you worked in the garment business, you'd know what I mean."

Steve nodded. "So where are you taking me?"

"A place called The Odeon. It's casual, the food's good, and most important it's near my house so we won't have to walk far. Have you ever been there?"

"No."

"Great. This place is always open, and the food's a lot better than at all-night coffee shops. This time of the year, when I work late almost every night, I know I can always stop by for a bite."

"Good to know."

They reached the restaurant, whose cavernous dining room had a feeling of the cafeterias of the thirties—all black-and-white tiles and chrome poles.

They were seated right away and Steve ordered a bottle of a California wine.

"Do you know much about wines?" he said.

"Not really. I just know when I like something."

"Well, that's all that really matters. I got into wine-tasting a little when I lived in San Francisco. Napa Valley is so close."

"I've heard fabulous things about San Francisco. Why'd you ever leave?"

"Let's just say I had an offer I couldn't refuse. So here I am."

"How long did you live out there?"

"Twelve years. I got a job there right out of UCLA Law School. And I loved it right from the start."

"Any regrets about leaving all your friends? I know I wouldn't have been able to do that."

Steve laughed. "Come on, Maxie. What you're really

asking is did I leave anyone special behind, right?"

Maxie laughed back. "Well, I *am* curious."

"Actually, there wasn't anyone. I've had my share of relationships over the years, but nothing that ultimately amounted to anything." He took a sip of his wine. "You know, attractive women with okay personalities, but when it got right down to popping the big question, I just couldn't. There were no sparks."

"They couldn't *all* have been the same."

He paused a moment. "Now that I think about it, that's really what they were. The same."

"Freud would have a field day with that."

"Probably. What about you?"

"I was married once for a couple of years, but that was a long time ago." Maxie smiled. "Now? I believe the expression is 'unencumbered.'"

"So how long have you lived in New York?"

"My dog, Buddy, and I have been here since college."

"Where'd you go to school?"

"Parsons School of Design—to my parents' horror. They wanted me to stay home, go to Ohio State, marry, and give them grandchildren. But that scene just wasn't for me. I was arty in a town of football jocks."

He laughed again. "That's Columbus, all right. My parents gave me everything, but Columbus just wasn't enough. I wanted to see more of the world."

Their food arrived. While they ate they joked and reminisced about Columbus. It had been a long time since Maxie had felt so comfortable with a stranger. Most of her first dates were a series of awkward stops and starts.

They each had a cognac after dinner, and then another one, trying to stretch the meal out as long as possible.

Finally they strolled back toward Maxie's apartment.

"I've got to walk my dog," she said when they reached it. "Want to come with me?"

"Sure."

"Okay, I'll be back in a minute."

Five minutes later, she and Buddy got off the elevator. Buddy cautiously went up to Steve, sniffed him all over, then jumped up and down several times. Buddy, who was an even better judge of character than Maxie, seemed to like Steve.

Maxie laughed. "Buddy, calm down! Steve, I guess you've got yourself a fan here." She snapped on Buddy's leash.

"I've always loved dogs." Steve stooped down and patted Buddy a few times.

They walked around the block. When they got back to Maxie's building, there were no more excuses. The evening was over. She looked up at Steve, feeling awkward for the first time all evening.

"I had a really nice time."

"I did, too," he said. "I hope we can see each other again."

"I'd love to."

"How about next Saturday night?" Maxie nodded. "Then I'll call you during the week and we'll set it up firmly."

"Great," she said.

Steve hesitated, then gave her a kiss on the cheek. Maxie found it a refreshing change from the pounces and gropings she sometimes encountered on first dates.

Back upstairs in her apartment, she was too exuberant to fall asleep. She kicked off her clothes, did some stretching exercises, but still wasn't sleepy. Finally she called Susanna.

It was almost midnight, but Susanna would understand. After all, they had gone through so much together. Art school, then rooming together for the first couple of years after graduation. Susanna had always been there for Maxie even through all of her troubles with Martin. And for several years now, she had assured Maxie that she would again find someone to share her life with.

"Yes?" Susanna's voice sounded muffled.

"Susanna, it's me, Maxie. Wake up."

Susanna was probably looking over at her bedside

clock. "Do you know what time it is? What the hell are you doing calling me so late?"

Maxie laughed. "I know, I'm sorry, but I couldn't sleep. Too excited. I just had my date with that guy, Steve Levine."

"Who?"

"You remember the lawyer from Columbus my mother fixed me up with? Steve Levine?"

"I remember. And—?"

"And he was really nice—wait a minute, who am I kidding? He was terrific! I really like him."

"That's great. Now be a good girl and call me in the morning when civilized people are awake."

"Okay, okay. And sorry I woke you."

"'Bye."

Maxie was still wide awake. She got into bed and stared at her TV. By the time she finally fell asleep, *CBS News Nightwatch* was already repeating its earlier broadcast.

Nine

JUST AS MAXIE was getting to sleep, Judy was waking up. She had slept for more than twelve hours. Even though it was still the middle of the night in New York, she knew she was done sleeping. She got up. After an hour of stretching and meditation, she felt refreshed.

Judy believed in ignoring jet lag and time changes. She had no plans to pamper herself by staying at home to rest for a day or so the way most designers did after these long flights through time zones. Judy believed in functioning immediately in whatever time zone she was in. Now she took a shower and dressed for work.

She arrived at the office before any of the other designers, so she checked in with Luigi to see how he was getting on with the samples. He and his crew had been hard at work for some time. This last week before the show, everyone could expect to work long, long hours.

Judy had just put her Osaka souvenirs at each designer's desk when Liz showed up.

They caught up on office news, then Judy spent the next hour recounting her experiences in Osaka—especially the Japanese restaurant treat. She knew Liz, a fellow Japanese foodaholic, would appreciate that story.

Maxie, glowing but tired, dragged in at about nine. Judy had already told her saga once, so she just gave Maxie the highlights and then showed her the swatches she had brought back for resort.

But Maxie shoved the swatches aside. "I just can't sit here and look at these right now. Fall is looming closer by the second, and I'm panicking a bit. What if everything isn't finished by Friday morning? At this

point, that's all I can think about. Sorry, Judy, the next
line will have to wait. The swatches look beautiful but
I just can't concentrate on them."

"No problem. You just let me know when you're
ready, and they'll be here."

The week raced by. The fall shows on Seventh Avenue
had begun, and Candace Evans's on Friday would be one
of the last. *Women's Wear Daily* gave reviews of the
preceding day's major collections. So far this season,
they were unimpressed.

Which only made the atmosphere at Candace Evans
even more tense. The sales people needed the uncondi-
tional support from *Women's Wear* that had eluded every
other house so far this season. That support would eliminate any last-minute hesitancy the buyers might feel.

Luigi was calmly moving everything along in spite
of everyone's hysteria. He and his department worked
day and night, and by Wednesday it looked as if the
show was actually coming together. All the models had
returned for their second fittings of the gabardine outfits.

Pamela was running nonstop, getting all of the last-
minute fiascos cleared up in time for the show's production. Maxie was settling last-minute design problems.
Jason was mostly pacing, showing up in everyone's
office. Even Candace put in a few hours every day.

Meals were brought in. No one had time to go out
for lunch, and nearly everyone worked straight through
dinnertime. They all arrived in the dark and left in the
dark. Nobody really knew what the weather was like,
although it was rumored that spring had come.

Friday came in a burst of brilliant sunshine, buoying
everyone's hopes and expectations. The air was so dry
and clear that the New York skyline could be seen from
miles away.

Everyone was in the office by seven A.M. The sewers
had stayed Thursday past midnight, putting the finishing
touches on everything. They had spent the night in a

nearby hotel so they wouldn't have to travel too far so late at night. The excitement was beginning to mount.

Since six o'clock the warehouse crew had been loading the samples onto trucks headed for the Plaza. Luigi hovered over the samples as if they were his children. Actually, they were guarded carefully every step of the way to prevent any last-minute glitch such as theft or damage. Show samples had been stolen before—grabbed right from a showroom or even off a truck on Seventh Avenue. And if samples were swiped, the season—and therefore a company—could be wiped out.

Pamela was waiting for everyone at the Plaza. The lighting and sound crews had worked there with her until past midnight the night before, setting everything up. She was having brown paper laid down everywhere, both on the runway and in the back where the models dressed, to prevent anything from getting scuffed or dirty.

If only she could pull herself together. Her eyes were bloodshot, her nose was runny, her hands were shaking. The pressure on her right now was immense. For the past ten days she had been going nonstop, getting practically no sleep. By the time she got home last night, it was almost time to get up again. She had been strung out on coke all week and would definitely need more just to get through the rest of the day.

Maxie, the assistant designers, and the sample hands were all at the Plaza by eight A.M. The show was at noon, but they needed to double-check each rack of clothes to make sure that no outfit was missing any piece, including its assigned accessories. Since the models had only a minute or two between changes, they needed help. The sample hands, the assistant designers, and some of Pamela's friends would all serve as the models' dressers.

Pamela saw Maxie and ran up to her. She kept wiping her drippy nose on a handkerchief that she shoved into her pants pocket.

"What do you think?" she said. "Everything look okay to you?"

"It looks fine, Pamela, fine. You've done a great job. Now look, there's nothing more for you to do right now, so go sit down and relax . . . In fact, why don't you go to the bathroom and pull yourself together."

"Why? Do I look that bad?"

"Let's put it this way, I've seen you look better. Go on, take your time, I'll see to anything that comes up."

"Thanks. Be right back."

Liz came up to Maxie after Pamela left. "Is she going to make it, do you think?"

"She'll be fine. She's just had so much on her mind for the past couple of weeks."

"On her mind or up her nose?"

"Well, let's not say anything, okay?" Liz nodded. "Now get back to setting up for the models."

The models started arriving at nine. To get eighteen girls made up and their hair done took a lot of time. Michael, the head hair stylist, Linda, the head makeup artist, and their three assistants were able to handle only a few models an hour, so they needed to be there early.

The steamers were going full blast, sprucing up all the clothes after the ten-minute ride over from the workroom. The cigarette smoke in the back room was growing ever thicker. Models were in various stages of undress. Snatches of conversations rose and fell over the room, the noise level increasing as more and more people arrived. The trays of croissants, rolls, fresh fruit, and cheeses, and pots and pots of coffee were almost empty. Used coffee cups were strewn over every available tabletop.

Candace and Jason had walked to the Plaza from their apartment. Candace, as usual, looked perfectly put together. She too had been made up and had her hair done. She seemed impervious to the carnival-like atmosphere, and was calm, as though everything in her life weren't riding on this event.

She double-checked all the girls' makeup and hair as they were finished. Any model who didn't look exactly as Candace had envisioned was sent back for touch-ups.

Finally, it was noon. The members of the press and key buyers were all taking their assigned seats—nearer or farther from the runway, according to their power and influence. The models were only now putting on their first outfits, waiting until the last minute so as to keep the clothes as fresh as possible. So many guests were arriving that even the standing-room areas in the back and along the balconies were jammed. Pamela kept running back to check on everyone's readiness.

At 12:15 she motioned for the lights to dim and the music to begin. A hush fell over the audience. The spotlights came on and the models moved along the catwalk. The Candace Evans Fall Show had begun.

Backstage, the models tossed their outfits in all directions before changing into the next one. The atmosphere on the runway was elegantly, smoothly professional; in the back, chaotic. Candace gave each model the once-over before returning to the stage.

Twenty-two minutes later, it was all over. To bursts of applause and a standing ovation, Candace walked down the runway surrounded by her models, acknowledging the accolades. Jason handed her a huge bouquet of white roses and called for another round of applause.

Backstage, everyone was running around hugging and kissing each other, light-headed with relief as well as genuine pride on a beautiful show. Minutes after Candace and Jason left the stage, the dressers were sorting and rehanging the clothes. They had to get them back to the showroom as soon as possible to be pressed yet again in preparation for Monday, when the real selling of the line would begin.

Candace and Jason, beaming, worked the room, graciously thanking everyone for all their help and support. Jason ordered the champagne poured, and everyone stopped working for a moment to enjoy a glass.

All the work and trauma of the past few months had been for these twenty-two minutes of show biz. And they faced it at least twice a year. Was it worth it? Yes. When the reaction was this positive and everyone had worked together to pull it off, the sense of pride and elation took a long time to wear off. And the reward could be millions of dollars in revenue.

Pamela had the workmen dismantle the platforms and runway, take down the wiring and speaker system, and send the clothes back to the showroom. The models all rushed off to their next show of the day. And slowly, still holding onto the high from the show's success, Maxie, the other designers, and the rest of the employees packed up their gear and headed back to the showroom.

Pamela alone remained behind. She stared vacantly at the remnants of the show, kicked at the cigarette butts and trash that hadn't been picked up yet. The makeup she had used to cover her blotchy skin was gone. Her ever-present handkerchief was rolled into a ball she kept clenching and unclenching.

That bitch Candace hadn't said a word to her all day. Hadn't even thanked her when she was going around to everyone else. Nor had Jason. Pamela had given him the best show ever—and nothing.

Her fist kept clenching and unclenching.

Ten

THE CELEBRATORY ATMOSPHERE continued in the showroom for the rest of the day. The design and pattern departments shared a more intimate party in the back, toasting each other with even more champagne.

Candace gave Luigi a beautiful monogrammed silver box to store his chalk and straight pins in, Maxie a Fendi wallet, each assistant designer a leather box to hold colored pens and markers.

Jason came into the back and called out to everyone to gather around.

"I just wanted to tell you again that this was the best show ever. And without each and every one of you, it wouldn't have happened."

They all looked at each other, nodding and smiling.

"I just found out about the best news of all. Pamela just informed me that *Women's Wear* is calling ours the collection of the season." Everyone hooted and clapped. "In fact, we'll be Monday's cover and there'll be a center spread on us in Wednesday's edition. They'll be coming to the showroom on Monday to conduct some interviews."

Candace moved over to him, beaming. "Jason, this is fantastic! I told you this collection would put us back on the map."

"I think it just might." He gave her a quick hug. "Let's get some more champagne in here and really start celebrating."

He asked Sarah to arrange for a restaurant to cater an impromptu party for the entire staff. As exhausted as everyone was, no one wanted to leave the office. They all wanted to savor their success a little while longer.

Music blared from the speakers high up in the corners of the showroom. The party went into full swing. Some people moved off occasionally to an inner office where cocaine and other drugs were being served. Pamela, by now exhausted, was one of the organizers of this side party.

Boosted by coke, she bounced back into the scene, seeking Jason out. She received so much praise as she made her way through the crowd that she was feeling particularly buoyed by the time she reached him.

Jason took in her dilated pupils and involuntary twitters, then maneuvered her off to one side.

Pamela sounded almost hysterical. "Well, honey . . . I told you I could pull this off and even you'll have to admit it was flawless. You know, I did it all for you, just for you. I wanted you to be proud of me."

Jason glanced around, hoping no one could hear this conversation. "Oh, I am, Pamela. Believe me, no one could be prouder. I know how great a job you did for us—"

"You know Candace had me running all around, couldn't make up her goddamn mind about anything. I tell you it's a miracle the show ever came off. If I hadn't just decided things for myself, it would never have happened. Candace just couldn't make any decisions. Thank God Maxie and I were there."

"I don't think this is the time or the place for this, do you?"

"Why not? Without me, sweetie, this show wouldn't have happened."

"Yes, we all know that, Pamela, you did a great job." He put his arm behind her back and tried to steer her toward the front door. "But I think you really should go home now and relax. Unwind a bit. In fact, why don't you take next week off? You deserve it."

Pamela shrugged herself free. "But I don't *want* to go home. I'm not tired, in fact I feel great. All I want is to see you. Remember, you promised to find time for me and now that I'm free, we could get together. Tonight, even." She wrapped her arms around his neck in plain view of everyone and attempted to kiss him.

Jason finally wrestled free. "I really think you must be exhausted, Pamela. Go home—you're making a fool of yourself." And he stalked off in the opposite direction.

It was probably his tone of voice more than the actual words, along with the drugs she had been taking all week, but Pamela snapped. Everything she had done for the past year had been done with the aim of snaring Jason—if he didn't want her, she was worthless.

She ran after him and grabbed his arm, spinning him around to face her again.

"If that's all the appreciation I get from you, then who needs it? You're nothing but a low-class boy from the Bronx, and no matter what you do and who you surround yourself with, that's all you'll ever be! You're not worth wasting another minute on—you hear me, Jason Gold?" And with that, she left the party.

The hush that fell over the room lasted only until tongues started wagging over this latest episode in the love life of Jason Gold.

Candace merely continued her rounds, thanking every employee. Finally she reached Jason, who was talking to Vince. She smiled sweetly at both of them, then moved close enough to whisper in Jason's ear.

"I told you before, see anyone you want but don't let it interfere with our life. You've humiliated me in front of the whole staff *for the last time*." Then she smiled again at Vince and turned away.

"Excuse me, Vince," Jason said. "Candace needs my help with something right away." He ran after her and led her off to a corner. "Candace, I'm so sorry, but she was so wired she didn't know what she was saying. I was trying to get her out of here— Believe me, I dumped her long ago, but she won't take no for an answer. I'll fire her soon, I swear it. I'd have done it already but we needed her for the show."

He put his arms around her, trying to get close, and felt her wince.

"Look, Candace, I really *am* sorry. Let's enjoy tonight, let's celebrate our triumph."

With his arm he encircled Candace's waist and held on, resisting her attempts to break free and dragged her to the center of the room. "In fact, I want to make a toast—come close, everyone!"

Jason surveyed the group for a moment. "Everyone, I want to take this opportunity to thank Candace for the fabulous line she's given us." He paused to allow the applause to die back down. "It's going to make our jobs that much easier. The word on the street—as you've all heard by now—is that Candace Evans is the hit of the fall season. And it wouldn't have been possible without this woman's vision."

He looked straight into her eyes. "Thank you, Candace . . ." She nodded her head in gracious acknowledgment of his praise. " . . . and thanks also to your design team and to Luigi."

Again, everyone clapped and cheered. The party kept on rolling. And the incident with Pamela was almost forgotten.

Eleven

ON SATURDAY, MAXIE didn't wake up till long past noon. Buddy had tried to rouse her several times, but to no avail. The strong April sun streaming through her tall windows finally got her up, but she decided to spend the day relaxing and puttering around the apartment.

Steve would be taking her to dinner that night at Bouley, one of her favorite restaurants. With no plans or obligations until then, she had the rest of the day to look forward to the evening.

Steve held open the heavy wooden door to the restaurant and Maxie slipped in ahead of him. The tunnel-like entrance gave the impression of an old stone storehouse, but the dining room was cozy and elegant. The tables were far enough away from one another to allow for intimate conversation.

They enjoyed a leisurely dinner, talking as much as eating. A lot had happened in the week since they had seen each other. Steve listened attentively to Maxie's account of the week's drama at Candace Evans. Never having been to a fashion show, he found it hard to believe all the work that went into it. Then Maxie described last night's party, culminating in the Pamela/Jason exchange.

"I can't believe the backstabbing that goes on at your place," he said.

"I know."

"No, I mean, you see a fair amount of it in mergers and acquisitions—one minute a guy is on your side and you're counting on his support, and then he jumps ship—but at your place it's so personal and vindictive. It has nothing to do with business, it's all for personal gains or losses. How do you stand it?"

"For a long time, I couldn't. Believe me, growing up I never dreamed this kind of bullshit existed. I thought Seventh Avenue would be about art and design and beautiful clothes, and sometimes it seems that's the least of what we do here. Actually, Candace Evans is just like all the other places, except we have to deal with partners who are married to each other. Occasionally we get dragged into their marital drama. And God knows there's enough of it."

"Better you than me. Candace Evans makes my work seem dull."

Maxie laughed. "I'm sure it's not. What's been happening with that account you were telling me about?"

Steve's week, in contrast to hers, had been calm. He was putting together the finishing touches on a secret takeover attempt by one of the biggest Japanese conglomerates for an American electronics firm. It would go into play this coming Monday, with the world totally unsuspecting.

While Steve couldn't talk to Maxie about the particulars, she easily grasped the concepts and nuances. She had a good head for business. In fact, she was like a sponge, trying to soak up as much of the detail as possible.

"This stuff is fascinating," she said. "I always read the business section of the *Times,* and you're right in the middle of it! It must be incredible—sort of like espionage or something."

"Hardly that," he said, but she thought he looked pleased. "And it's not nearly as interesting as the garment business."

"Not true—you have information before anyone else does that can change so many lives."

"But so do you."

"Whoopee. I assume you mean my inside track on skirt lengths and shoulder pads for the next season. That's hardly crucial information. Steve, you're involved with decisions that affect people's livelihood. That's significant."

"I'd never thought of it that way. And it is exciting when the play begins."

"I'll bet."

"Starting Monday, till it's over, we'll probably be working round the clock, trying to make it happen just the way we want it to." He reached for her hand. "You know, Maxie, it's nice to be out with someone who's really interested in what I do."

Maxie looked at him. "I feel the same way."

After dessert and cognac they took Buddy for a walk, then listened to some quiet music. Finally Steve got up to leave. After he invited her to brunch the next day, there was a moment of awkwardness as he put on his coat.

Maxie reached up and kissed him. He pulled her close and kissed her back—thoroughly. Finally she broke the embrace with a laugh.

"You'd better leave now or I won't let you out the door."

Steve smiled. "See you tomorrow at one."

"I'll be there." She closed the door and leaned against it, a contented smile on her face.

Maxie arrived at Steve's Upper East Side apartment building shortly after one o'clock. It was an all-glass design that housed a health club, pool, and all the services its tenants could possibly want. Yet the building had no real personality.

The concierge made her wait while he announced her, then let her proceed to the elevators. Maxie rode up twenty-nine flights and stepped out to see Steve at the end of the hall, leaning up against his apartment door, a grin on his face.

"What mischief do you have planned for today?" she said from down the hall.

"Nothing. I was just enjoying the view."

"Oh, God!" Maxie gave him a quick hello kiss, then walked past him into his apartment. "You have a helluva security system in this place. I hope it's a bit friendlier up here."

"Why don't you see for yourself?"

"I already am. And all I can say is—wow!" She could see the East River and Queens, completely unobstructed, as well as the downtown skyline and the view to the west. There was even a terrace. The furnishings were attractive but definitely geared for a bachelor—lots of hi-tech stereo equipment and glass and chrome. It was a perfectly decorated apartment that lacked any personal touches.

"You should see it at night—it's even more dramatic," he said. "At least I thought so the few times I actually stopped and looked at it on my way to pass out after another eighteen-hour day. It's a lot different from my place in San Francisco."

Maxie continued her tour of the apartment. From the kitchen, she called "Oh? How?"

"Well, there I had my own house with a view of the Bay. It had character and I spent a lot of time fixing it up. This apartment is fine for now, but I like a feeling of warmth in a place—like yours."

Maxie came out of the kitchen. "Thanks. I've worked hard to make my loft into a real home. I know what you mean about wanting character in your place."

"This has none. But that'll come in time. Listen, I had a great idea for brunch. Since the day's so gorgeous, why don't we have a picnic in the park instead of fighting the crowds in the restaurants?"

"Great idea! I haven't done that in ages. And after being cooped up all week, it'll do both of us a world of good."

"Glad you like the idea."

"Well, let's go get some food."

"It's all done already."

"What do you mean, all done?"

"I got up this morning and went to Zabar's—"

"Zabar's? On a Sunday morning? Are you crazy? How crowded was it?"

"Let's put it this way, by the time I got there, some people had been waiting an hour already. But it wasn't too bad. And I love watching the people." Steve opened his refrigerator and began taking out containers of goodies.

"Did any fights break out between any of the old ladies?"

"Not quite, but a few did get testy. It's unbelievable, the scene there."

"And some people do it every week. They love it! I could never do that." Maxie sneaked a peek into one of the containers. Steve slapped her hand lightly.

"But the food is so terrific."

"That it is. Well, you seem to have this all organized. Let's go."

Finding a quiet spot in the park was impossible—the entire city appeared to be there. Everyone was letting loose on this first beautiful Sunday of spring. Frisbees, roller skates, bicycles, and boom boxes made the park come alive.

Steve looked around. "This isn't exactly what I had in mind. I hoped for some peace and quiet."

Maxie laughed. "This is fun! And just what I needed after the week I've had. Come on, I'll show you a spot where we'll have some quiet yet still be a part of it all."

"Just lead the way."

They found a spot behind the Metropolitan Museum of Art and spread out their meal. They talked and ate and watched the passing scene, letting the sun repair what the many weeks of being inside had done to their souls.

Eventually they headed back to Steve's place. The sun, just setting when they entered the apartment, cast a rosy glow. Maxie stood in awe in the middle of the living room, admiring the view of thousands of windows reflecting the sun across the river.

Steve moved toward her and turned her toward him slowly, the view of him replacing the view of the city. Maxie looked up into his face—now that rosy glow came from him.

In each other's arms, kissing, Maxie felt at home. Steve led her over to the sofa and they snuggled up together. He massaged her temples, neck, and shoulders, while they watched the light change. There was no rush, they had all the time in the world.

"You know, Maxie, I feel like I can tell you anything and you'll understand."

"I feel that way about you, too, and it scares me. I haven't felt this way since Martin—"

"Your ex?"

"Uh-huh. And I don't know if I'm quite ready for that yet."

"Take as much time as you need." He tilted her face so he could look directly into her eyes. "Just know I'll be here waiting."

They stayed together on the couch as the sky darkened into night and the city lights began twinkling in the sky. Finally Maxie got up to go. At the door she kissed him one last time, then walked out.

In the cab speeding downtown she hugged herself, shivering in the chill of the night after the warmth of Steve's arms around her.

Twelve

CANDACE AND JASON were so besieged by congratu-
latory phone calls all day Saturday that Jason suggested
they escape to the Hamptons. When Candace agreed,
they cancelled their dinner plans and headed out to their
house in East Hampton. With no summer traffic, they
made it in under two hours.

In the kitchen of their sprawling clapboard house on
Dune Road, with a pool as well as an ocean view,
Candace started putting together a simple dinner from
the supplies they had brought along.

Jason sat on a stool near her, sipping a glass of wine.
It had been a long time since they had spent this kind of
time together. Lately they had both seemed to run from
one engagement to another, always surrounded by as
many other people as possible. The running helped them
to avoid dealing with their real problem—each other.

But now, after Friday's triumph, Jason was determined to try to smooth out the rough spots so they could
move on with their lives together. First he apologized
again for Pamela's behavior the night before. "Nothing
like that will happen again. Believe me," he said. He
spoke long into the evening of his plans; Candace listened and responded in kind.

Candace again mentioned opening a showcase boutique on Madison Avenue. Jason was no longer totally against it—in fact, they even discussed the timing
they would need to have it ready for fall merchandise.

Jason shared his longing to produce the play written
by Marcus Putnam, a new playwright he had discovered. He even dreamed of taking it from Broadway to

Hollywood. Candace understood this dream—it could remove him further from the Bronx tenements of his boyhood than being a success on Seventh Avenue could ever do.

They discussed at length their strategy for handling Andrew—actually, Jason proposed and Candace accepted. In these matters she always yielded to Jason. Unlike Maxie, Candace had neither a head for business nor the desire to learn it.

In the morning, with the sun warming the sand, they took a long stroll along the almost deserted beach. Jason stood close to Candace and stared out at the ocean with its gently breaking waves.

They turned to each other at the same moment. Jason squeezed Candace's hand, they smiled at each other, and they returned to the house.

They drove back to Manhattan in a companionable silence, warm with a new resolve to move forward together.

By eight o'clock Monday morning, the showroom was jumping. The sales force had worked over the weekend—Larry had held a sales meeting and pep rally. The crew was pumped up to sell the collection.

Maxie arrived after nine, late for her. Liz and Judy took one look at her and then grinned at each other.

"Okay, who is he?" Liz said. "Tell all."

"Oh, come on guys, I don't know what you're talking about."

"Well, we do. You're positively radiating."

"I am?"

"Yup. So tell us all about him."

Maxie hugged herself. "Not yet. I'm going to keep it to myself for a little while longer. I'll tell you when I'm ready . . . So what have you two been up to? Get any rest this weekend?"

"I did, sort of," Judy said. "But Liz didn't, I can tell you that."

"Ah-hah, Liz! What sinful things have you been up to, pray tell?" Maxie shrugged out of her jacket and sat down.

"Well . . . first off, a bunch of us went to Mars after the party here Friday night—"

"You're kidding? You actually went out even after the week we'd gone through? I don't know how you do it!" Maxie shook her head. "What am I talking about? Of course I know how you do it—I used to do the same thing."

"Anyway," Judy said, "Liz met this absolutely gorgeous hunk. Turns out he's a musician on tour. He's all cranked up and drags our Lizzy away from us and onto the dance floor." Judy smiled at Liz. "And from there, you'd better take over, because we didn't lay eyes on you after that."

"Well . . ."

"Come on, Liz," Maxie said. "Tell me—I'm dying to hear about this hunk."

"We ended up going to his hotel—Morgans, no less. Not just any ole sleaze joint for this gal." She took a sip of her coffee. "We partied all night Friday and then he had his concert at the Garden on Saturday. He even got me a front row seat for that. Then I went backstage afterward, and from there we partied the rest of Saturday night."

"And—?"

"Well, he left for Boston yesterday, so I guess that's it."

"And—?"

"Oh, you mean, how was he?"

Maxie nodded.

"Let's put it this way, he and his moves were—shall we say—musical? And that, my dear, was my weekend."

The *Women's Wear Daily* copy was finally delivered. Maxie flipped through to the page that reviewed Friday's showings. It was even better than they had expected.

She stood up. "So it looks like all our hard work has paid off. On to resort."

Everyone groaned.

Over the next few hours, the designers purged all remnants of fall—charts, sketches, swatches—from the room so they could mentally begin to devote themselves to the next line.

Jason stopped by to share Larry's news that the buyers were thrilled. The phones rang nonstop with buyers trying to see the line before it was all sold out. Three days ago these same buyers were barely taking calls from Candace Evans salesmen.

The energy level was at an all-time high. When the reporter and photographer from *Women's Wear* arrived in the early afternoon, they saw how busy the showroom was.

They grabbed Larry for a short interview in between meetings. Buyer reaction, he told them, was unprecedented. Paper was promised from most stores by the end of the week—unheard of in today's market. Normally the actual orders didn't come in for several weeks at the earliest, and even then only after the sales people pushed the buyers. But this time the buyers seemed afraid that the line would be sold out if they didn't act quickly enough. Even the reporter was impressed by *that* news.

They interviewed Jason, who said that Candace Evans intended to increase its volume at least fifty percent over last year. This was total hype—Jason hadn't even had time to sit down with Larry to review their projections—but it would keep the momentum going.

Then they met with Candace and photographed her at her desk and with her clothes in the showroom. The reporter left without interviewing anyone else in the company. The Candace Evans story would be the center spread of Wednesday's edition.

Jason finally grabbed Larry early that evening. The place had been a zoo all day, and Jason wanted to sit down with all of the sales force to get their feedback. He had Sarah order in a platter of deli and scheduled the meeting for eight.

Tired or not, everyone stayed late for the meeting. Jason heard positive news from each salesman. Something was definitely happening at Candace Evans—something that didn't happen often at any designer house.

Jason wanted to hear specific buyer's reactions. At this point, with no actual orders in hand, this could be a little dangerous to project. After all, stores were famous for promising everything and delivering nothing. Nonetheless, Jason felt truly optimistic.

With the *Women's Wear's* promotion, even the stores that had dropped Candace Evans would be back. The key was the gabardine and silk group. These styles were the base on which everything else was built. Without the group, they wouldn't be able to move anything else.

Jason asked everyone to stay to help edit the line, cutting down the total number of styles that would actually be produced. If a collection opened with over a hundred items, the orders would be spread out over so many selections that there would be no volume for any particular item and production would be much too slow and expensive. So editing a new line was standard practice in the industry. Some designers even added auxiliary pieces just for the show, knowing they'd never actually get made.

But editing was never easy. There was a lot of screaming and hollering as styles were hung up and reconsidered. Everybody had their favorite item. In the end, the line was culled down to manageable proportions and Jason was pleased.

When everyone got up to go home, Larry pulled him aside. "Look, these guys don't know how big this is going to get, but I do. I met with management today, and they were throwing out serious numbers."

"How serious?"

"I don't know for sure, but I think we'll be able to do twenty million. I mean, I had these guys scared that they might miss out on the line if they didn't give us substantial increases. And they were buying it!"

"Shit, that's terrific! How soon before we see any paper? A month?"

"Are you kidding? Plenty will be in by the end of the week, beginning of next, latest."

"Who would have thought, huh?"

"I know."

Jason walked with Larry over to the elevators. "Look, don't discuss any specific numbers with anyone yet—in or out of the company—until the picture is clearer. I mean *no one*. Got it?"

Jason couldn't wait to get home and share the news with Candace. They had to discuss how to get Andrew out of the picture before he realized how big the fall line's potential might be. That would mean wrapping things up with him this week. If Larry's numbers were right, Andrew's last offer was too much of a bargain.

"Guess what?" Jason said as soon as Candace came into the room. "Guess how many millions we're gonna do for fall."

"Oh, I don't know. You know I'm not very good with numbers."

"Take a guess, anyhow."

Candace fell into a leather recliner across from Jason. "Ten?"

"Ten million? Baby, we're flying . . . Try twenty. Twenty million big ones! At least five in outright profits, based on the way I costed the line this season. We're back in the fucking big time!"

"Does that mean we're out of the woods?"

"Not yet, but we could be real soon if we continue like this. Listen, I have an idea." Jason got up and started to pace.

"What?"

"You know Andrew has submitted an offer for us to buy him out of the partnership?"

She nodded.

"Well, his figures are based on when we were doing lousy, and it was really a reasonable offer then—which means now it would be a steal. We'll have to pay him three million bucks immediately and then pay him two million over the next three years. With the way things are going, that would be a snap."

"Good."

"And if the orders come in the way I think they will, no bank will turn me down for financing. We won't need Andrew and his bank contacts anymore."

"And you'll still have Maurice . . ."

"Your brother? He ain't gonna be much help with the banks, my dear."

"Sure he will, if you just give him a chance."

"Yeah, right. I'll give him a chance. Anyway, the way I figure, we get rid of Andrew and then it'll be just the two of us to split the money when it starts rolling in again."

"Great."

Jason stopped pacing and looked directly at Candace. "I assume you know not to talk to *anyone* about all of this?"

"Don't worry, I don't understand any of it anyhow. Except that I've turned things around for us again."

"Yes, sweetheart. We're a team again."

Thirteen

THAT NIGHT MAXIE had dinner with Susanna. She had to talk to someone about Steve—she'd explode if she didn't—so she asked Susanna to cancel her own plans and meet her at Quatorze, a small French bistro on Fourteenth Street. The tables there were fairly close together, but they could still have a quiet conversation.

They sat at the bar waiting for a table and caught each other up on the latest garment center gossip. They had a lot to talk about. No manufacturer—be it on Seventh Avenue like Candace Evans or on Broadway like Susanna's firm, a large volume dress company—was devoid of intrigue.

Whenever designers, pattern makers, merchandisers and sales people are congregated, each with his own creative ideas, drama is sure to follow. Susanna's company had just as many secrets as Maxie's but the participants' names were not as well known to the public.

When Maxie described the encounter between Jason and Pamela at the party Friday night, Susanna broke into laughter.

"No!" she said, between spurts. "You're kidding! I'd have loved to be a fly on the wall, just to see Candace's face."

"I must say, she held her composure pretty well. I expected her to kill him on the spot, though God knows what she did to him later."

"Any strange bruises on him today?"

Maxie laughed. "None where I could see."

"What about Pamela?"

"I don't know. Come to think of it, I don't remember seeing her at the office. Maybe she quit. I sure would if

I had to take the abuse she has. It's just not right."

"The first thing she's got to do is dump Jason. Then maybe she'll feel better about herself and start moving forward from there."

"I think Jason's already told her it's over but she just won't accept it." Maxie shook her head. "I don't know how she can throw herself at him, especially when he dumps on her like that. No wonder she has a low opinion of herself. And it's not like she isn't good at what she does, either."

"I know."

"I mean, look at our show. She pulled it off without a hitch, even with all of Candace's bullshit. I just don't get it—she could get another PR job anywhere." Maxie took a long pull on her drink.

"The thing is—and I hate to say this—she's acting like a typical female. Thinking with her heart instead of her head. Neither of us would stand for that kind of treatment from anyone. We'd walk, the first sign of trouble. Look at you and Martin."

"Yeah, well . . ."

"Yeah, well, right." Susanna gestured grandly with her plastic drink stirrer. "He went for you once and out the door you went. Most women don't have the guts, whether the abuse is physical or mental. Pamela obviously doesn't."

"Well, I hope she gets her act together soon. She's still got a great reputation and she knows everyone who counts. But it's getting around that she's been doing a lot of drugs. I know for a fact about the coke. God knows what else."

"Well, we know what that can do. For her sake, I hope she straightens out."

The maître d' called their names and led them to a table along the wall.

"Okay, Maxie," Susanna said as soon as they ordered their food. "Now that we've talked about everyone else, what's up with you? Somehow I don't think you made me cancel a dinner date so we could gossip about the latest doings at Candace Evans."

Maxie grinned. "Well . . . I saw Steve again this week-end."

"And?"

"And, it was fabulous. He's absolutely wonderful . . . and I'm scared to death."

"What do you mean? What happened? Tell me everything."

"Saturday night he took me to Bouley. And we talked and talked and then went back to my apartment and we cuddled and talked some more."

"That's it? That has you scared?"

"Susanna, I haven't felt this comfortable with a man since the beginning with Martin. You remember how that was?"

"I sure do. You two were really terrific together."

"Exactly. Well, I'm feeling like I could be as totally in sync with Steve."

"So what's the problem?"

"If you'll just let me talk, I'll explain."

Susanna nodded her head to go on.

"On Sunday, I met him again up at his apartment. We were supposed to go out for brunch, but instead Steve put together a picnic."

"A what?"

"A picnic. Come on, even your sophisticated New York childhood must have included a picnic or two. And it was lovely! Really. Romantic, too. We walked to the park and sat near the Metropolitan, ate and drank and people-watched. It was just so relaxing. I mean, when I'm with him I feel . . . at home."

"But that sounds wonderful. I've never heard you talk like this."

"Because I've never felt like this before. Even when we got back to his apartment, I felt as though being with him was where I belonged. And then he told me he knew I was someone very special and that what we seemed to be developing was important to him—and of course I panicked. I couldn't get out of there fast enough.

Although once I was in a cab, all I wanted was to be with him again."

"Why?"

"I don't know . . . I'm afraid of getting hurt again, yet being with him is where I want to be. Does this make any sense to you, at all?"

"It makes perfect sense. It's been a long time since you've felt anything for anyone, and you associate loving a man with being deeply hurt. So your survival instincts make you afraid to leap into another relationship."

"Steve seemed to understand, too. He said for me to take my time, that he'd be waiting."

"My God, grab him quick, girl. He sounds positively divine. When do I get to meet him? Are you going to see him again?"

Maxie nodded. "Wednesday. You know, he sounded relieved that I'd called."

"You see, he's just as scared as you are. But he's willing to give it a shot. You've got to be willing to do that, too. Maxie, you're so caught up in the drama at Candace Evans that you've missed a lot of chances for happiness. Don't blow this one."

"I know, I know. I just needed to talk things out with someone." Maxie reached over and took Susanna's hand. "Thanks for letting me dump all of this on you."

"You've done it for me so many times, I've lost count. So what does your mother have to say about all of this?"

"Oh, I'm not telling her a thing. You know how she gets, she'd be planning the wedding if I told her."

"That's your mother, all right."

Their food arrived, and they dug in. Maxie already felt better, after only half an hour with Susanna. Thank God for friends.

Very early Wednesday morning Jason and Andrew met for breakfast at the Regency Hotel, surrounded by others having power breakfasts.

Andrew signaled to the waiter for two fresh cups of coffee. "Looks like we've finally got a winner on our hands again."

Jason shook his head. "Still all talk, no paper. Larry's over the moon about the reaction, but until we have the orders in our hot little hands, I'm counting on *nothing*."

"I suppose you're right."

"Look, even though I'm ecstatic about the reaction, I don't want to be left holding my dick in my hands. So till we start seeing paper, Larry and I have decided to hold the budget to the figure we gave the banks."

Andrew put down his coffee cup. "Really? Don't you think we could be a little more aggressive than that?"

"No . . . We're still walking on eggshells with the majors. We've killed them the past few years and they don't forget easy. And with them being under the gun from their top brass to hold the bottom line, I ain't exactly sure of them." Jason was so convincing he almost began to believe it himself.

"How about new buyers?" Andrew said. "With all this hype, shouldn't we be able to attract some of them?"

"Absolutely. But again, my feeling right now is sell out, be clean." Jason looked skyward. "That should only happen. No inventory, nothing. The banks would love us."

"That they would."

Jason popped the last piece of his sweet roll into his mouth and eyed another one in the basket.

"I had to twist Larry's arm to get those numbers we gave the banks, so better that we have some cushion in there. It's enough for me that we might actually sell out."

"I understand. It's just that it's been such a long time since we've had a line worth anything, I was sure you'd really want to move on it. I thought I'd be the one holding *you* back."

"I've learned my lesson the hard way," Jason said. "The stores just aren't going to give us carte blanche like they used to. We're gonna have to earn it from them, season by season. So while I definitely think this is a start, we're gonna have to come back with a great resort line and a super spring line before we'll see any real jump, if ever."

"So then what did you want to discuss this morning?"

"I've been thinking about us—I mean, the partnership. Now that the show's over, I can put that at the top of my agenda."

"Okay, so what do you think of my last offer?"

"I had our boys review it and while it's a fair offer—and don't misunderstand me, I really think it's fair—you know how strapped for cash we are."

"What are you saying, Jason? I think I'm being very reasonable."

"You are, you are." Jason could resist the second sweet roll no longer and tore off a chunk. "I know you need to settle with Christa and get that over with so you can move on to new things. So let's—just the two of us—hammer out a deal. Quick, easy, and clean enough so we can both walk out satisfied."

"Tell me where you've got a problem with my last offer. Maybe I can think of an alternative way of financing it for you."

"It's the three mil up front."

"So how about you pay two million up front and three million over the next three years?"

Jason finished the roll. "Make it two million up front and two and a half million over the next two years? And I'll take over all personal liability from you starting with this fall instead of later. You'll stay liable with us just through summer."

Andrew took a sip of his coffee, then drank the rest of it down. "Sounds reasonable," he said finally. "You know I received an anonymous letter a few weeks ago saying you were stealing from the company."

"What? You don't know who sent it?"

Andrew shook his head. "But I checked and it was just as I thought—bullshit. We've had a good, fair partnership, one that I want to end that way as well."

"So do I. Do we have a deal?"

Andrew reached across the table and shook Jason's hand. "We have a deal."

"Good. My lawyers will have a draft to yours by this afternoon. Let's get this wrapped up this week—I know Christa's been pushing you to settle up quickly."

"You have no idea how much of a pain she's being."

"Well, Candace and I are gonna miss you. It really won't be the same without you. You know we wish you the best."

"I wish it for you, too. I'll tell my lawyers to be expecting the draft."

Jason walked back to the apartment, burst through the front door and went right to Candace's bedroom. She was sitting at her dressing table.

"He bought it!" Jason said. "Not only did he buy it, we're—"

"Slow down, slow down," Candace said. "Who he? Tell me what you're so excited about."

"Andrew! He accepted my counteroffer, which will ultimately save us half a million dollars—only four-and-a-half million, instead of five."

"Spare me the details. You're pleased?"

"I'm ecstatic."

"Then that's good enough for me."

"You should've seen him when I said we shouldn't chase fall business but be satisfied with selling out clean. At first he couldn't believe I'd be so tight. Then he fell for it."

"Great! So now everything's settled?"

"Absolutely."

"Just let me know when I have to sign all those papers, and I'll be there. But don't forget, I'm going down to the spa next week. Can it be finished before then?"

"No problem. Andrew and I plan to wrap this up by Friday." Jason let out a big sigh. "You know, I'm feeling so good about the company again. I know you're on the right track, too. It's like old times. Look at fall! Resort's going to look great, too. We're on a roll." Jason danced in a circle, like a carefree child, then went up to Candace and kissed her soundly on the lips.

He turned to leave. "I'm off. See you at the office shortly."

It wasn't until Jason let himself relax in the car headed downtown that the nagging thoughts began to surface. First that Chapter 11 rumor, now another one.

What was going on?

Fourteen

BY WEDNESDAY MORNING, the showroom was even
more crowded than it had been on Monday. The sales
staff had appointments nonstop from eight in the morning until seven at night, and the momentum showed no
signs of slowing down. Time was getting so tight that
certain buyers had even scheduled Saturday appointments. But the team showed no signs of fatigue. In
fact, they were revved up by all the attention.

The hype was feeding itself. Buyers knew that if they
hadn't seen the Candace Evans line, they'd better not go
back to their headquarters.

Maxie walked through the showroom, a copy of *Wom-
en's Wear* under her arm. She shook her head in disbelief
at the mayhem, chatted with some buyers who compli-
mented her on the line. It felt good to know her work
over the past months hadn't been wasted. She made her
way to her office. No one was in yet, so she would have
a chance to sit quietly and read.

Just as she sat down, Liz poked her head in the
door.

"Hi!" Liz said.

"Oh, hi there. Have you seen *Women's Wear* yet?"

"No."

"Come and read it with me—the article on us is supposed to be in today."

"That's right."

Liz walked around Maxie's desk so she could read
over her shoulder. Maxie thumbed through the paper to
the center spread.

"The photos aren't bad, but I wouldn't have picked
those outfits to represent the line."

They began to read:

FALL NOW

NEW YORK—Candace Evans has come back with her strongest collection yet. Skirts above the knee covered by jackets that hug the contours of the body . . .

   Ms. Evans cites her fast-paced lifestyle as the inspiration for the line. Clothes that go anywhere— day into night . . .

   She said it felt wonderful to come out of semi-retirement to do the line, to again be responsible for the direction Candace Evans will take. "Having taken some time off," she says, "I have a fresh approach to designing again." She feels strongly that this direction is necessary to the company's well-being . . .

"Oh, my God," Liz said.

Maxie slammed her fist onto her desk top. "That bitch! She's making it sound like I was the reason our lines didn't work. Now she comes out of retirement to save her damned company."

"She also makes it sound like *she* was the one who came up with all these new ideas for fall. We know it was you, Maxie."

"*You* might know. But the people reading this article won't. I've had to fight—"

"Calm down, Maxie. Candace isn't worth getting that worked up over."

"Don't you see?" Maxie flicked the back of her hand across the article. "She's insulted me in front of the whole industry. According to this, she doesn't need me anyhow. So if that's the picture she's going to paint, then she can do without me. I don't need this bullshit." Maxie paused for breath, then looked up at Liz. "Would you mind giving me a few minutes?"

"Sure. But really, don't let her get to you." Liz closed the door on her way out.

Maxie took a few deep breaths to quiet herself down. Liz was right, there was no point in giving herself a coronary. But this really was the last straw. She would resign; she had no choice.

She calmed herself enough to call Sarah to set up a one o'clock meeting with Jason. She would resign, but it would be to Jason, not Candace. Resigning to Jason would be a slap in Candace's face—the least Maxie could do under the circumstances.

She had money saved, she could afford to take some time off. And she was always getting calls from headhunters for jobs, so she figured she'd have no trouble getting another one when she was ready. That is, if people didn't take the article too seriously.

She was making the right decision, she knew it. Even though she'd worked nowhere on Seventh Avenue but at Candace Evans, the prospect of leaving wasn't frightening. And a vacation right about now didn't sound like the worst idea in the world.

Maxie opened her office door and walked into the design room. Liz rushed up to her, but Maxie waved her off.

"I'm fine, now, really. I'm just going to shop the stores this morning, take a little break."

"Good. You'll feel better."

"See you all this afternoon." And without waiting to hear if she was needed for any impending crises, she left.

At one o'clock, Maxie came back to the showroom and headed directly for Jason's office. She didn't even stop to check her messages, just marched in and seated herself across from his desk.

Jason got up and came around his desk with a huge grin on his face. He leaned over and actually kissed her cheek.

"Can you believe the showroom?" he said. "Isn't it

fabulous? I've never seen anything like it."

"Yes, it's terrific. I'm glad fall seems to be going so well."

Jason clapped his hands together. "Well, what can I do for you?"

She took a deep breath. "I'm here to resign, Jason. Effective today."

He sank heavily into his chair. "You're serious?"

"Perfectly."

"But why? Why on earth would you quit now that things are finally turning around? Don't you want to stay and be a part of it?"

"I'm glad things are finally going well, and I feel I had a lot to do with that turnaround."

"You have—we all know that. We—"

"I'd very much like to stay, under the right circumstances," she said. "But Candace and I are coming from two opposing points of view—a difference so apparent that I feel uncomfortable. And since it's her line, I'm the one who should move on to other things."

Jason got up and started to pace.

"You know, Jason, this has been the only company I've ever worked at. I need to see how other places operate, I need to experience some new things."

"Look, bear with me, this whole thing is quite a surprise," he said. "I'm still a little confused and I'm just trying to get it straight. Now if it's new challenges you want, you know with the line coming around again, there'll be plenty of new things to keep all of us busy. And as for finding out how other places operate . . . in the old days, people used to stay with one company for life, but that didn't mean they stagnated. You can innovate from within, experiment with new ideas—no one would discourage you from doing that here. In fact, we'd welcome it."

"But I've *tried*—"

He waved her words away with a sweep of his hand.

"You know, I think you're more than a little exhausted from all the work of getting the show together. Why don't you take the rest of the week off? The break will do you good, you'll see."

"No, Jason. This has been a long time coming and I've made my decision. Things aren't going to change here. The differences between Candace and me are making it impossible for me to remain."

"Differences? You keep talking about differences— what differences? This is the first I'm hearing about any problems between you two."

Maxie sighed. What good would it do her to expose Candace when she was going to leave in any case?

"Well," she said, "suffice it to say that Candace and I have different ideas on how to give the line newness and spirit. The things she likes I don't, and vice versa. Since this is her line, not mine, she should take direct control. Besides, that's what she told *Women's Wear* she was already doing. This way, there'll be one voice— Candace's. You don't need both of us here."

"Of course we do. This company's going to be expanding. There's plenty of room for both of you."

"Believe me, there isn't."

Jason picked up his pen and began tapping it on his desk blotter. "How about this? You and Candace can get together and see if you can't iron out all of these differences."

"They aren't 'ironoutable'; they're too basic for that. They're philosophical and taste differences, and those are always too subjective to change. Believe me, this isn't a sudden decision, it's been building for quite some time. I really want to leave, today."

Jason continued to tap his pen. "You have another job? From some schmuck who'll be out of business tomorrow? Is that it?"

Maxie smiled. "No, no plans yet. I'll probably take some time off, get my head screwed back on straight, then start looking for something else."

"And there's nothing I can say or do to change your mind?"

Maxie shook her head.

"Well," he said, "I have to say I'm going to miss you. I hope you won't regret this decision."

"I don't think I will."

"Well, then I can't hold you, as much as I'd like to. So, all the best to you."

"Thank you. I'll never forget everything you've done for me. And if Candace will work closely with the assistants, you'll find they're a very talented bunch."

They both stood up. Jason walked around his desk and embraced Maxie. She held back her tears, turned and walked out of the room.

Fifteen

MAXIE HEADED STRAIGHT for her office, ignoring everyone in her path. She had to calm herself before she could pack up, say goodbye to everyone and leave. She closed her door, then broke down and cried for quite some time. After all, Candace Evans had been her home for ten years.

When she regained her composure, she dialed Susanna's number.

"I've quit," she said without preamble.

"You've done *what?*" Susanna said. "I'm not sure I heard you right."

"I said, I've quit. I walked into Jason's office about twenty minutes ago and resigned."

"Hallelujah! But why? What made you finally do it?"

"Did you see the *Women's Wear* article on us today?"

"Yeah, I saw it. You—"

"That bitch made it sound like she walked on water, while I've been running the company into the ground. You and I both know she's a washed-up has-been. I just couldn't take that kind of bullshit anymore."

"Maybe I'm a little more objective, but in all honesty, I didn't take it quite that way. But if that's how you see it, then you'll never be able to get past it. You've been ready to move on for a long time anyway. So I'm glad you quit, no matter what the reason."

"Even if I could get past this incident, Susanna, there'll always be another one. I guess this was as good a time as any."

"How 'bout we have a drink tonight to celebrate?"

"Sure, but it has to be early. I'm meeting Steve at eight."

"No problem. Where and when?"

"I'll call you later and we'll decide."

"Sure, sure. Anyway, congrats! You've done the right thing. Now get the hell out of there. They're all gonna come in, one at a time, and pound away at your resolve till you give in and stay. Leave now before they have a chance!"

"Yes, ma'am!" Maxie laughed for the first time that day. She hung up the phone and started going through her desk, deciding what to do with ten years of accumulated odds and ends. This mindless task was actually therapeutic. She needed to be able to face all of her long-standing friends and say goodbye without breaking down, and by the time she finished the job she was wonderfully calm.

The first people she told were Liz and Judy, seated together at their adjoining desks.

"Liz, come in here a second, please," Maxie said.

Liz rushed in. "What is it? I've been so worried. You were all blotchy before."

"Well, I did it. I quit. Today's my last day."

"Why? I mean, I *know* why, but couldn't you have stuck it out anyway?"

"You know I couldn't. It's been getting tougher and tougher."

"I know. Just between us, I've been asking around a little, too. But now, without you here, how will I be able to stand it? I'm really going to start looking!"

"That's up to you. If I hear of anything I think you'd be interested in, I'll let you know. And I'll stay in touch, in any case."

"Good, that means a lot to me. And look, working with you has been wonderful. In spite of all the bullshit, I've learned a lot from you that'll help me when I leave here."

"Thanks for saying that. You've been a big help to me, too." Maxie stood up and hugged Liz. "Now I'm going to tell Judy, so could you ask her to come in?"

Judy came in, looking even more worried than Liz. "What's going on?"

Maxie waved her to a seat. "I just wanted to tell you that I've resigned."

"Why? Things are finally getting better here."

"True, but you know how frustrated I've been dealing with Candace's bullshit. Well, the article today in *Women's Wear* was just the icing on the cake. You heard me threatening to quit often enough. This was just the push I needed to get off my ass and do it."

"What'll happen to us? Without you here to act as our go-between, it's going to be impossible. Candace barely knows our names."

"Well, that'll be up to you. I've told Jason how talented I think you all are."

"I mean, I love my work here . . ."

"Then for the time being, you'll be fine. After that, you can see."

"I'm going to miss working with you." Judy's voice was shaky.

"Me, too. Anyway, we'll stay in touch."

"Promise?"

Maxie nodded. "Who knows? If I ever get another job, maybe I'll need someone as talented as you to work with me." Maxie wiped her eyes, gave Judy a quick hug and pushed her out the door.

Jason told Sarah to find Candace and get her here quick, then called Larry in and told him.

"Jeez, you can't let her quit, you just can't! We've finally got momentum going out there—we'll lose it all if she goes."

"Goddamn it, don't you think I know that? But no one—not Maxie, not you, not even me—is indispensable. I tried to talk her out of it, but she's adamant. She says she and Candace are going in two different directions, whatever the hell that means, and so she wants to leave. That's it!"

"Well, I'm going to try to stop her. Take it from me, we're screwed without her."

"Hey, give it a try, I'm all for it. If you can persuade her, great. And Larry, if this is a grandstand play for money, you tell her I'll make it work for her."

Larry headed for Maxie's office, Jason for the cookie cupboard.

Candace sailed into Jason's office a few minutes later, a big smile on her face.

"Can you believe the showroom? Isn't it fabulous to see it like that again?"

"You might not think so after the news I've got for you."

"What? What could have happened since your breakfast with Andrew? Everything's been playing into our hands perfectly."

"Maxie's resigned."

"Are you sure? Why on earth would she quit now that we're hot again?"

"She claims you two don't see eye to eye on the direction of the line and since it's your name on the label, it'd be best for her to step aside. Would you mind telling me what the hell she's talking about?"

"Well, it is true, actually," she said. "Maxie and I have had our skirmishes about what the line should look like. I mean, I had to fight her to put in some of the key pieces that are being applauded now, but she had some good ideas, too. I thought she'd grown up enough to understand that differences of opinion are okay—in fact, they can be inspirational."

"Apparently not."

"Well, no matter." Candace pasted a brave smile on her face. "I'll miss her, of course, but if she can't move on, then she'd just hold us back. And we don't want that, especially now that it's just the two of us."

"Are you sure? Maybe you should talk to her?"

Candace shook her head. "No, I don't think that's necessary."

"I just hate changing anything at this stage . . ."

"Don't you worry, I'll just work twice as hard and we won't skip a beat—you'll see. After all, it is *my* line, not Maxie's." Candace stood up and smoothed her skirt. "I'll go settle them down in the design room. And you, my dear, just relax." Candace gave him a winning smile. "We're going to be just fine."

Candace went directly to the ladies' room.

"Goddamn her!" She beat her fists on the sink. "Goddamn her!"

Mona walked in. "Oh, it's you. I thought I heard somebody . . ." She looked more closely at Candace. "Are you okay? Do you need anything?"

"No, I'm fine. I'm just fixing my face. Be out in a sec—"

"No rush. Just thought I heard somebody yell, that's all."

Candace washed her face with cold water, blotted it dry, then headed for the design room.

When she reached Mona's desk she straightened her shoulders, lifted her chin, and walked on.

Maxie, having said goodbye to everyone, was headed for the elevator. For the second time that day, she found leaving 550 Seventh Avenue to be a freeing experience. In spite of the heaviness in her heart, she knew she was doing the right thing.

She hailed a taxi and headed downtown, with nothing on her mind but getting ready for Steve.

Sixteen

BY EARLY EVENING, Maxie's departure had faded to just a faint ripple for Jason. He couldn't forget that he'd bested Andrew—that was the main thing. All these other little details would work themselves out.

Jason had called and asked Tina if she was free for the evening. It had been too long since they'd gotten together, and she'd agreed to meet him tonight.

He went directly from the office to the lobby of the Plaza Athenee. There, he sat back in a large armchair and ordered a double scotch on the rocks. With drink in hand, he watched the people coming and going, waiting for Tina.

He spotted her as soon as she walked into the room, looking fabulous in a stretch lycra minidress with dark tights. She spied him across the room and moved toward him, her briefcase in hand.

Jason stood, kissed her cheek, then whispered in her ear, "You look gorgeous! What a sight for sore eyes you are!" He assisted her into the chair next to his. "It's been way too long."

Tina just looked down at her lap. She was fidgeting with her hands.

Jason quickly ordered a drink for Tina. As soon as it arrived she immediately took a large gulp.

"What's with you?" Jason said.

"What do you mean?"

"You're acting as though you've got something on your mind. And every time I've called you these past few weeks, you've always been too busy to get together. What's the story?"

Tina shook her head, then took another large sip of

her drink.

"Come on, baby. Something's up. We see each other nonstop for a few months and then—wham, bam, out of the blue—nada. You're avoiding me."

"I'm not avoiding you—"

"What would *you* call it?"

Tina stared at the coffee table for a few moments, then let out a big sigh. "Well, all right. I'll tell you. A few weeks ago, I got this note in the mail."

Jason sat up. "Note? Anonymous?"

Tina nodded.

"What'd it say?"

Tina waved her hand in the air. "Oh, something about you and Candace having separate bedrooms, that you were gay, and that I should watch out about AIDS . . ."

Jason laughed. It took a while before he could collect himself enough to speak. "That's the funniest thing I've ever heard."

"Well," she looked confused. "You and I *don't* have sex—not in the normal sense anyway. You can understand how I might think that. God knows, there are plenty of marriages in our business like that—"

"Well, not this one. Sure Candace and I have separate bedrooms. We've been married forever. But gay? Hardly!" Jason took Tina's hand. "You have nothing to worry about my dear, honestly."

"I believe you. I guess I was just being silly."

"I'm glad we finally got all that straightened out. Friends?"

Tina nodded. "So how does it feel to be on top of the heap? It's gotta be so exciting."

"It is, but I'm not talking about it yet. Don't want to jinx it."

"Oh, come on, Jason. You're the talk of the town!"

"I know, I know, but the orders aren't in hand yet. Just between us though, we predict business will go through the roof!"

"That's terrific!"

"Guess what *else* is happening."

"What?"

"I'm buying Andrew out of the partnership. All the money for fall will be mine."

"Really?"

Jason looked at Tina sharply. "That's not for publication, my dear. The deal's not signed yet."

"I understand."

They chatted for a while longer, then Tina glanced at her watch and stood up.

"What're you doing?" Jason said.

"I've got plans and I don't want to be late."

"Plans?" Tina nodded. "I thought we'd be going out—celebrate my good fortune!"

Tina sat back down and took Jason's hand. "I'm sorry, Jason, but I really can't break this."

"I can't say I'm not disappointed, but I understand. We'll get together another night, right?"

"Absolutely!" Tina stood up again, gave Jason another peck on the cheek, and walked away.

They'd see each other again. He knew it. A small gift from Cartier's wouldn't hurt either. He'd get it tomorrow.

Maxie, still flushed from the drink she'd had with Susanna, walked up to the cashier at the movie theatre and bought two tickets. The ticket-holder's line was already around the corner, and Maxie followed it all the way back. It was one of the hottest movies of the season. Thank God it wasn't the weekend or they'd probably never get in. She and Steve had agreed that she'd get there early and he'd meet her as soon as he could.

Finally Steve strode up to her and planted a kiss on her lips.

He shook his head. "I still can't believe what you have to put up with here—the lines, the waiting!"

"It's not that bad. And this thriller's the perfect escape after the week you've been having. How *is* it going with that merger you're working on?"

"It's still not closed. We've been meeting round the clock, but still no deal. I've been at the office every night till almost dawn. Tonight I'd had enough and told everyone that we needed a break."

"You poor guy."

His eyes were red from lack of sleep, yet there was a sparkle in them nonetheless. "I'm exhausted, but excited, too."

"Tell me everything." Maxie leaned back against the wall.

"My client's offer was extremely generous. Already over half of the board members have indicated that they're behind us. Anyway, the American company is too exposed at this point. If it's not us, it'll be someone else. But with the majority of the board's support already in our pocket, I think we'll make a deal. Maybe by the end of the week."

"So soon? I thought these things took forever."

"They do when the deal's real big and there are other parties interested. But this isn't complicated. I don't think anyone else can top our offer—the deal's just too sweet."

"That's terrific."

"Believe me, this is not the way all deals go. Sometimes it's a nightmare! It's not often I get involved in one like this."

Finally, the line started to move. It was two hours later before Steve had a chance to ask, "Well, what's happening over at Candace Evans?"

They were walking out of the movie. "No big deal—I just quit today," Maxie said.

Steve stopped walking. "You're kidding, aren't you?" Maxie shook her head. "How come?"

"It's a long story. You see, for the past couple of years, whenever I've proposed an idea for the line that's even a little avant garde, Candace has nixed it. After a while, it's kinda gotten to me."

"I see what you mean."

"After a while, I just stopped fighting her. I've been

designing by rote for the last few years—it felt as though all of my creative juices have been slowly drying up."

"But I thought this new line was a whole new look for you?"

Maxie nodded. "That's just it. It was. Business had gotten so bad that Candace had no choice but to try something different. She actually let me use some of *my* ideas—and without a fight!"

"So then why quit?"

"My look is making front-page news in *Women's Wear*. People are already trying to copy it. And now Candace is taking all the credit."

Just then a cab jumped in front of them as they crossed the street. Maxie instinctively threw out her arm to pull Steve back to the curb. The driver sped away, his expletives echoing in his wake.

Maxie caught her breath and continued. "Why should I stay with her, letting her use my creativity for her own benefit? I should do it for myself! I'm going to finally get up off my ass and start my own company. Set the world on fire! Design the way I dreamed I would when I was in school!"

"You never told me any of this," Steve said. "An operation costs money. How are you going to get it?"

"I really don't know yet. Guess I'll start talking to some people in the industry, see where that goes. And if I have to, I'll start small. I absolutely don't want to overextend myself."

"This is some piece of news."

"Well, I feel better already."

Steve grabbed Maxie's hands and squeezed them affectionately. "Go for it! I know you're gonna have the best damn line out there."

Maxie stopped walking and looked at Steve. "I sure as hell am going to try."

They walked on a while, a warmth Maxie had never felt before passing between them.

Steve could not stop talking about it. Maxie laughed at his enthusiasm.

"God, you know, I wasn't sure how you were going to take my news. I was afraid you'd think I was nuts."

"Why? I can tell you've thought about this for a long time. And with your energy and enthusiasm I don't see why you can't make this work."

Steve pulled her to him and lifted her chin with his finger. "I'll always try to understand and support you, whatever you do."

For Maxie, the cars whishing by and pedestrians walking past faded into the background. She wrapped her arms around Steve's neck and kissed him with all the happiness she felt.

Later as they stood in Steve's darkened living room, the lights of New York twinkling all around them, Maxie leaned toward him, their lips and bodies pressed together as one.

Steve swept Maxie up into his arms and carried her off to the bedroom. Later she wondered how he had negotiated the doorway, but she just remembered being on the bed, Steve looking down at her. Her eyes communicated her willingness, her defenses finally abandoned.

They were tender and wild together, savoring every mounting delight. Maxie drank in his scent, his feel, and his touch.

They made love for hours, then dozed off, arms and legs entwined.

In the early morning light, they drifted awake. Maxie glanced over at Steve. Here was a man she could count on. They made love again. Last night's magic had disappeared with the dawn, but somehow that was even more reassuring.

Steve left the warm bed reluctantly to get dressed for work. His deal was awaiting him. But Maxie just lay there, in no hurry to get up. She had no need to rush anywhere.

She didn't feel the least bit awkward in Steve's apartment, even after he left. In fact, everything about Steve and their budding relationship seemed perfectly natural to her.

But then inactivity finally got to her. She found the kitchen, looked in the refrigerator. It was empty save for the baking soda in the back, a few bottles of white wine and champagne, and a jar of instant coffee. Not even a quart of milk. Typical. Maxie chuckled to herself.

Back in the bedroom she threw on last night's clothes. She stepped out into a day so beautiful she couldn't resist it. Buddy would be fine for a couple of hours yet— she'd arranged with her neighbor to walk Buddy late last night—so she decided to enjoy the weather a bit.

She headed into Central Park. Softball games were already being organized, so she stood behind the fence and watched. The men seemed to take the results of their play very seriously, as they probably had in Little League. They even wore official-looking uniforms, T-shirts with matching logos to identify themselves.

There were mothers pushing strollers toward the carousel. Maxie headed in their direction. Toddlers were lined up, fidgeting with anticipation—the carousel had opened for the season. In the playground nearby, nannies gossiped while their charges ran off to the swings and jungle gyms. Drifters hung around on the benches. No one was rushing anywhere. Spring had truly arrived.

Maxie had never imagined New York could feel so friendly. All she had ever noticed was the grind and the rush. But today the city wasn't nearly as hostile as she'd always thought. She vowed to return to the park sometime soon.

At home again, Maxie faced her first day—well, half day—of having nowhere to go and nothing much to do. Her answering machine was flashing more times than she could count. The word must be out, and everybody was curious to know what had happened. She'd return the calls eventually—contacts were important.

She decided to call her mother first. Her mother would probably panic—it was daytime rates.

"What's wrong?" Mrs. Siegel said. "Are you hurt?"

Maxie smiled to herself. Right again. "Ma, Ma. Calm down. Everything's fine."

"Thank God for that. You gave me quite a scare."

"I'm actually surprised you're home. Nothing's wrong with you? Dad?"

"No, no. In fact, I was just on my way to a luncheon, and then I have to pick up Stephanie and Adam at school because your sister's baby-sitter is sick today. I think I'll take them to the park. It's such a gorgeous day. Is it nice in New York?"

"Hm? . . . Oh, it's gorgeous here, too. In fact, I was just in Central Park this morning—"

"Central Park? Don't you have to work?"

"Actually, that's why I called."

"What do you mean?"

"I've quit Candace Evans."

"You've what?" Maxie had to move the phone away from her ear. "Why on earth would you quit?"

"Candace and I just don't see eye to eye anymore. It was getting too frustrating for me there, and I just couldn't take it anymore."

"What will you do? You have another job, don't you?"

"No, I'm gonna take some time off, relax. Who knows, maybe I'll come back to Columbus for a visit." Why did she say that? Maxie regretted the words the moment they'd escaped her lips. "But we'll see. Right now, I'm making no plans."

"Are you sure you've made the right decision? This wasn't just artistic temperament or something?"

"No, Mom. This has been building for a long time. I wasn't being hysterical at all."

"Well, I'm sure you know what you're doing, even though it makes no sense to me. What will you do for money? Do you need us to send some?"

No matter how old or successful Maxie would get, she'd always seem like a little girl to her mother. Maybe it was because she was "artsy," with her feet supposedly several feet off the ground.

"No thanks. I don't need money. I've got enough saved so I won't have to make any quick decisions."

"Are you sure you're okay?"

"Yes, I'm fine. Don't worry. And send Daddy my love."

"Okay. But call if you need us."

"You bet. Now, bye."

That wasn't as bad as she'd expected. Before she could return the first of yesterday's calls, her door buzzer rang. Flowers were on the way up. Steve had interrupted his busy schedule to send her a fabulous bouquet. The card said, "Go for it! Love."

Toward the end of the day, her phone rang.

"Hello."

"At long last! I've been trying to get you for hours."

"Steve—hi! The flowers are lovely."

"Good, you got them."

"You shouldn't have bothered, what with your crazy day at the office—"

"Just wanted you to know I'm behind you."

"Thanks, really. It means a lot. So how's the deal coming?"

Steve let out a long sigh. "Still crazy and still not done. I'm exhausted."

"Well, I hope it's over soon."

"Me, too. Listen, how 'bout dinner Saturday—that is, if you're free and my deal is done."

"I'd love to. In the meantime, call me whenever you want, especially if the deal gets to you. I'm here for you, too."

Seventeen

THURSDAY WAS DAMAGE control time in the design room. Candace went out of her way to appease the assistant designers' fears. She even took them to lunch at Bice, hoping to impress them and bring them over to her side. She knew they were all more loyal to Maxie than to her, even though the company was hers. At this point, she needed them working full tilt, not worrying about job security.

The restaurant attracted the rich and famous. The tables were a bit too close for private conversation, all the more reason why Candace chose it. She ordered a bottle of wine and they all studied the menu, an uncomfortable silence enveloping their table.

Then Candace held her glass high for a toast. "To our next line. I know it'll be as good as fall."

The designers exchanged glances which didn't escape Candace. "Listen, the reason I invited you all out for lunch was so we'd have a chance to get to know each other better. I feel as though I don't really know you. But then, Maxie always wanted to be the only one dealing with you before." She saw the surprised looks on each face. "Really, it's true. She thought it would be less confusing for you all if only one voice told you what to do. And with my hectic schedule, she felt she'd be more available."

"Well, what exactly did you have in mind for us?" Liz asked.

Candace toyed with her knife and fork, then looked up at Liz. "I think you all should continue doing what you have been doing. That seems to be working out nicely."

"Normally, Maxie helped steer us," Liz said.

"Well, I'll be doing that now."

"How?" Liz said.

"I don't quite know yet, I haven't had a lot of time to think about it. I suppose I'll set the concept and tone for each line and then you all will expand on it—Judy by finding the right fabrics and colors, Elliot with the knitwear, and you, Liz, with the wovens. But I want you all to have more control over your areas. It'll be a big growth step for each of you. And I wouldn't be opposed to any suggestions you might have for the general look of the line." Candace gave them a wide smile. "I'm always open to new ideas. And I'll be in the office and available to you at all times."

Judy said, "Hm . . . sounds fine—"

"And I think you all should travel more." Candace looked around the table and saw everyone perk up, if a bit warily. "Really, you will. Maxie thought it was an unnecessary expense, but I think it's an important part to being creative as a designer."

"Well, I agree with that," Liz said. "When and where are you thinking of sending us? Europe?"

"Oh, I don't know yet." She waved her hand. "I'm just throwing out some ideas now. We'll play it by ear. And if you work hard, believe me, it won't go unrewarded."

They stopped discussing business when the food came. But the small talk was embarrassingly stilted. As they were finishing up Candace glanced at her watch.

"I've got to run. I have an appointment uptown." She stood up and they followed her.

As Candace made her way through the restaurant she had to stop, kiss cheeks, and chat with several society matrons along the way. The three designers just trailed behind her until they reached the sidewalk where Charles was waiting.

Candace stopped at the car door and turned to the designers. "I'm looking forward to working closely with each one of you. Remember, I'll always be available for any and all problems. I'm giving you an opportunity that you would never get anywhere else."

Candace then got into her car and it glided into traffic.

Liz, Judy, and Elliot stood in front of the restaurant, feeling a bit lost.

Liz shook her head. "Well, what was that all about? I mean, did you see her eyes, even when she was saying all those wonderful things? Ice cold. Like rocks. And sure—she'll be there to help with all our problems. Like right now?" She looked skyward. "Maxie, Maxie, where are you now that we need you?"

She looked back at Elliot and Judy. "What the hell are we supposed to do now? Go back to the design room and follow her lead? I guess that means long lunches, weekly manicures, and midafternoon exercise classes, right?"

"I think, Liz, I might finally start following your advice," Judy said.

"Oh, what advice is that?"

"Start looking for a new job. I mean, *she's* going to set the tone for each new line? I'd like to know what startling new concepts she's had recently."

Elliot, though talented, was much softer-spoken than either Liz or Judy, and didn't have the same drive to succeed.

"Oh, I don't know, guys," he said. "I think we should give her a chance. Maybe Candace really will improve now that she's only got herself to fall back on. And she did say we're going to have a chance to grow as designers."

"Yeah," Judy said. "Maybe it *will* be a good opportunity." She shook her head. "I just don't know."

"Well, *you* can believe her all you want. I don't trust her," Liz said. "Really, Judy, can you picture her yelling at one of your fabric suppliers like Maxie used to when there was a disaster? I doubt it."

"You've got a point."

"What about my Hong Kong trip in two weeks?" Elliot said. "I wonder if I'll still get to go."

"That's right," Judy said. "I wonder . . ."

"Maxie and I always sketched everything out real rough before I went, and then I'd detail them over there. I don't see Candace taking that kind of time to help do that. Watch, she'll tell me to go and do it all myself and then she'll hate it. Then I'll really be screwed."

"You know, Candace mentioned earlier in the week that she was going to that Florida spa next week to recuperate from the show," Liz said. "So she won't be around to help you get ready for Hong Kong, even if she could. And what are we supposed to do while she's gone? Twiddle our thumbs?"

"Let's not panic, guys," Elliot said. "We have some time and we can see how it goes."

"You do what you want, Elliot," Liz said. "I, for one, don't intend to be around here when the line goes downhill again. And mark my words, it will. Let's face it, it's a whole lot easier to get a new job while the world thinks Candace Evans is hot and we were a part of it. When it goes cold, no one will care that we had ideas that fell on deaf ears."

"I understand what you're trying to say," Elliot said. "But at this point, there's not much we can do about it. So let's head back to the office. We've still got jobs to do."

Back at the office Sarah waylaid them, saying Jason wanted to meet with them. He gave them a pep talk, too.

And though not one of them truly believed Jason's little talk, they were all enjoying this sudden attention. Since they were "only" assistants, their opinions had always been ignored. But now that they were needed, even the powerful were taking the time to stroke them.

Friday started as a truly dreary spring day, the kind of day best spent indoors. After so many beautiful days, Maxie had expected the weather to turn sooner or later. She set about reorganizing her kitchen and decided impulsively to make Steve some of her famous (to her friends, at least) homemade hearty soup. Today was a perfect day to eat it, and he would certainly be surprised.

When Liz called, Maxie was slicing carrots.

Liz laughed. "Is this the Maxie I know? You always were the first to suggest takeout or delivery, even for your own dinner parties."

Maxie laughed, too. "I know. Can you imagine, one day out of a job and already I'm June Cleaver? But don't spread it around or my reputation will be shot."

"Gotcha."

"So what's doing at Candace Evans?"

Liz described the lunch with Candace in glorious detail.

Maxie was furious. "She's such a liar! I would never have discouraged any of you from moving on or upwards. I've helped lots of designers do that in the past ten years. She's just trying desperately to alienate you all from me, and I'm not even there anymore! Incredible!"

"I know that, don't worry. Everybody saw through her act pretty quick. I mean, until yesterday we were totally ignored and now we're worthy luncheon companions? Please!"

Maxie had moved on to the potatoes.

"Well, just watch your back. Have her initial everything she approves or it'll come back to haunt you later."

"I will. But I don't expect to be around too long—"

"Until you do, remember—"

"Can you believe she also hinted that she might give us raises—"

"Go for it! You've obviously got her running scared. Take that bitch for everything you can." Maxie banged her cooking spoon on the counter to emphasize her point. "You're in the driver's seat now. She thinks she can get you to work twice as hard for just a little more money and a token lunch now and then. Unbelievable! You know, I'm now doubly sure walking out was the right thing."

After Liz hung up, Maxie's stomach was still churning and her hands were shaking too much to use the knife. She sat down at her kitchen table to recover. How could Candace try to sabotage her relationship with the other designers? How? Maxie should know better by now. This was typical Candace behavior and she'd seen it plenty of times before.

But not even Candace's destructiveness could spoil Maxie's plan to surprise Steve with the soup. By late morning, it was done, and she dropped it off at Steve's office. She left instructions with his secretary not to disturb him. When he came out of his meeting, there it would be, a surprise.

A few minutes after one o'clock, Steve threw open the conference room door where he and his clients had been holed up all week.

With meetings round the clock, Steve had been living for days on food catered by some of the finest restaurants in midtown, but he needed a break. He moved down the hallway almost at a run and shouted to Catherine, "I'm grabbing a sandwich downstairs. Back in a little while."

Catherine jumped up and ran after him. "Steve, wait . . ." She finally caught up with him at the elevators.

"Christ, what is it now? Can't I be left alone for twenty minutes?"

"You've got to pick something up in your office before you go."

Steve cursed under his breath, but he headed back to his office. There he saw Maxie's jauntily wrapped gift in the center of his large chrome and glass desk.

Steve tore off the wrapping paper and saw the still-warm soup in its mayonnaise jar. On the card, Maxie had drawn a cartoon of an all-American family at home and had written a joke to go along with it.

Suddenly his good humor was back. He was still smiling to himself when he dialed the phone to thank her, but got her machine instead.

He tasted the soup, which was thick and delicious, a real stick-to-the-ribs type. Twenty minutes later he went back into the conference room, refreshed and ready to wind up the deal.

Five blocks from Steve's office, Candace, Jason, and Andrew were meeting at Andrew's lawyer's office to sign the final papers that would end their fifteen-year partnership.

Most of the terms were as Jason and Andrew had outlined, despite the lawyers and accountants on both sides who still disagreed over various points. Jason was so convinced of the company's ultimate future that he was unconcerned. He dwelled only on the up side of the deal—less cash to Andrew. He never once thought of the down side—that if problems occurred, he could lose everything. Jason was to deliver a cashier's check for the first two million by the close of business next Monday. Andrew had understood that Jason needed a few days to get the money together.

On the other hand, Andrew's accountants felt he was settling for less than his share was worth. But he just wanted the deal done so he could move on with his life. They had all made a lot of money from Candace Evans during the past fifteen years, and now Andrew wanted to walk away with enough to satisfy his soon-to-be ex-wife and have some capital left over to fund another project.

The three of them sat at a long, rectangular conference table, the contracts in front of them.

Every one of the myriad pages had to be read and initialed by each person until they reached the end, where their full signature was required. Candace merely followed Jason's instructions, saying nothing and trying not to show her ignorance. No one explained anything to her. Her lawyers and accountants—whom she shared with Jason—had reviewed each point with him. They simply assumed Jason had gone over everything with Candace.

Finally, Jason and Andrew reached across the table and shook hands, wishing each other the best. This moment was the only evidence of genuine emotion felt in the room that day.

It had taken one hour to dissolve a partnership of fifteen years.

Jason and Candace clinked their glasses of chilled Chardonnay and toasted their future together. Candace looked around and wondered if Jason came here with his mistresses. It was small, dark, intimate. The perfect restaurant to rendezvous before going off to his hotel suite.

These thoughts still could arouse extreme rages of jealousy in her. Why just last year she had actually slapped one of his tartlets. The girl had appeared unexpectedly at a function that Candace and Jason had attended, and that bitch had actually tried to make advances on Jason in public. How dare she! And, of course, there had been the steady stream of assistant designers in the beginning of Candace Evans; she had set him straight about that. Jason had finally learned not to mix business with pleasure. Until Pamela, that is.

But Candace pushed those thoughts aside. She looked up at Jason, a practiced smile on her face. "I'm so excited about all the possibilities we have now. Where do we go from here?"

"I feel as though the whole world has opened up for me again. With fall as successful as I think it's gonna be, I can do anything. For instance, I've got to get that play to happen."

Candace patted Jason's hand. "You will, Jason, you will. But what do you want for us?"

"To make Candace Evans a really strong company. It's all there for us to grab."

"You're right. The opportunities are—"

"But are you sure you feel okay with Maxie gone?"

"Oh, absolutely. I can handle it." She reached over to pat his hand again. "Remember, I had no one to help me in the beginning, and we didn't do so badly."

"That's true . . ."

"But maybe a seasoned professional to help me would be a good idea. Someone who could manage all of those assistants for me. They definitely need guidance and you know I'm not too good in that department. Of course, I'd still be the one setting the tone for each line." Candace drank from her wineglass. She really needed someone to help her, to give her the ideas she couldn't come up with anymore.

"But if you're willing to work full-time again, you'll be there to guide them. Anyone else would just confuse the situation. Remember, you did all the guiding in the beginning . . ." Jason looked up at Candace and held her hand momentarily. "No, let's leave it the way it is for now. We can see how it goes and then if you need more help, we'll get it. Let's face it, we don't know if these kids are what we want, either. So let's not make any changes for a while. Okay?"

Candace wanted to push him further on the subject, then decided against it. "Okay."

"Don't worry, it'll all work out. Look at the winner fall is, and resort's looking good, too. You'll be able to keep the momentum going for us."

But would she? Would she be able to motivate the assistants to come up with the new ideas? And would she even know the right idea when she saw it?

They paused long enough to eat their lunch. Actually, Jason wolfed down his food while Candace pushed hers around on the plate.

Jason, chewing, said, "Now I think we could discuss the space on Madison with the realtor."

"Oh, do you really think so? That would be terrific! You know how much I want that store."

"I know. And this is the perfect time to cash in on it."

"Exactly. But we'll really have to push to get it opened in time. You do agree we should be ready to open for fall?"

"Absolutely. It's gotta be ready by August."

"Oh, I have so many wonderful ideas for it—"

Jason chuckled. "It's not finalized yet, so slow down. I'll get on it next week."

"You know I was thinking about what else we could be doing—like licensing. Now that we're so hot again, we should be able to revive some of our licensing agreements and get some new ones on board."

"Very good thinking, Candace. I don't see why not."

A rosy glow suffused Candace's complexion.

Jason looked closely at her. "You know, it's been ages since I've felt so positive." He took her hand. "In this last week, I feel we've gotten back so much of what we had. Don't you?"

"More than you know. In fact, why don't you come to the spa with me? You need a break as much as I do. It would be wonderful. Why don't you?"

"I'd love to, believe me. But fall isn't wrapped up yet, and I've got to stick around to finalize it. I'm sorry, I'd really like to."

"Well, when I get back, I'll be ready to pull my full share in this partnership."

They raised their glasses and toasted each other one last time.

Jason stood up and pulled up his pants that had fallen below his belly. He sucked it in.

Candace laughed. "I saw that. You really should be coming with me to the spa."

They walked each other to the front of the restaurant. Candace gave Jason a kiss on the cheek. "Have a good day, partner." And she turned to walk uptown. She had a million things to do before she went away.

Jason got into the limo. Things with Candace were definitely better than ever. It was wonderful to feel this close again. But moments like these made Jason feel particularly cheated and lost. Because as intimate and loving as they were, as positive as they were to each other, they would never have it all. There would always be one part of life that Jason would have to find elsewhere.

Eighteen

THE NEXT DAY Candace called the office to touch base with her designers. Elliot reminded her that he was leaving next Friday for Hong Kong to do the resort knit collection. Should he postpone it, he asked, since they hadn't had time to work together yet?

"No, no, not necessary, you'll do a fine job. I've seen some of your sketches—"

"You have?"

"They were sitting out on your desk last time I passed by. I think they're terrific."

"Thanks, Candace, I appreciate that. Which ones exactly caught your eye so I can expand on those?"

"Oh . . . I don't remember *exactly* . . ."

"Oh . . . well . . ."

"Look, I have an idea—why doesn't Liz go with you?"

"Are you kidding?" Elliot waved frantically to Liz to pick up her extension.

"Not at all. That way you two could work together and really come up with a strong, cohesive resort line."

"That's an absolutely great idea, Candace."

"Good, then it's settled. You'll both go."

Candace hung up, sure that she would get more out of Elliot with Liz monitoring him. And Candace had actually settled all the design problems by phone. Maybe Jason was right—directing the staff was easy. Why, she could even do it long distance from Vail or the spa.

But what Candace didn't realize was that no one was really following up on anything. Maxie had always given her assistants check lists to follow. But now, cracks in the schedule were opening, and widening daily as details were left undone. The apparent calm in the design department was only an illusion—if all was going well, disasters would be happening daily, and then fixed. But Candace never thought about details, and her staff was still too young to know.

Liz leaped for joy. She took hold of Elliot and swung him around. She had never been to Hong Kong before.

"Christ! Hong Kong! You lucky devil, Elliot. You get to have me as your understanding travel companion. I've always wanted to go there!"

"You know, I'm glad you'll be coming. This way if she hates everything, she'll blame both of us."

"Oh, Elliot! You're such an old lady. You'll see— we'll come back with fantastic stuff."

Elliot chuckled. "You wait. You've never seen what these factories can do with even the simplest ideas. You can give them sketches as detailed as blueprints, and the samples will still come back with three sleeves. *You* can explain that to Candace."

Liz couldn't suppress her grin. "Okay, Mr. Gloom and Doom, I will. In the meantime, let's book this trip before she changes her mind."

"Okay. I think we'll need about three weeks. That'll give us enough time to bring back corrected samples. Candace doesn't seem the type who can imagine long sleeves instead of short ones."

"Sounds reasonable. And we'll stay at the Regent, right?"

"Of course—if we can get in. I'll fax them tonight."

Liz looked at Elliot, a teasing expression on her face. "Hey, don't worry, I'll stay out of your hair, really. I'm just thrilled to be going."

Exhausted from a marathon week, the men sitting around the conference room had their jackets off, ties unknotted, and sleeves rolled up. No one was actually working at the table any longer. Cigarette smoke hung in the air, mixed with the smell of old coffee. The tension in the room was almost as thick as the smoke.

Just then, the phone rang.

Steve answered it, and a moment later whooped for joy. "Gentlemen, it looks like we've got ourselves a deal! They're on their way over right now to bang out the final points."

Steve looked around the room. Assembled here were some of the most influential Japanese businessmen in America.

The Makiyama Corporation was one of those large Japanese conglomerates with hands in many pies—shipping, car manufacturing, textiles, electronics, banking, construction, real estate. During the past few years, as the Japanese yen gained in strength against the dollar, they had been pursuing direct footholds in America. This electronics deal was one of several they'd completed in the past few years.

With each acquisition, Makiyama America was fast becoming a power in its own right. Yukio Tanaka, the president, was a genius at seeing which deals to go for and which would never happen. He picked and chose carefully, disregarding most of the suggestions for acquisitions that came across his desk. He was determined to make it to the very top of Makiyama someday and wanted his term in America to be well regarded.

Now Tanaka walked in, straightening both his tie and his Armani silk suit. He headed toward Steve, his hand outstretched. His thick, graying hair, normally so neat, was a mess.

Steve had a hard time not laughing at the sight of him, normally the epitome of Western style and elegance.

"It's been a helluva week, Steve," Tanaka said with only a trace of an accent. "But I knew we could pull this off."

"Me, too."

Tanaka nodded his head. "I think we've gotten it at a fair price, too. I'm very pleased. Thanks for your help."

"My pleasure." Steve bowed his head slightly.

"Now, if you'll excuse me, I'll call Tokyo with the news. We can fax them the details later."

Everyone else awkwardly clambered out of their seats, stretching their limbs. Though the hours had been too long over the past few days and they were exhausted, they still good-naturedly celebrated this news. Everyone hit the bathrooms to freshen up and try to revive themselves for the coming finale.

Half an hour later, the "opposition" arrived. They looked battle weary, too, but over the next couple of hours, everyone hammered out the final rough agreement. The sale would be announced by Makiyama's PR people on Monday morning at nine o'clock, before the market opened.

Finally, at midnight, the deal was put to bed. Someone opened the windows—the cigarette smoke was so thick, Steve feared the smoke detectors would go off. The secretaries shredded every piece of scrap paper and sent the last fax to Tokyo.

Steve and Tanaka were the last to leave. On the street, Tanaka turned to Steve and shook his hand, pumping it up and down. "Please join me for dinner tomorrow evening," he said.

"Thank you for the invitation, Tanaka-san, but I have a previous engagement," Steve said. "Perhaps we could make it at your next earliest convenience?"

"Is it a lady, Steve?"

Steve smiled in embarrassment. "I'm afraid I've been rather neglectful lately."

"Why don't you bring her with you?"

"I wouldn't dream of imposing—"

"Nonsense, I insist. Please, both of you come tomorrow at eight to the Four Seasons."

"My pleasure." Steve helped Tanaka into his waiting limousine. "Have a good rest, Tanaka-san. See you tomorrow night."

Steve waved goodbye to the car headed for Westchester. He walked the few blocks home to wind down, both mentally and physically. Twenty minutes later, still half dressed, Steve flopped onto his bed and was asleep in seconds.

By Saturday morning, it had been three days since Maxie had seen Steve and two since they'd actually had a phone conversation. She didn't know what was happening with him, or even if they were still on for dinner that night.

She didn't want to call him at home and possibly wake him up, so she tried to busy herself, pretending that she wasn't just waiting for his call. But by three o'clock, she was stir crazy. She started getting angry at Steve, then stopped herself abruptly when she realized she was putting back up the walls that Steve had been breaking down.

Finally at four the phone rang. Steve bumbled an apology, afraid he had slept through all of Saturday and their date, too.

She chuckled. "Earth to Steve, come in Steve. It's still Saturday, four in the afternoon."

Steve let out a big yawn. "Oh, God. I've slept almost fourteen hours. Guess I needed it."

"I'll say. I didn't want to call you at home 'cause I figured you'd be sleeping, and I'm glad I didn't."

"If you had let me sleep through tonight, I would've killed you. I can't wait to see you."

"So I take it the deal is done?"

"Yep, we wrapped it up last night about midnight. Then I stumbled home, threw myself on the bed, and passed out. I still have half my clothes on."

Maxie laughed. "Hold on. I'll be right over. Don't move!"

"Believe me, you don't want to be anywhere near me right now. I desperately need a shower and shave and gallons of coffee. This has been a helluva long week."

"Well, maybe we shouldn't go out tonight—"

"Are you kidding? No way!"

"Why don't I just bring over some food? That way you won't have to push yourself so much."

"Sounds good—oh, damn, I just remembered—"

"Remembered what?"

"Now don't kill me. I forgot that we—you and me that is—have been invited to dinner tonight at the Four Seasons by my client."

Maxie groaned.

"I tried to get out of it," Steve said. "Believe me, I did. But he wouldn't take no for an answer and I couldn't embarrass him."

"Say no more. Of course I'll come. I can imagine how awkward a situation you were in. We can be alone later, right?"

Steve laughed. "I like the way you think!"

Maxie hung up the phone and stormed into action. Finally, she had a specific task—to look as stunning as she could for their date tonight.

She looked through her closets and flung aside one outfit after another. Nothing would do. She was almost desperate when she spied a silk dinner suit in the very back. It was a peacock blue and black number that she'd designed several years ago and Luigi had made. She was a knockout in it.

But first, she had to clean up the mess in her apartment. What if Steve came back here? Then she took a long, hot bath with the works. She couldn't wait to see him.

Steve and Maxie walked up the staircase at the Four Seasons, and the maître d' led them to a table near the pool.

As they approached the table, Steve looked questioningly at the three place settings.

Tanaka stood to greet them. "I wanted this to be a celebration of thanks for you, Steve. You did a great job for us and I saw no need to include anyone but ourselves." He turned toward Maxie. "And, of course, this beautiful woman."

"Tanaka-san," Steve said, "please meet Maxine Siegel. Maxie, this is Mr. Tanaka."

Tanaka bowed his head slightly. Maxie did the same. "Ms. Siegel, a pleasure."

"Oh please, call me Maxie. Everyone does."

Maxie saw that Tanaka wore his Western attire with assurance and ease. Maxie was drawn to him immediately because he had an aura of self-assurance and confidence.

They sat down and Tanaka turned to Maxie. "Your friend has done a remarkable job with the deal he and I have been working on."

"I can imagine. He's told me a little about the deal and it sounds like a real coup."

"Oh, I'm sure you wouldn't find it very interesting—"

"But I do. I love all the nuances of making deals, the bigger the better!"

"Tanaka-san," Steve said, "Maxie's a fashion designer, but she really is fascinated with big business."

"A designer?" He raised his eyebrows slightly.

"Yes, she's been working for the Candace Evans house."

"They're the ones making big news recently, yes?"

Maxie laughed. "You could say that! Fashion has been dead for so long that when we offered something new this season, every paper and magazine sort of jumped on it."

"Tanaka, don't let her fool you. It's being called the collection of the season."

"Really?" Tanaka said. "What about this dress you have on? It's lovely. Is it one of your designs?"

"Yes, it is. Actually I designed this years ago."

"You're kidding? It looks so au courant. I believe that is the proper expression?"

Maxie nodded. "That's just it. For me fashion should be timeless. If women are going to pay the kind of money we're charging, they've got to feel that the clothes will be as new and stylish next year and the year after."

Tanaka looked around for the waiter, who took their order.

Then Maxie went on, "Of course, I've heard of the Makiyama Corporation. In fact, I've bought a lot of their fabric—"

"I'm not very involved with the textile division. Of course, I oversee it, but I'm more involved with new acquisitions and setting general policy."

Maxie looked over at Steve. "Yes, Steve said this isn't your first merger together."

"And always they have been my smoothest deals."

"Oh, come on Tanaka-san . . ." But Steve smiled broadly and bowed his head slightly in acknowledgment of the praise.

Dinner was served with a flourish, several waiters in attendance.

Tanaka said to Maxie, "What exactly do you do at Candace Evans? Doesn't she do her own designing?"

"Well, yes and no. I've been her number one assistant for the past ten years. And at this point, Candace has pretty much removed herself from the actual designing of the line. She's more involved with the overall scope of things."

"That's not how you described it to me, Maxie." Steve pointed to her and said to Tanaka, "She's the one who did the actual designing of this fall line that's being so talked about."

"Steve—"

"Well, it's true."

"I like to think that things are a team effort," Maxie said to Tanaka. "I'm not the type to nitpick about which styles I actually did and which I didn't."

"Well, maybe you should." Again Steve turned to Tanaka. "You see, Candace has been doing a lot of interviews claiming she alone designed the fall line—"

"I think Candace is just trying to promote herself better. The company has been in a slump lately and now she has a golden opportunity to get some good press."

"She did so much that you quit this week after ten years there," Steve said.

Maxie stared down at her plate.

"Really?" Tanaka said.

"Uh-huh." Maxie forced herself to raise her head and put on a cheerful grin. "But let's talk about something more pleasant. A toast to the newest Makiyama acquisition."

They all raised their glasses and drank, then finished their dinner after several more courses and toasts.

Tanaka looked at his watch. "It's after eleven already. This evening has flown by." He nodded to both Maxie and Steve. "I have to admit, I'm exhausted after this week's events. I hope you'll understand if I take my leave now."

Outside the restaurant, Maxie said, "Now I've got you all to myself again." She grabbed Steve's hand and pulled him close to her.

They started walking uptown.

"I might as well have been invisible for all that you and Tanaka noticed," Steve said.

"Oh, Steve—"

"No, I'm not kidding."

Steve pulled her to him even more closely. "I'm glad, too. With you such a hit, maybe his opinion of me'll improve, too."

"Are you joking? It's obvious he thinks the world of you. I bet you'll get all their U.S. legal work pretty soon. Face it, Steve. Tanaka likes you. And what's more, he respects you. Don't underestimate the significance of tonight."

On the drive back to Westchester, Tanaka made a mental note to check up on Maxie Siegel. Perhaps Makiyama's textile division would be interested. She seemed good at selling herself, projecting an air of competence as well as creativity. She had so much energy that he could still feel it now, and knew how contagious that could be. And she was stunning. That didn't hurt either.

Yes, Maxie Siegel had definitely impressed Tanaka.

Nineteen

EARLY MONDAY MORNING, after a glorious weekend with Steve, Maxie sat down to call Luigi. He'd been out of town the week before, and she wanted to tell him about her resignation herself, before anyone else had the chance.

She called the Candace Evans number and after an interminable number of rings—it was *very* early—the call was picked up and she was transferred. The sales crew must be in early again, which meant their appointment schedule was still jammed.

Maxie heard Luigi's heavy Italian "hello" on the other end of the wire, and almost lost it.

"Oh, I'm so glad to catch you."

"Maxie? You sick? No come work today?"

"Actually, that's why I'm calling . . ."

"Why? I no follow you."

Maxie told him she'd resigned.

He seemed surprised, then said, "Well, I'm gonna miss you. You always help me. You know Candace she don't like to follow up, but you always took the time. It's not gonna be the same here without you. I have to say, no matter how many times I think it be better you leave, I never want you go."

Then the phone started ringing with new job offers. Obviously the news had spread fast, and it seemed that Mona had given out her home telephone number.

Some of the callers were Candace Evans's direct competition. Others were lower-end people who wanted to rip off sophisticated designer styles at cheaper prices. Maxie listened to them all. The one thing she had learned in her years in the business was that it never hurt to go on an interview. At the very least she could pick the brains of the interviewer and possibly learn something new. Who knew? Anything could happen.

So Maxie scheduled meetings for the next two weeks.

Jason arrived at the showroom ready to work. Today was the day he would start all the new projects he and Candace had discussed. First, he wanted to write an announcement—a combination company memo and a press release—that Candace Evans was now solely owned by Candace and himself.

He dictated a brief memo that said Andrew was moving on to other personal projects and that Candace and he would be sole owners by fall. There would be continuity of all financial arrangements so the change would be virtually unnoticeable except of course, they would all miss Andrew. He concluded by saying that Candace and he were looking forward to taking the company to new heights in the near future.

Jason tried to gauge Sarah's reaction to this news as she wrote it down, but her face was impassive. Sarah didn't like to seem gossipy in front of Jason, but as soon as she got back to her desk, she'd spread the news.

Next he wanted to see Pamela. He had to fire her, yes, but first there were still so many things he needed her to do.

Strike while the iron was hot, Candace had said. Well, finding and breaking in a new PR person at this critical juncture would be nuts. All the magazines were clamoring to take pictures and run articles, and they wanted them *now*. He needed Pamela for that. And as Candace had suggested, he wanted to push for more licensing agreements, another area of Pamela's expertise.

He would just make her understand that she had a job here as long as she behaved herself. Candace would have to understand, too, and get off his back. After all, the company should be their paramount concern right now.

Sarah was back, holding a large handful of messages. "Mr. Gold, Pamela still isn't around, so I took the liberty to go through her messages. I think we've got a problem here. Most of these are from last week—they're from all the stores and manufacturers that she'd borrowed accessories from, and apparently she never returned them. Everyone is threatening us."

"Let me see those." Jason flipped through the pile. "What do you mean we didn't return the stuff? What kind of shit is this?"

"From what I gather, it was all to go back last week, but Pamela wasn't here to organize it. So I guess it never got done."

"Goddamn it!" Jason slammed his fist on his desk top. "I told her to take last week off but it never occurred to me that she hadn't organized everything already. All right, what now? Does anyone know where the stuff is?"

"I believe it's all marked and bagged in Pamela's office. Probably we can just messenger it all back."

Jason waved his hand. "Okay, you handle it then. Don't bother me with the details, I've got a lot to do right now."

Sarah left, but was back ten minutes later.

"Mr. Gold?"

Jason looked up from the pile of papers on his desk, an exasperated look on his face.

"Some of these people are insisting that we pay them full price for the merchandise. Others want a rental fee. We're talking about almost twenty-five thousand dollars here."

"What? What do you mean, twenty-five thousand dollars? They've gotta be outa their minds!"

"Well, some of the shoes are three hundred dollars a pair and we did have eighteen models. Some of the bracelets are one-of-a-kind. It adds up pretty quickly."

"Let me see these figures." Jason scanned the page of numbers. "Get these schmucks on the phone for me and I'll deal with them myself."

He spent the rest of the morning chasing down all of the suppliers and working out compromises. The accessories were going to cost him eight thousand dollars. Not free, but at least not twenty-five thousand dollars, either.

Before he knew it the morning was gone and he hadn't had a chance to call the real estate broker about the Madison Avenue retail space. Now that would have to wait as well.

Jason headed out to Bill's. His lunch was with three of his oldest cronies in the business. They'd all started out together about the same time and had made and lost millions several times over in the decades they'd been at this game. Each was in a different aspect of the business—fabric, budget sportswear, and ladies' dresses—and Jason was meeting with them to see if they wanted to go in on some outside ventures with him.

Jason had some high-risk ideas, but he wasn't interested in sinking all of his hard-earned money into them. He figured a limited partnership would spread out the risk. These friends were all flush with cash right now. In the garment business, when you're hot, the money rolls in fast and furious, and when you're cold, you're bankrupt.

Now Jason pitched his ideas and got three definite maybes. At least the lunch wasn't a complete bust. He figured that if he could get one in quickly, the others would come on board that much easier. Jason was still thinking about which one to pitch to first when he arrived back at the showroom. Sarah was waiting for him.

"Mr. Gold, I'm awfully sorry but Luigi says he really must speak to you. He called all morning."

"Okay, okay, get him in here."

Luigi strode purposefully into Jason's office, unlike his usual nervous and quiet self.

"What's on your mind, Luigi?"

"Mr. Gold, we got a problem." Luigi leaned toward Jason's desk and splayed his hands on it. Chalk dust remained behind. "Today, I plan redo all fall patterns for production. Now, some I can do, and I already do that, but lot I no can do. They brand-new style, you see. What am I to do? Candace no here and no back all week, I hear. How I gonna keep the room busy? I no got enough."

"Now let me get this straight. You don't have enough work to do? Is that it?"

"Uh-huh."

Jason started tapping his desk with a pen. "What do you normally do at this time? 'Cause this is the first time I've ever heard you've got no work."

"Normally, I make photo samples for Pamela, but she not around. And I start production pattern, but no Candace and no Maxie here. I also do few things for the next line, but I got nothing. No one here. It sorta mess back there."

"Okay, I'll see what I can do. I appreciate your letting me know. Pamela will be in any time now and I'll have her get working right on it. And I'll speak to Candace, too, to see what you can do for fall. By tomorrow, you'll be swamped again. Just do what you can in the meantime."

"I wanna give you honest work for my money."

Jason smiled. "Well, I'm glad someone does. Thanks for letting me know."

Luigi left and Jason slammed his fist on his desk top. "Goddamn it! What the fuck is going on here!"

He got out his spread sheets and saw that this week alone would cost him ten thousand dollars if the pattern room sat idle. And that was ten thousand dollars of his profits.

Normally, Jason never heard about problems like these. Who knew how many more there were? It was only because this concerned Candace that Luigi had even come to Jason. What could she be thinking? How could she go off to Florida without once remembering her responsibilities to Luigi and his people?

No one understood that if one person sluffed off, the whole house of cards would come tumbling down. Jason decided that organizing the company would be his top priority, or there wouldn't be any company left.

Just then Pamela walked in, looking more rested and in control of herself than at show time. The jumpiness and jitteriness seemed to have disappeared, and she seemed more like her old self.

Jason decided to forget the accessory fiasco—after all, he was partly to blame. And there was still so much to be done.

"Well, Pamela, you're looking much better. Rested. I hope the week off did you some good?"

"Oh yes, I needed the rest." Pamela matched his businesslike demeanor. "Thanks for the time off. I apologize for the scene I made at the party. It was uncalled for, and I'm really embarrassed."

Jason waved his hand in the air. "Don't even think about it. We're just glad you're back and feeling better. We've got a lot ahead of us to do, so I'd like to get down to that."

"I've already lined up appointments with *Vogue, The New York Times, Elle,* and other regional papers for this week to show them the line again. Everyone is super excited. They'll want to interview Candace as soon as possible."

"Good. She'll be back next week."

"Next week? You mean she's not here?"

"Right. She's down at the spa in Florida."

"Oh, God! How could she be away? All the press is clamoring to meet with her!"

"Well, they'll just have to clamor a little while longer, won't they?"

Pamela's foot jiggled rapidly.

"Don't get me wrong," Jason went on, "I'm not dismissing the importance of having the press on our side, but there's been many a time when we've had to wait for them. So now the shoe's on the other foot."

Pamela noticed her foot's movements and shifted in her seat. "But I've worked so long and hard cultivating all of these people! And look at how *Women's Wear's* paid off. I just hate to lose the momentum."

"Well, so do I, believe me, but we can't do anything about it now." Jason took a deep breath. "So can we move on? We've got a lot to discuss today."

They spent the next ten minutes on licensing possibilities and plans to get Luigi more work. Then Jason stood up, their meeting over. "That's all for now. Glad to see you're feeling better, Pamela. You had us all worried there for a while. We need you in good shape here at Candace Evans so don't let yourself get so strung out next time."

"Yes, it was stupid. Thanks for your vote of confidence. I won't disappoint you again." Pamela breezed out of Jason's office, her face a study of calm and confidence.

Pamela closed her office door and fell back against it. Her mouth started to quiver. Her eyes filled with tears and she began to weep.

That goddamn bastard! Sure, let that bitch go off to her spa and fuck off for a week while I hold down the fort here. And I should try to stay calm? Bullshit! He didn't even say if he ever wants to see me again. If he really thinks I care about this goddamn company he's the one who's crazy, not me.

Pamela needed a fix. In fact, she was coming apart. She was crashing and needed another hit soon.

She couldn't go back to Charles anymore because he might tell Jason. She would just have to go outside the company, that's all. Everyone had to think she was clean.

Where could she get more coke? Think . . . think. She started going through her Rolodex, her hands still shaking. Maybe a name would leap out at her that would lead to some coke.

This past week, Pamela had not spent her time resting and relaxing at all. She'd toyed briefly with the idea of flying out to visit her family in Wisconsin, but she'd quickly nixed that idea. They'd take one look at her and know something was terribly wrong. They'd heard nothing but horror stories about New York and she didn't want to prove them right.

She kept flipping through her file to see if any of her "friends" would be able to help her now.

In the quickly changing art and fashion scene, drugs proliferated, boosting the highs and buffering the lows. Pamela had hurled herself into this world and loved every second of it.

But she couldn't control her recreational drug usage the way the others did. Whatever they did, she did more. And when Jason suggested they indulge in it, she went overboard. If he gave it his blessing, then she had permission. Of course, the difference was that she couldn't stop.

Pamela had spent the past week holed up in her apartment. She watched TV, paced the floors, listened to music, and snorted coke round the clock. Alone. She pulled herself together only when she needed more—a party here and there just to score. Other than that, she'd seen no one and spoken to no one. In fact, it had taken an incredible amount of energy this morning to pull herself together and make it to the office. That was why she was so late.

All week she'd plotted her new strategy against Jason. She was not ready to give him up, and the drugs reinforced her obsession. She'd fight for him.

She would be subtle. No more begging. She'd be cool and calm, unemotional. Just like she was today. He acted businesslike, fine. So would she. She would take her cues from him. He would get aroused by her aloofness, she knew he would. And he'd be back.

She drummed her fingers on her desk incessantly and continued to flip through her Rolodex. She wanted someone who could get her a large amount, not just a gram or two. Finally, she found two candidates.

She wiped her nose, then tried the first number, a photographer friend. He answered somewhat sleepily, even though it was already after noon. She sounded as composed as she could, and asked if he could get about half an ounce for her—for a friend's party, she said. Bill said he'd get back to her right away.

Ten minutes later he called Pamela back from a pay phone—he never did drug deals on his own phone—and they agreed on a price.

Pamela took several deep breaths, wiped her eyes and nose again, and walked out. She had to get to her bank and withdraw money. Then to Bill's and back in an hour and a half for her next scheduled appointment. It would be possible if there wasn't a long line at the bank. But she wasn't going to worry about that now.

All that mattered was getting what she needed. Everything else could wait.

Twenty

JASON WAS STILL plowing through paperwork when Larry came in, a big smile on his face.

"What are you so happy about?" Jason said.

"I've just checked out a few key orders and they're more than double last year's buy. It's unbelievable!"

"Let me see." Jason grabbed the papers from Larry's hands. A huge smile spread across his face, too. "Fabulous. Larry, my man, you have just earned yourself the biggest bonus you've ever had. What's the catch?"

"Well, yeah, there *is* a catch. Ain't it a bitch? It's always something." Larry shook his head.

"Always has been, always will. I knew it was too good to be true. What do they want?"

"Well . . . of course the stores feel solid about the line and want to go after it in a big way to show it properly."

"Now that's the first smart thing I've ever heard those bastards say."

"But—and here's the catch—they want some sort of guarantee from us."

"Guarantee? Since when is anything in this world guaranteed? If they want guarantees, they should be in the food business. People always have to eat." Jason held up his hands. "So what kind of guarantee are you promising them?"

"Believe me, I've been fighting this with all of them. They're willing to take full responsibility—within the usual guidelines, of course—up to twenty-five percent above last year's levels. That alone is fantastic! And a lot more than we ever dared hope for. But the rest they want on consignment."

"Consignment? They've got to be kidding!"

Consignment was the way some high-volume manufacturers and one-of-a-kind designers operated with the
stores. Whatever the store couldn't sell at the agreed-to
bottom price would then be returned to the manufacturer.
Candace Evans—not the store—would be stuck with the
inventory, a disaster if a lot of the merchandise came
back. The stores figured the jump in volume would be
a fair trade-off.

"I've been back and forth with them since last week,
and that's the only way they'll go for these numbers."

"If only they had just agreed to a fifty percent increase
with the usual conditions, I wouldn't even consider this
proposal. But, I'll think about it. If we don't agree to the
consignment deal, then what's the magic number we'll
hit for fall?"

"I'd say twenty million, easily."

"You feel confident with that number?"

"No problem."

"How should we buy it?"

"I've been looking at the trends so far and I've worked
up a budget based on that."

"Good." Jason put his hand up. "Hold that thought.
Let's get Vince in here right now. We might as well
do it all at once. That way he'll know what we need
for piece goods and production space before we go off
half-cocked."

Candace finally called while they were waiting for
Vince. Jason signaled for Larry to step outside for a
moment.

"I got a message that you called," Candace said. "Is
anything wrong?"

"Last I heard, you were planning to pull your full
weight in this partnership of ours. You've sure got a
helluva way of showing it!"

"What are you talking about?"

"Luigi came back today and he's sitting here with his
thumb up his ass."

"What?"

"You can't just think of yourself, Candace. People

depend on you for guidance and leadership. How can we plan any long-range goals if you fall flat on your present duties?"

"Jason, just what are you talking about?"

Jason swiveled his chair so that he was facing the window. "Luigi needs to be told what patterns to put through his room. He wanted to start working on fall production, but he doesn't know which he can do. So here he is, stuck."

"Oh, Maxie used to handle all of that—"

"Well, Maxie ain't here anymore. Did you forget?"

"No—"

"Now you've got her responsibilities as well. You'd better get that into your head and switch into high gear with this part of your job. Is that clear?"

"Fine, Jason. I'll take care of it."

"It's not that simple. Do you realize that your forgetfulness has cost us not only the few thousand dollars you're spending at the spa, but also ten thousand dollars by not having organized Luigi before you left?"

"Do you want me to come back? I'll fly right back. Really, I will. I'm truly sorry."

"No, no, just stay there. I'll get Luigi's room set up myself. You stay and have a good time. Don't worry about a thing. I'll just add this to the millions of other things I've already got to do."

"Oh—well, great. Thanks a lot."

"And have a good time."

"Oh, Jason, I'll be better at these things in the future. I promise."

"Right. Listen, got to go. Bye." Jason hadn't mentioned that Pamela was back and would be giving Luigi plenty of work soon enough.

He took several deep breaths to control his frustration. Maybe taking over this company without Andrew or Maxie here was really too much for him alone. And now he would have to keep an eye on Candace, too.

Larry and Vince waited outside Jason's office door.

"How 'bout Andrew and Jason?" Vince said.

"Yeah, it took me by surprise." Larry said.

"You, too?"

Larry nodded. "Only last week Jason told me not to talk to anyone in the company—even Andrew—about buyer reaction to fall. Now I know why. He probably didn't want Andrew to know how great we're doing."

"Naah. Andrew's no dummy. We don't know when they actually settled on everything. Maybe it was a while ago and they didn't want to say anything until the line opened, or maybe Andrew took fall's increases into account. We don't know. In any case—"

"Yeah, in any case, it doesn't matter, if all the financing remains intact."

"I would assume so—"

Just then Jason's door opened and Sarah motioned them in. They took seats opposite his big desk.

Jason rubbed his hands together. "Vince, did Larry update you on the fall projections?"

Vince shook his head.

"Then I'll give you a quick rundown. Larry thinks we're gonna do twenty-five million, but we're buying now for twenty million. We'll decide in a couple of weeks if we're gonna chase the balance."

"What? Hedging your bets?"

"You could say that. If we went for the rest, it'd be on consignment."

Vince whistled. "Whoo boy. Consignment, huh? That could hurt."

"You're telling me. They're tempting me by such big increases, but I'm scared if the shit doesn't sell."

"Let's see how the buy breaks down," Vince said.

Jason got up. "Why don't we do this at the conference table and Larry can then give us the breakdowns."

The meeting went quickly. Jason reviewed each item with Larry, checking the buy quantity compared to the trend that item was charting to date.

"Well, what do you think?" Jason said to Vince. "See any problems?" Jason tilted his chair back.

"Only a time problem. I hope I can get all the additional piece goods in time to make August garment delivery. All of these are specially designed for us and not stock items. It's already almost the end of April, so delivery could be tight."

Jason waved his hand in the air. "We have this problem every season, but I see no way around it. We don't want to buy wrong by buying early."

"I know, I know."

"Anything else?" Jason said.

Vince smiled. "Actually, with these increases I'll finally be able to give some decent production runs to my factories here. And finding more production space is always easier than cancelling orders. The only problem will be the gabardine—the quantities are so big."

"The gabardine and silk group is the focus of the whole line," Larry said. "Without it, we're dead."

Vince groaned.

Jason looked over to Larry. "Can you believe this? He always complains that our dinky little quantities kill his factories and no one wants our orders. Now he's got the quantities, and still no one wants our orders."

"You don't understand," Vince said. "Sometimes gabardine is such a pain in the ass to manufacture, the factory would rather not have the business."

"Well, just remember, quality has got to be A-number-one."

Vince let out a big sigh. "Don't worry. I'll just plan it really carefully." Vince looked at the orders again. "As far as the overseas production is concerned, I'll telex our people in the Orient and get back to you. Sweater production is very tight. Almost all the actual knitting is done in China now. And these days with the political instability there, we might not be able to get reorders."

"Well, do your best and let us know."

"My final thought is that with so much of the business in the gab and silk group, I'd sit tight and maybe not chase the consignment business. I'd hate to see you stuck holding the bag."

"I'll keep that in mind when I make my final decision."

Vince walked back to his office, shaking his head in despair. Why couldn't he be chasing the wool group instead of the gabardine and silk one?

He called Shoji to come over by six o'clock to discuss potential reorders. Shoji wasn't the type to leave his office at five, and he'd be more than happy to come by for any reorder business.

Most of the New York reps of the European mills were long gone by five o'clock, so Vince would telex the reorders directly to the mills. That way, the mills in Europe would have the orders in their hands first thing tomorrow.

Slowly and methodically, Vince added up each item, careful to make no mistakes. He was astounded by the quantities. An error in either direction would spell disaster. Either Candace Evans would own excess piece goods or be too short to complete their orders. Vince knew how important this menial task was. For just that reason, he chose to do it himself, rather than delegate it.

By the end of this exercise, he figured they'd need a total of almost three-and-a-half million dollars' worth of fabric, not an insignificant quantity. Shoji arrived and Vince gave him the total revised order. Even Shoji seemed impressed by the quantity. That kind of yardage was usually given by bridge lines or lower-priced houses, not a designer house. And the piece goods were top of the line, too. This was not an order to sneeze at.

Then Vince wrote every telex to every mill in Europe. Even though it was already rather late, the company telex operator was still hard at work and was able to send them all out right away. Finally, Vince had done all he could that night for the company, so he headed for the elevators and home.

Pamela had been hard at work for hours since her rendezvous with Bill. Late into the evening, buoyed by occasional jolts of coke, she was still catching up on all of her messages and setting up press appointments.

The feedback she was getting was astounding. Magazine editors were committing to two-page spreads or more for fall issues without even personally eyeballing the line. She had never seen things jumping like this before. Normally she had to twist someone's arm to just come back up to the showroom and see the line again, but now they wanted those samples rushed over to them for their review and consideration.

Finally, Pamela was able to wrap things up for the night. She peeked out her office door to see if anyone was around. No one seemed to be; even the cleaning service was already gone. She stealthily made her way toward Jason's office.

Her heart was pounding against her chest and her stomach was doing somersaults as she came closer to Jason's office. Finally, she reached it and walked in and over to his desk. Somehow it seemed even bigger to her than usual. For a second, she stood immobilized, listening for even the smallest sound. Nothing. She moved her eyes and hands to the many drawers of his desk, opening and closing each one, carefully flipping through the papers and objects she found in them.

Pamela knew Jason kept a spare key to his apartment somewhere in his desk. She wanted to make herself a copy. One never knew when it might come in handy. She continued, sweat crossing her brow, her nervousness growing. She paused to wipe her forehead with her sleeve and again stopped to listen intently. Nothing.

She resumed the hunt. Only the bottom right drawer was left. Below the Pendaflex files, in the empty space of the drawer, she found the key. Triumphantly, she clutched it in her clammy hand. She ran out of his office, straight for the ladies' room. She stood there, shaking uncontrollably, heart pounding.

She had to get herself under control. She took several deep breaths and then once she felt better, she went back to her office and gathered up her belongings. She needed to find an all-night locksmith in the area to make a copy of the key. Then she'd return it early the next morning before Jason could discover it was missing.

Pamela paced back and forth, jabbing the elevator button every few seconds. She kept thinking she heard someone. The cocaine was working overtime, making her paranoid.

Finally, the elevator arrived. She checked inside to see if it was safe, then pushed the first floor button.

This part of town was not an area to wander around late at night, but Pamela wasn't thinking about that. She finally found a locksmith and had the copy made. Then she was undecided—should she return to the office now or come back early the next morning?

She realized she would be too nervous to sleep; the key would probably stare at her all night. So she decided to go right back to the office.

Luckily, she met no one on the way back to 550 Seventh Avenue. She opened the outside gates to the Candace Evans floor and raced to Jason's office. She paused yet again to listen. Nothing. So she moved quickly to his desk and put the key back where she'd found it, then left his office for the second time that evening. She was relieved that she had obtained the key successfully and began whistling.

And almost crashed into the telex operator.

"Jesus!" Pamela said. "I didn't think anyone was still here."

"Neither did I. You scared me to death!"

Pamela ran her hand through her hair nervously. "Oh, I was putting a note on Mr. Gold's desk and then I was just leaving. I've had so much to catch up on since I was out all of last week. You know how crazy it can get when you've missed a day, let alone a whole week . . ."

"Yeah, sure. Relax." The telex operator reached out to pat Pamela's shoulder, but Pamela jumped back.

"Hey—easy, easy. It's only me. Are you okay? You seem so . . . so—"

"No, no. I'm fine, honest." Pamela tried to smile.

"You just startled me, that's all."

"Look, I'll go push the elevator button. Why don't you turn on the burglar alarm?"

"Sure, whatever you say. I'll be right back. But don't leave without me."

Twenty-One

JASON HEADED UPTOWN to his suite at the Mayfair Regent. After the kind of day he'd had at the office, plus the frustrations of pitching his limited partnerships at lunch *and* cocktails, he needed a quick dose of Tina.

He unlocked the door to the suite and pushed it open. Tina stood in front of the living room window, her straight blonde hair cascading down over her ivory satin robe. She turned toward him with a welcoming smile.

Jason crossed to her in a flash and grabbed her roughly. He smothered her face with kisses.

Tina pulled away and giggled. "Slow down, Tiger. We've got all night."

She moved to the bar area and said over her shoulder, "Do you want the usual?"

"Sure." Jason collapsed into the plush sofa and leaned his head back.

Tina handed Jason's drink to him along with a greeting card.

"Open it!" she said. "You sounded so frazzled on the phone this afternoon, I wanted to perk you up."

Jason opened the card and chuckled. It was a sketch of a man sinking under the weight of a dozen people partying on top of him and said, "To life's little pleasures . . ."

"Thanks, honey. I needed that."

Tina sat down near him on the couch and then Jason leaned against her so she could massage and relax him. Small moans of pleasure escaped from Jason's lips.

"So what happened today that was so awful?" Tina said.

"Oh, I don't want to talk about it."

"Come on . . . tell me. You'll feel better."

"It's just so much bullshit. Everything's falling apart at the office lately and I'm the last to know. The specifics aren't important. What *is* important is how disorganized the place has become. It's gotten away from me, and now I've got to set it all straight again." Jason let out a sigh. "What a bitch!"

Tina tickled the back of his neck, easing the last bit of tension from him. "You'll make it fine again. I know you will."

"I will 'cause no one else can—particularly Candace."

"Well, then you will."

"The good news is that we really are gonna do a gangbuster business for fall and now I'm not afraid to say it. I've seen some of the paper. Unbelievable!"

"I figured it was true. Everyone's talking about it at the magazine."

"Can you imagine? A month ago I was pushing my sales staff to hold last year's volume, and now everything's changed. I'm on top again!"

Jason turned and pulled Tina to him. He moved his hands and lips hungrily all over her body.

But Tina resisted his demands and stood up. "Why don't we take a bath together? I've been dreaming about that tub for ages." And she moved away from him toward the bathroom.

This was a rather spectacular room of black marble, with a shower, steam attachment, and a jacuzzi. She turned the jacuzzi on and then turned around, almost bumping into Jason, who had brought an opened bottle of champagne and two glasses.

"I was just going to come and drag you in," Tina said. "But I see you've gotten into the swing of things!"

"I'm a step ahead of you." Jason handed her a filled glass. Her nose twitched from all the bubbles. "Shall we?"

Tina shook her head. "You go first. I want to put my hair up."

Jason stripped and slipped into the tub. He watched

Tina gather her hair atop her head, a few strands eluding the knot, undress, and then slide into the soothing warmth. Their bodies were completely immersed except for their heads and their hands holding the frosted champagne glasses.

"To us!" Jason said.

Tina clinked her glass with his.

They lazed in the tub for about half an hour, Jason refilling their glasses as needed. A Beethoven string quartet filtered through the suite. Jason hadn't felt this content and relaxed in a long time. And then he jumped. Something fluttered against him.

He looked at Tina, who wore a devilish grin. He smiled, too. "What're you doing?"

Her toes were slowly and methodically rubbing and circling his inner thighs. Jason reached over and grabbed Tina to him.

Water spilled out of the tub.

After they were sated, Jason continued to hold Tina close, the hot water swirling about them.

"God, Tina, you make me feel so good . . . But now you're gonna get your ass up and outa here—because we're going out on the town!" Jason squeezed Tina's wet bottom as she scrambled out of the tub.

He paused for a moment before he heaved himself out. What a perfect lover Tina was! A life of her own, a career. No problems, no excuses, no demands. This was a perfect arrangement for Jason.

What a mistake he'd made getting involved with Pamela. He should've recognized the signs long ago and ended it then, but he hadn't. And then it had just gotten out of control. But now, finally, Pamela seemed to be over him. The week off must have done her some good.

Pamela walked into her office at seven-thirty the next morning. She hadn't slept all night, but that didn't bother her in the least. Her breakfast was a Bloody Mary and a couple of Valium to quiet the shaking caused by all that coke. Fifteen minutes later she did a few lines of coke to counteract the grogginess caused by the Valium. To the untrained eye, she now looked in perfect balance.

Her early appointments with key magazine people were going very well. She had even gone over the list of samples she needed immediately with Luigi. Now she tried to focus on what the editor from *Vogue* was saying.

" . . . and actually, we want to do a whole article, not just a double spread."

"Really?"

"We always cover everything that's important. And, this season, Candace Evans is it!"

"Of course I'll do all I can to help with the article. Just let me know what you need and I'll get it to you."

"Thanks, Pamela. You always do. And we'll have to set up an interview with Candace."

"She's on vacation—can you imagine anyone taking off now, right in the middle of all this?"

"Well, when she comes back will be fine."

Pamela nodded and tried to finish up this meeting; her next appointment was due any minute.

Vince had to wait almost all day to get the responses he needed from the fabric suppliers. The answers weren't all favorable, and prices had increased noticeably. He had a tough fight ahead of him with the mills for better delivery dates and lower prices, but if he pushed like hell, he could get it done.

Vince knew enough about how these mills operated. They would push back the less important customers to give the needed space to Candace Evans. It was at times like this that Vince *loved* working on a hot line.

The week sped by for Maxie. Even without a job she didn't have a spare moment. Over the years, she'd put off so many things, and now she was finally making progress on her mental list.

First, she attacked her closets and shelves. She was going to make a clean sweep of her life, and that includ-

ed her closets. She was ruthless, tossing out anything she
hadn't worn in a year.

Next on her agenda were museums and galleries, many
of which she had never visited. She could linger in a
particular room with no thought of time, and allow her
mind to rediscover her original ideas about color and
shape. She formed the kernels of future design concepts,
to retrieve later on her sketch pads at home. Dozens of
ideas tumbled forth.

Maxie also had several job interviews. None seemed
really interesting, at least not yet. But it was important
to keep her name hot in the garment world—after all,
out of sight, out of mind. And Maxie was not ready to
be counted out yet.

One interview was to be the head assistant designer
for Joseph Long, one of Candace's direct competitors.
She'd met Joseph socially many times. He was another
older designer whose star was waning. The stories that
had always circulated about him were that his herd of
young male designers served him in many ways, only
one of which was in a business capacity. At Joseph
Long's, clothing wasn't the only objective. Maxie wanted
no part of that situation. She'd agreed to meet with him
only as a courtesy, but by the end of their meeting, they
both knew she wouldn't fit into the setup there.

Another interview was with Michael Lipmann, chairman of the board of Clothco, which was the largest
apparel corporation in America. It had ten different divisions making ladies' sportswear and dresses in all price
ranges. Michael wanted to see if Maxie would fit into
his organization as head designer overseeing all of the
divisions. Her title would be corporate vice president,
with all the perks that went with it.

It would be a huge job and could make Maxie a very
powerful force in the business. But she wasn't sure. Was
being in such a large company right for her? What if
all her innovative ideas had to be sold to a committee
before they could be implemented? How could you cre-
ate fashion there? Ideas would get bogged down in the

bureaucracy until they were out of date.

Besides, Maxie had been unemployed for only one week. She wasn't ready to abandon the dream of starting her own company. She did agree to meet Michael again the next week to continue their discussions.

The Clothco interview was important for Maxie's self-esteem, but she didn't believe she was ready for another job yet.

As the news of her resignation got around, all her friends were calling to get together and find out how she was. These people had shared her Candace Evans horror stories for years; now they wanted all the gossip.

So Maxie committed herself to dinner with someone else every night. While she wasn't avoiding Steve intentionally, she didn't actually have time for him. She managed to keep in touch with him daily by telephone. He was still busy with the Makiyama deal and all the other projects that had been put on hold during the takeover. Still, she could hear the disappointment in his voice when she told him she had plans every night of the week, so she promised him the entire weekend.

Jason had finally contacted the real estate broker for the Madison Avenue store and they were haggling over the final terms of the lease. He was getting frustrated by how long it was taking. After all, he had a meeting with his bankers—his first without Andrew—on the following Monday. Not only would he have to sell them on the increased fall budget, he also wanted their approval for the store. He would need a new loan to finance that operation, and he wanted all the details wrapped up before then.

Jason called Jose Alvarez to his office. He took a seat in front of Jason and then continuously shifted to and fro.

"Would you cut that out, Jose. You're making me crazy!"

"Sorry. I'm just trying to get comfortable."

"Well, *you* picked out these chairs—"

"Yes, well—"

Jason signaled for no more interruptions. "Look, I wanted to review the store concept once more. I'm going to need a formal written proposal on it with your anticipated budget."

"Okay."

Jason stared him right in the eye. "By Friday."

"Friday? That's impossible!" Jose flayed his arms.

"Impossible? Nothing's impossible. Now let's begin."

Jose readjusted his suit jacket one more time, sat up straight, and pulled out his rough sketches. They reviewed the general feeling once more.

"Your ideas look great." Jason then looked straight at Jose as he continued. "But I mean it, Jose. If you take this project on, it better be on time and on budget. We cannot afford for you to go off half-cocked and screw up the budget and the timing. I won't have it. This store must open on a certain date or we might as well not open at all. Is that clear?"

"Yes."

"Do you think you can handle that?"

Jose let out a sigh. "Really, Jason. I am not a child. I am a professional."

Jason chuckled. "Sure you are. Then talking as a professional, you screw this up and you're history. Remember, aesthetics are one thing, but reality and practicality have to remain uppermost in your mind. By Friday I want—in my hands—a written proposal with numbers you know are attainable."

"This is really too rushed for the way I like to work."

"This is business, Jose. Are you in or out?"

Jose tossed his head back. "I'll do it, but for *Candace's* sake only. I know how much this store means to her and I promised her I'd see it through." Jose looked straight at Jason. "For Candace only."

Jason waved him off. "Fine, fine. Whatever your reasons, just so the plans are here on Friday. See you then."

"Hmmph." Jose stood up and stalked out of the office.

At least the store was off the ground. Now Jason could move on to his more pressing problems.

Luigi was working full steam ahead on Pamela's samples, so he was taken care of. And their production fit model was booked for Monday morning, so Candace could proceed.

Vince had promised to give Jason a revised cash flow plan by Friday, since their monthly Letters of Credit requirements would now have to be increased. Jason decided to have Maurice at that meeting, as well. If Maurice was to emerge as the new CFO, Jason had to give him a chance.

Finally, after a hectic start, the week was falling into place.

Just then Jason got a phone call from the agent of the young playwright whose play he had optioned. The terms of the option gave Jason only one more month to disclose his financial plan and production schedule for the play—or he'd lose it. The playwright was pushing to get his work developed, and other parties were interested if Jason couldn't meet the deadline.

Jason and Marcus Putnam, the playwright, had the same dreams for the play—produce it off-Broadway, then take it on to Broadway, and finally make a movie of it. But where was Jason going to get the million dollars he would need?

He would have to make one last push with his friends to get the money together quickly. He would set up meetings for the rest of this week and into the next to see if there was money out there. If not, he would think of some other way. He was going to get his dream, too. No matter what.

Twenty-Two

CANDACE FELT COMPLETELY relaxed after only four days of pampering. She was awakened early each morning for a nature walk, followed by daily facials, massages, whirlpools, and exercise classes. She could already see a difference in herself. She had more energy than she could remember having in years. Her body appeared firmer, and her skin seemed so much more youthful that she decided to put off her plans for a face lift. She would look terrific for all of the upcoming publicity shots.

Best of all were the other women at the spa—they seemed quite impressed to meet *the* Candace Evans. She felt like a celebrity instead of a has-been. And that, more than anything else, contributed immensely to her new vigor.

Candace called the design department toward the end of the day on Thursday to see how everyone was coming along. She hadn't actually spoken to anyone but Jason all week because she had been so caught up in the schedule at the spa.

Liz and Elliot said they had sketched all week, working on their concepts for resort. They told her they'd leave copies on her desk for her return. If she thought they were going in the wrong direction, she could always call them in Hong Kong to discuss it. They would be leaving Friday. Judy was putting the final touches on the resort fabrics, which would also be ready Monday.

Candace assumed that everything was okay, that there were no problems. In fact, she wouldn't have known which questions to ask to discover any potential disasters, anyhow. Then she switched over to talk to Jason who told her that Vince had finally been able to confirm the reorders and everything else with all of their suppliers. They'd be going for at least a twenty-million-dollar fall season. And Pamela had lined up quite a few interviews for her over the next few weeks.

"Pamela? What on earth is she still doing there?"

"Hold it, Candace. Let me explain—"

"I thought you were firing her! You promised! You said I wouldn't have to be embarrassed by her ever again. Didn't you? *Didn't* you?"

"You're right, of course, I did. But you don't know what's going on here!"

"What do you mean?"

"The showroom is still jammed! And the press is lined up at the door. If she was gone, who would work with them? The sales people are all tied up with buyers. We're getting offers for minimum two-page editorial spreads from everyone. Free publicity, Candace, free!"

"Well . . . that *is* good news. But why can't you get someone else to deal with them?"

"Look, they're used to working with her. If I let her go right now, they might get nervous. What if they pulled their coverage? I don't want to risk that, and I'm sure you don't either, right?"

"Well, no, no. But she makes me very uncomfortable."

"When you get back, you can pick her replacement. Then we'll get rid of her, simple as that."

Then Jason told her about the call from Marcus's agent about his option. The time was almost up and they wouldn't allow Jason to extend his option any longer. Other people were interested in putting together a package if he couldn't. Jason sounded upset—but what could she do about it?

That night Jason was meeting with Michael Lipmann, one of the friends who he'd lunched with at Bill's earlier in the week. Jason figured if he could get Michael to commit some money, the others would surely follow.

Now Charles picked Jason up in front of 550 Seventh and they headed downtown. As they pulled away, a figure that had been lurking in the corner of the building, near the deli, ran out and frantically tried to hail a cab.

Jason had agreed to meet Michael at their favorite southern Italian restaurant in Little Italy. They'd been going there together for years, and while it wasn't fancy dining, it was off the beaten track. They wanted to be sure their meal and discussion would go uninterrupted.

Once they'd ordered a bottle of wine, they studied the menu. Since Candace wasn't around, Jason was going to have it all—appetizer, pasta, and main course. And he would enjoy every bite.

Jason turned to Michael. "Well, what do you think? Can I count on you?"

Michael let a sigh escape. "I wish I could be more supportive right now, but things are still pretty tight."

"Tight? I've seen your financial reports—"

"Look, even though the business is finally back on track, we're sinking all of the profits back into the company to recapitalize after the mess of the past few years."

"But all I need is a measly hundred thou. Frankly, I'd hoped to bring in fewer guys with bigger wallets so that not as many people would be involved, but for you, I'd accept a hundred thousand."

"You know I'd love to be in. I'm sure this play will be a winner—but I just can't do it right now." Michael stared into his wineglass. "I'm sorry. After all these years, when we've always given each other our last nickels, I hate this. Maybe next time."

Jason waved off his apology and tried to cover his own disappointment. "Don't worry about it. I'll get it elsewhere. Now let's eat."

Finally, Jason stood, hoisted up his pants, and let out a huge groan. "I'm stuffed."

Michael laughed and they walked to the door together. "By the way," Michael said, "I met your Maxie Siegel this week."

"You met Maxie? Where?"

"Well, actually, I interviewed her. She's something! I was impressed."

"Yes, I'm just now discovering how talented she really is. I miss her already."

"How'd you let her get away?"

Jason paused a moment and stared out into the congestion on Mulberry Street. "You know sometimes when a person grows up right under your eyes, you miss it. She's been with us since she got out of school and I think she just wanted to break free from Candace and try things out on her own. I know where she's coming from, and I told her she could expand with us, but she was determined to go. And believe me, we're sorry she's gone. So what were you seeing her about?"

"We're thinking of putting all the design departments together under one roof, with one head designer. This way, Clothco would project one taste level, and we might be able to cut back on a lot of duplication of effort, too. I'm thinking of Maxie for that position. She has great taste and would give the company a fabulous look. What do you think?"

"She's good with people and very organized, which would be essential in that job. I'm just surprised she'd be willing to go with your level of merchandise. She's really too sophisticated for you, no matter how much you want to upgrade your customer. What does she say?"

"Actually, pretty much the same thing. She wasn't exactly thrilled by the idea, but she didn't say no either. I'm meeting her again next week. Who knows? Maybe I can talk her into it."

"Good luck. Let me know how it comes out."

They shook hands and were about to walk off when Michael said, "There's something else . . ."

"What?"

"I wanted to get you alone for a sec—"

"What's up?"

"I just thought you should know I've heard a lot of disturbing rumors about you and the company recently."

"Rumors? What kind of rumors?"

"Oh, this and that." Michael looked directly at Jason. "You're okay, aren't you?"

"Of *course* I am!"

"Well, okay then."

Michael turned to his waiting limo. Jason stared after him a second before he proceeded to his own.

What was going on? First Andrew commented about stealing, then Tina got an anonymous note, then Joe from *Women's Wear* heard a Chapter 11 rumor, and now Michael says more rumors are circulating. Just when everything was finally falling into place. Jason shook off the uncomfortable feeling and headed for the car.

He slid into the backseat, then remembered Michael's refusal to join the partnership. He pounded his fist into the cushiony softness of the leather seats. "Damn it!"

Charles turned around. "You say something, Mr. G.?"

"No. Take me to the Mayfair Regent." Then Jason punched in Tina's home number on the car phone as they made their way slowly through the congested streets of Little Italy and Chinatown. He prayed she'd answer even though they had no plans for this evening.

In fact, Jason hadn't seen her since Monday. They had talked on Tuesday, but Jason had just been too damn busy all week. He let the phone ring and ring.

Finally, a breathless Tina answered.

"What're you doing now?" Jason said. "Busy?"

"No, I just got in. I ran all the way up the stairs when I heard the phone ring."

"How 'bout meeting for a drink?"

"Now? Isn't it kind of late? Besides, I'm already home. I don't want to schlepp all the way back uptown."

"I'm downtown, so why don't I just pick you up and we can go somewhere nearby? How does that sound?"

"I'm really not in the mood. I'm pooped—I just came from a truly boring party. But since you're down here already, why don't you stop by? We could have a drink—or whatever—here. Okay?"

"Great! See you in five minutes or so."

Tina's building was in the middle of a peaceful Greenwich Village block with a huge maple tree on the sidewalk outside. Jason looked around the unfamiliar neighborhood and felt as though he had found a quiet, peaceful oasis in New York City. He dismissed Charles for the night.

A cab stopped halfway down the block and someone got out just as Jason disappeared into Tina's Federal-style brownstone.

He slowly climbed up the three flights of stairs to her apartment. At last, slightly out of breath, he reached her open door where she was leaning against the frame. She looked terrific in a striking body-hugging suit in black and white, her long blonde hair framing her face. As always, Jason was excited just at the sight of her.

With more jealousy than he intended to show, Jason said, "Where were you tonight so dolled up?"

"Oh, come on. I told you, I was at a party. Boring, boring, boring. You know what I mean—a mandatory publication party, no exceptions. Terribly crowded, terribly boring. No one really talking to anyone else." Jason smiled at her description.

He was at her apartment for the first time, so he looked around. The place had high ceilings, a working fireplace, and the original detailing found only in older buildings. It was a rather small one bedroom, but the rent, Jason was sure, was steep. After all, in Manhattan people paid dearly for atmosphere and there was plenty of it here.

"So what brings you down to my neck of the woods?" Tina said.

"I had a business meeting down in Little Italy."

"In Little Italy?"

"Yes, with an old friend. But he couldn't help me, so I got feeling sorry for myself. Actually, mostly frustrated. I was riding along wondering how best to get rid of it, and voilà, here I am."

Tina fixed them each a drink while Jason paced. Then she beckoned him to the couch. Tina swung his legs up

onto her lap and began massaging each foot. "Relax,"
she said. "Tell me all about it."

Jason rambled on for some time. Her voice and her
hands relaxed him.

Late in the night, after many drinks and many more
words, Jason fell asleep, thoroughly exhausted, but
relieved.

Tina roused him long enough to undress him and drag
him with difficulty into the bedroom, where he fell onto
the bed and passed out.

All week Pamela had been spying on Jason. She'd
gotten hardly any sleep, at most a couple of hours a
night. And the week before she had barely slept either.
Plus she wasn't eating. All she could think about was
getting Jason to come back to her. As the week wore
on, she saw she was getting nowhere.

By Thursday, at her wit's end, she realized there must
be someone else in Jason's life, since Candace was out
of town. Pamela was sure there had to be someone else.
It was beyond her comprehension that Jason just didn't
want her any longer. Their affair couldn't be over. It
couldn't!

She followed Jason from work. As he got into his car
and headed downtown, she'd grabbed a cab and followed
him. In rush hour traffic it was almost impossible, but
her cab driver hadn't lost the car.

Then she had waited for hours across the street from
the restaurant. Charles never saw her as she hid in
the shadows. Hours later, Jason headed back uptown.
Pamela had found a cab with difficulty and had almost
lost Jason yet again when Charles turned around to go
back downtown. Then Jason entered a brownstone.

And didn't come out.

Twenty-Three

PAMELA WAS FURIOUS. All she could do was wait. Wait for Jason to come out again. But he never did, not all night.

Jason had never spent the night with her. Not once! Not ever! Not even when Candace had been away. In fact, they'd always met at the suite, never even at Pamela's apartment. And now Jason was not only visiting someone's apartment, they were spending the entire night together!

What Pamela felt now was more than simple jealousy. It was rage. It was uncontrollable and growing with every passing minute. All night she had paced and paced up and down the block, sitting on a stoop occasionally to do some more coke.

Now she was out of control. When Jason finally emerged at daybreak, Pamela almost ran down the street and attacked him right then and there. But just then a taxi came by, and he got in. She hid in the shadows again, but he never looked back. Calmer now—after all, he had to be heading home to change—she grabbed a cab and followed him back to his apartment building.

Pamela had been there many times, often working with both Candace and Jason late into the night. So now the doorman wasn't at all surprised to see Pamela at such an early hour. And when she said that she was with Mr. Gold, whom the doorman had just admitted, he didn't even bother to buzz her up. After all, she had been there before.

Pamela quickly let herself into the apartment with the duplicate key she'd made, then paused with her back to the door to listen. She heard the shower running and followed the sound down the hall. She peered inside the bathroom door, then backed off. She closed the bathroom door silently and waited.

Jason towel-dried himself vigorously and then walked naked from his bathroom toward his bedroom. Suddenly he was attacked from behind by a raving lunatic who was screaming incoherently and pummeling him relentlessly.

Even out of shape, Jason was still a strong man. But now he was fighting a maniac. Blow after blow landed to his stomach and groin areas.

He heaved with all his might and pushed his attacker across the floor, giving him just long enough to see who it was.

Actually this creature barely resembled Pamela. Her hair was a ratty mess. Her complexion was so yellow, it looked as though she hadn't seen sunlight for months. She had huge dark circles around her sunken eyes, and they darted around insanely.

"What the fuck are you doing?"

All Jason heard was an inhuman growl.

And then she was back on him. Jason tried with all his might to fling her aside, but she kept coming back for more. She didn't loosen her hold on him for a second. And in her eyes Jason could see the determination to kill him.

Frantic, he tried crawling over to the silent alarm system panic button. The crawl was interminable, but with one final burst of energy, he pulled away and punched the button just as Pamela lunged for him again. This time she was at his throat, choking him. And then blackness descended.

By the time the police broke down the door, he was unconscious. But Pamela was still mauling Jason's body. The police had to pry her off his inert form.

When Jason arrived at the hospital, the emergency trauma unit worked him over, checking for broken bones, contusions, and internal bleeding. While he'd be severely black-and-blue, and had some minor cuts and scratches that needed dressing, no other outward signs of his struggle existed. But his insides were badly battered. There was extensive internal bleeding, most damaging to his lungs. He needed to be on a respirator until they could stifle the flow of blood to them. Both his EKG and EEG were erratic, but they were gradually stabilizing.

Half an hour after his arrival at the emergency room, Jason recovered consciousness, but he was still very confused. He couldn't focus and didn't know who or where he was. The doctors pronounced him out of immediate danger, although still critical, and admitted him to the intensive care unit.

Pamela, in restraints, had been taken directly to the psychiatric ward. By now she had withdrawn completely from reality. Unable to speak or hear anyone, she was in a catatonic state, rocking back and forth, sighing and mumbling to herself. Her eyes were glazed over, and her hair was wild and unrestrained, emphasizing her look of insanity.

The doorman had accompanied Jason and Pamela to the hospital in one of the police cars so he could positively identify them. The police tried to contact their relatives, but that proved difficult for both of them. Pamela's neighbors knew nothing about her, and the same was true for Jason. Since Candace was away at the spa, the building had no idea how to find her. It was only when Charles arrived at their building at eight-thirty for Jason that they learned where they could reach Candace.

By now the apartment building was swarming with cops, not only in the apartment, but in the lobby as well. At least five police cars, lights flashing, were parked at the entrance. It looked like a big drug bust—not exactly what the residents of this exclusive Fifth Avenue apartment building usually saw. Most of them remained behind their locked doors, wishing to avoid the spectacle.

Meanwhile Charles rushed over to the hospital and stayed there with Jason.

*   *   *

Detective Third Grade John O'Reilly, though small in stature, had the body of a bull. He approached Charles in the intensive care waiting lounge, identified himself as the detective in charge of the case, sat down, and pulled out his note pad. He asked the questions and Charles told all he knew.

"Yes, Mr. G. and Pamela had an affair."

"Are you sure?"

"Hey, man." Charles pointed to his own chest. "I see everything. But it was over, and it *had* been for a good long time. I mean, I haven't picked that witch up at the Mayfair Regent in months. That's where Mr. Gold has a suite."

Detective O'Reilly didn't seem at all surprised. "Well, what do you think led Miss St. Clair to do this?"

"I can only guess . . ."

"Guess all you want. I'd be interested to hear."

"Well, Pamela's been pretty strung out for a while now. I mean, she's a mess. She even caused a big stink at the company party a couple of weeks ago—"

"Really?"

Charles described the party in all its detail. Finally he said, "I guess she had one too many hits of whatever it was made her do this, huh?"

Detective O'Reilly put away his note pad and stood up. "Guess so. Thanks for your time. We'll be in touch."

By this time, the company was in an uproar. Several police cars, lights still flashing, could be seen ten floors below at the entrance of 550 Seventh Avenue. People from every building on the street were rubbernecking from their windows or the sidewalk.

The police had cordoned off Pamela's and Jason's offices to search them thoroughly. In Pamela's, they found her cocaine stash—what was left of it. They planned to interview everyone in the company individually to see who knew what might have precipitated this event.

Under the circumstances it was impossible for Larry and his sales staff to try and sell the line with all the commotion, so he cancelled all appointments for the day and closed the showroom.

Sarah, the first to be interviewed, broke down halfway through. She had worked for Mr. Gold a long time, she told them. She was too concerned with his well-being to concentrate on their questions. Frankly, it was all she could do to arrange for Candace's flight back to New York.

Candace had just returned to her hotel room from breakfast when the phone rang. She grabbed it, thinking it was the spa calling to switch some of her day's appointments.

Candace had to take a big gold earring off to bring the phone closer. "I'm sorry, I didn't quite hear you. Could you repeat it?"

"I said this is Detective John O'Reilly of the New York City Police Department. Your husband has had an accident and he's in Lenox Hill Hospital."

Candace fell into the chair that was near the bedside desk. "Oh, my God! Jason?"

"Yes, Ms. Evans, but he's okay—"

"I've got to see him. Oh, my God, what can I do?"

"Ms. Evans?"

But Candace had hung up. She was having trouble breathing and her legs were trembling uncontrollably. Detective O'Reilly called the spa back and spoke to the director, informing him of what had happened and suggesting that perhaps Ms. Evans would need assistance.

By the time the director and the resident physician had arrived, Candace had pulled herself together, spoken to Sarah to book the next flight, and was throwing everything into her suitcases.

Throughout the long flight back to New York, Candace felt more and more guilty. All she could think about was how Jason had given her everything, and she'd given him nothing. No warmth, and certainly no happiness.

If he survived—and please God, he would—she desperately wanted and needed the chance to make it all up to him.

Charles met her at the airport and took her immediately to the hospital. She was so intent on seeing Jason that she pushed past all of the doctors and nurses in her path. And when she saw him lying there, hooked up to so many machines, her legs buckled beneath her. A nurse assisted her into a chair.

But Candace wouldn't allow herself to show any weakness. She would be strong for Jason now. She leaned over him and grasped his hand tightly, praying her presence would strengthen him.

His eyelids fluttered open and he almost smiled. Perhaps he knew Candace was now at his side. Then he slipped back into unconsciousness.

The doctors assured Candace that his brief awakening was a good sign, that his appearance—his face and neck already a deep purple color and swollen almost beyond recognition—was a lot more frightening than his actual condition. They were most concerned about his internal bleeding, particularly in the lungs, but they were confident Jason would recover completely. He would float in and out of consciousness for some time yet, but that was to be expected.

Candace stayed at Jason's side all day. If he should awaken, she wanted him to see her there.

Jason had always been her tower of strength. Now she would have to be his.

The showroom now had a carnival-like atmosphere. No one could work, as people were called one by one by the police to be interviewed. The phone never stopped its incessant ringing. The avalanche of calls was even greater than during market week.

As soon as the police were finished, Larry called a company meeting. He tried to allay people's fears and concerns, although he didn't know anymore than they did. Afterward, everyone was given the rest of the day off, with instructions to be back bright and early Monday morning.

Larry and Sarah had managed to hold the news media at bay to give Candace a break for a few days. Maybe by Monday Jason's condition would be a lot clearer.

Candace remained by Jason's bedside the entire weekend, going home only to shower and snatch a few hours of sleep. Actually, Candace was holding up beautifully. It was at times like this that her survival instincts—which had been so finely honed during the Soviet invasion of her homeland—came to the fore. She was able to carry on quite effectively, making rational decisions and plans. Her body and face still glowed from the four days at the spa. And this sudden attention brought out all of her hidden reserves.

It was this strength that Jason must have felt, because by Sunday night, he was demanding to go home. He was still extremely sore and bruised, but his internal bleeding had stopped, and his vital signs were back to normal.

Enough already. Jason had a business to run.

Twenty-Four

THE WESTERN CONNECTICUT inn was only a two-hour drive from Manhattan, but it seemed farther away in terms of atmosphere—it was very quaint and relaxed. Steve and Maxie had left the city at the crack of dawn on Friday to spend as much time as possible getting reacquainted. They stopped at anything that looked interesting along the way, and pulled up to the inn at about four o'clock.

It was in the middle of town but set back over several acres of pretty hills and gardens. The hedges were precisely clipped, the inn freshly painted white, the lawn recently mowed.

The owner led them to their room, which was full of English antiques and decorated in chintz and lace. Its centerpiece was a huge four-poster bed. When Maxie saw it, she broke out into giggles. Steve glared at her, as if to say, Control yourself until we're alone. Meanwhile the owner was showing them the sitting area with its small fireplace that could be lit upon request.

As soon as their host left them, Maxie headed straight for the bed and bounced up and down on it like a little kid. "Oh, Steve, how fabulous! A four-poster bed!"

"I *thought* you'd like it." He grabbed her and silenced her with a barrage of kisses. "I've missed you this week, Maxie Siegel. I really have."

They rolled around on the bed for a few minutes until there was a knock on the door. They scrambled off the bed as their afternoon tea arrived. Since they had absolutely nothing urgent on their agenda, they just sat back and relaxed.

Their room faced west and as the day settled into the

last flames of rose before dusk, they ordered up drinks and hors d'oeuvres.

The entire weekend was more of the same. They relaxed, talked, cuddled, and loved each other. They ate in the restaurant at the inn, walked around town, and explored the nearby lakes and woods. There was no rush, no pressure.

Finally, by late Sunday afternoon they headed back to the city. Steve looked over at Maxie and smiled. "I had such a great time this weekend."

Maxie covered Steve's hand on the stick shift. "Me, too, but now it's back to the real world."

"No—please—anything but that!"

"I'm serious, Steve. You've got to go back to work, and I've got to decide what I'm going to do with the rest of my life."

"Well, don't be afraid to use me as a sounding board. I'd love to help, if you'd let me."

"How can you help me? You're a lawyer and I'm a garmento."

"That doesn't matter. I want to be there for you, that's all." Steve glanced at Maxie, then turned his eyes back to the road.

She leaned back and smiled. "Thanks, that makes me feel really good." And she reached over and kissed him on the cheek.

Monday's banner headline in *Women's Wear* was about Jason. They reported that he was fighting for his life after a strangulation attempt by a disgruntled employee. The slant they gave their story was favorable to Jason and the Candace Evans company. After all, *Women's Wear* had promoted the new fall line vigorously, and they had their reputation to protect. Other New York dailies also ran front-page articles, and the wire services picked up the story. They all revealed that Pamela St. Clair had been a habitual drug user and was now in the hospital under psychiatric evaluation.

Candace was still in Jason's hospital room. No matter

how much he protested, his doctors insisted he stay for a few more days. Candace had brought newspapers from all over the country, and now they were strewn haphazardly across the bed. Jason was still not supposed to be reading anything as hard on his eyes as a newspaper, but he wanted to see what they had to say.

He was not a pretty sight. His bruises had changed from purple to varying shades of yellow and green, making him look even sicker than he was. His face was still swollen, and his lips were puffed out even more. His eyes were still slits, but at least the swelling there had begun to subside. Reading and even talking were difficult, but Jason didn't care.

He scanned the articles as quickly as he could. At last, weakened, he had to lay back and let the last paper slip through his fingers. Candace gave him a sip of water, then blotted up the dribbles that had escaped from his swollen mouth. He drifted back to sleep.

A little while later he awakened. He said, as though no time had passed, "Well, the articles don't seem too bad. Look at all the trouble I went to for all this free publicity. It sure has kept Candace Evans in the news."

"Oh, Jason, really."

"I betcha all of this is gonna be a big help."

"Don't be ridiculous!"

"No, really. The more our name is out there, the more customer recognition we'll have and then the more the buyers will feel obliged to carry the line. Good news, bad news, what's the difference?"

"If this is what we have to resort to to get on page one, then forget it! I just thank God you're alive."

Jason took hold of Candace's hand and tried to smile. "I love you, Candace."

Her eyes prickled with tears. "I love you, too, Jason Gold. I even made a vow to God that if only you'd get better, I'd make up to you for so many things. And I will, you'll see!" She squeezed Jason's hand tightly.

Just then the nurse came in to take Jason's blood pressure, and Candace was sent from the room.

*   *   *

Candace sat in the visitor's lounge for a long time, trying to read. Suddenly she looked up and saw two people, a couple. The man was tall and strong-looking, his face tanned and weathered as though he'd spent his entire life outdoors. He held a well-worn brown cowboy hat, which he shifted from hand to hand. The woman had gray, brittle hair pulled back into a bun. She wore a faded shirtwaist dress that had definitely seen better days.

"Ms. Evans?" The woman seemed hesitant.

"Yes?"

"I'm Pamela St. Clair's mother and this is her father." He nodded his head. "We're very sorry for what happened and hope Mr. Gold makes a speedy recovery."

"Thank you. And how is your daughter?"

"No change yet. We're thinking of taking her home— that is, when the doctors say it's okay." Mrs. St. Clair's eyes filled with tears. "They don't even know if she'll recover. This whole thing is such a mess. We can't believe our Pammy was capable of doing something like this."

Candace just stared up at them.

Mrs. St. Clair twisted the cotton handkerchief she held. "They told us we could find you here. We just wanted to let you know how truly sorry we are. I hope we haven't bothered you."

"No, no . . . not at all. Thank you for stopping by and I do hope Pamela gets better. Both Jason and I hope so."

Candace headed back to Jason's room. "You'll never believe who I just met!"

"Who?"

"Pamela's parents! Real country folk. They wanted to apologize for Pamela."

"That takes guts. It was very nice of them."

"Yes, it was." Candace made herself busy fluffing up Jason's pillows.

"Oh, cut it out, will you! You're making me feel like a sick old man. And I'm *not*." Jason hit the bed in anger. "I want out of here already!"

Candace really smiled for the first time all day. "Sorry to be the one to tell you, honey, but they're just not letting monsters wander the streets of New York today. With that face, you'd probably be arrested. Oh, speaking of arrest . . . the police want to know when you can make a more complete statement and if you'll be pressing charges against Pamela."

"Soon, soon—but I don't want to press charges. She needs a detox, not a prison."

"That's what I thought you'd say and you're right, of course. I'm very proud of you." Candace leaned down and pressed her lips lightly against Jason's still swollen mouth. "I'll let you rest now."

Sarah stopped by the hospital later that morning. She brought the paperwork Jason had insisted on having—the budget from Jose and the revised financial requirements that Vince had put together. She'd cancelled his meeting with the banks indefinitely. They would reschedule when they heard from him.

Jason thanked Sarah, but as soon as she left, everything fell from his hands. He couldn't concentrate at all. His head throbbed.

The atmosphere at Candace Evans was as chaotic as it had been Friday. The phones were ringing nonstop, and it was impossible to get any work done.

The sales force was calling accounts to push for their orders, but the buyers were only interested in the front-page story. Larry refused to close the showroom again. They would do whatever little work they could.

When Jason woke up again, Detective O'Reilly was there to take his statement. Jason reported everything he could remember, but was baffled how Pamela had gotten in. He was sure he had locked the door.

"We're sure you did, too," the detective said. "We found a duplicate key in Ms. St. Clair's handbag."

"Really?"

"There was a key to your apartment in your office desk. As near as we can figure—and of course we haven't spoken to her yet—we think she took it and made a copy of it."

Jason shook his head. "Jesus."

"It seems last Monday night your telex operator bumped into Ms. St. Clair coming out of your office. Apparently she was acting very suspiciously. Ties in with our theory. We found an all-night locksmith who remembered someone answering to Ms. St. Clair's description coming in late Monday night to have a key made."

"I can't believe—"

"That's not all."

"What do you mean?"

"Normally we wouldn't give out so much confidential material—but in your case we think you should be aware of the full extent of the danger you were in." Detective O'Reilly paced around Jason's bed, his hands behind his back. "When we were going through Ms. St. Clair's desk, we found a diary—and boy were there crazy things in it."

"Crazy?"

"Yeah, crazy. It seems she'd sent notes and made phone calls—all anonymous—to various associates of yours. We believe she was trying to cause trouble."

Tiny goosebumps broke out all over Jason's arms. Who would've thought Pamela was so sick?

"Now it's all beginning to make sense," Jason said.

"You knew about it?"

"Of course not, but a few people had mentioned they'd received some anonymous calls or letters. But why'd she do it?" Jason's head was really pounding now.

"It seems—from what the police psychiatrist can make of it—that she was obsessed with you. If she couldn't have you, then she wanted to destroy you."

For the first time, Jason realized how he flirted with danger every time he took up with a new woman. He'd always been totally upfront with them, letting them know that permanency with him was not in their future—but maybe that wasn't enough. How many women would be able to settle for a casual, fun, physical relationship with no potential?

Jason closed his eyes. He knew that this aspect of his life was over, but right now he couldn't deal with it. He couldn't deal with anything. His head still throbbed.

Twenty-Five

MONDAY MORNING, MAXIE was still glowing from her weekend with Steve. She lazily opened her copy of *Women's Wear* to read with her coffee. Then she saw the headline.

She dialed the showroom repeatedly, but the lines were busy. It was her only link to Jason and Pamela. Finally she got through to Mona who didn't have a whole lot to add, but she did know that Pamela's parents were taking her back to Wisconsin to recover. Since Jason still refused to press charges against her, the doctors had no choice. But they insisted on a few more days of observation before she would be permitted to leave.

Maxie had difficulty focusing on other things all week. The crisis at Candace Evans seemed such a contrast to her own aimless life right now. Maxie was a doer, and right now she wasn't doing anything. Sure, she had a few more job interviews, including the follow-up meeting with Michael Lipmann. But he didn't want to talk about the job any more than she did. They spoke mostly about Jason, then set up another meeting for the following week.

Toward the end of the week Steve got a call from Tanaka, who requested a meeting—just the two of them—for lunch.

Now they sat opposite each other at Il Nido.

"We've got only a few small details left to iron out on the deal and then it's done," Steve said. "You should be able to sign off on it by the middle of next week."

"Good. I'm most pleased by the whole transaction—as is Tokyo."

"I'm glad, Tanaka-san. Coming from you, that means a lot."

"I was most impressed by how you handled yourself. Everything you've ever done for us has been smooth. When you cautioned us against something, we avoided it and you were right. When you felt it was doable, it always paid off exactly as you said it would."

"Thanks." Steve knew Tanaka hadn't arranged this lunch just to compliment him. Tanaka had something important to say.

So Steve took a sip from his water glass and waited.

"What would you say to becoming Makiyama's chief counsel in the U.S.?" Tanaka said. "I think you've got a talent that we could really put to good use. We'd make you happy with us."

Steve held up both hands. "That's a fantastic offer, but—"

"Let me tell you exactly what I'm talking about—"

"Before you do, Tanaka-san, I think you should know that while I'm sure the offer is unbelievable, I can't possibly accept."

"Why not? Give me a chance to explain."

Steve waved Tanaka off. "No, let me. I've just moved here from San Francisco for my firm. I like my job and I really like the people—they're my partners and have treated me very well. So far, the work I've been getting has been diverse and very challenging." Steve looked directly at Tanaka. "While your offer is very flattering, at this point, I just can't accept. I hope you understand."

Tanaka let out a long sigh. "I do. And I respect you for it. Actually, it's how we Japanese would act, but I didn't expect to see it here. Not everyone in this country feels such loyalty to their partners. It's nice to see."

"Don't get me wrong, I want to make money as much as the next guy, but I'm being compensated well enough where I am."

"I think your actions are quite admirable."

Steve nodded his head in acknowledgment.

Tanaka said, "Let's forget we've even had this conversation and enjoy our meal."

When they rose to leave, Tanaka said, "And how is that friend of yours, Maxie Siegel?"

"Fine."

"I was very impressed by her. She's quite a woman."

"I agree one hundred percent."

"In fact, since that dinner of ours, I've had occasion to speak to quite a few people in the garment business. They've all spoken highly of her."

Again Steve wondered where this conversation was heading, and again kept silent.

"Well . . ." Tanaka said, "I was quite impressed with her. Please send her my regards."

"I will."

By now they had reached Tanaka's limousine. He turned to Steve and grasped his hand one last time. And continued to pump it. Why was Tanaka shaking his hand so long and not releasing it?

"Since you've turned down my job offer," Tanaka said with a sly smile on his face, "what would you say if I offered your firm the exclusive to handle all of Makiyama's outside legal work?"

Now Steve understood. Tanaka wasn't finished deal-making yet.

"What would I say?" Steve grinned. "I'd say we'd give you the best advice and service you could get anywhere. You wouldn't be disappointed, believe me!"

"I thought so. Well, Steve, you've got yourself a deal! And we've got you! You see, I just had to have you one way or another." Tanaka chuckled, then he slid into the backseat of his car.

Steve looked after the disappearing car. What a coup! All of Makiyama's outside legal work! Back at the office, Steve met with the managing partner as soon as possible. The news spread quickly throughout the firm, and in one afternoon, Steve's position rose several rungs on the corporate ladder.

That night he met Maxie for dinner at her apartment. He was so excited he couldn't wait to share the wonderful news with her.

"I *told* you that dinner we had with Tanaka was significant," she said.

"And you were right. God, you're so smart!"

"Oh, come off it."

"No, really—you guessed all his moves." Steve took a bite of the roast chicken Maxie had prepared. "This is delicious! By the way, we didn't just talk about me at lunch."

"Oh?"

"It seems I wasn't the only one Tanaka was impressed with that night."

"What do you mean?"

"He asked about you, and let it drop that he'd heard from other people in your business that you were highly regarded."

"So?"

"So, why would he have spoken about you to other people unless he had a reason?"

Maxie put down her knife and fork. "I see what you mean. What do you think he's up to?"

"I'm not sure yet, but my guess is he's thinking of bankrolling you in your own company."

"Oh, Steve, do you think so? That'd be fantastic!"

They speculated about that for a while, then spoke about a lot of things that evening, including the business with Jason and Pamela.

"I just can't believe Pamela could've done something like that," Maxie said.

"But you said she had a drug problem. If, as you say, she'd been taking all of those different drugs together, they can do crazy things to a person."

By this time they'd finished dinner. Maxie was curled up on the sofa, hugging a pillow to her chest. "I know, I know. But she was my friend. I should've seen the signs and helped her before she got this out of control. And I didn't."

"*No* one did. You can't beat yourself up. A person like that has deep-rooted problems. Anyway, she was a master at covering it up. You would never have seen it."

"But you forget, I've been this route before."

"With Martin?"

Maxie nodded. "I should've seen it coming." She hit the pillow hard. "I should've."

Steve moved over to the sofa and wrapped Maxie up in his protective arms.

"There's absolutely nothing you could've done," he said. "It's time to move on with your new life and not let this incident sideline you the way it has all week."

Maxie wiped her eyes and blew her nose. "You're right. Candace Evans has been my life for so long that even when it's not anymore, I still think it is."

Steve hugged her and they stayed that way for a while.

Two days later, on Sunday, Jason was released from the hospital. He was still black-and-blue—yellow and purple, actually—and his face was slightly swollen. He was still suffering from occasional dizzy spells and throbbing headaches. But he was determined to leave.

The doctors issued strict orders that he was not to go back to work for at least two more weeks and to only work at home for a little while each day. He was not to push himself.

Candace hired nurses to stay with him, but Jason fired them immediately. Their housekeeper and Candace would be enough. Too many people around made him even more cantankerous than usual.

Jason made repeated attempts that week to read the financial reports Vince and Maurice had prepared, but he just couldn't. Instead, he had Maurice come over to talk it through with him.

Maurice sat in the chair opposite Jason's in the library. His bulk dwarfed the chair. He was riffling through the papers, front to back, back to front.

"What's the answer, Maurice?"

"I'm looking for it, Jason. Give me a chance—"

"But *you* prepared the report. Shouldn't you know it in your head?"

"Here it is." Maurice shifted his weight and the chair legs squeaked in protest.

"Watch it, don't break the goddamn chair."

"See, this shows we need a large cash infusion by June to cover all the fabric orders that'll be ready to ship by then." He knocked over an empty coffee cup as he reached across to hand Jason the papers. "Sorry."

"Jesus, Maurice. Watch what you're doing." Jason grunted and then focused on the papers. "What kind of profit estimates do you show?"

"If all goes well—and that's a big if—we should make about three million on the year."

"Great!"

"But I'm sure this doesn't include what we owe the banks. They'll insist you partially pay down their loan. And you still need to talk to them about a loan for the store."

"I know, I know. But these numbers should eliminate any problem getting the additional credit line and loan."

"Seems like a sure thing to me."

"Okay, Maurice. That's it for now."

"Anytime Jason."

Later that day Jason also met with Larry about the incoming orders. They were coming in, but only sporadically, much slower than expected. But Larry was still confident he'd meet his targets.

Jason wanted more than promises. Right now, though, he just didn't have the energy to push Larry further. He knew he had to get back to the showroom to see for himself what was going on. But he couldn't even dress himself without getting so dizzy he had to lay back down again.

Jason had no choice but to rest, read, and sleep. The only pleasure he had was reading the get-well cards that poured in from friends and associates.

He received a note from Tina, written on the inside of a funny get-well card:

Just wanted to let you know I've been thinking about
you. Good friends are hard to come by.
So you get well, get strong.
If you have time when you get back on your
feet, we could always have a drink.
My best,

Tina.

Yes, Tina understood him. No pressure. They were
friends now—nothing more—and for that, Jason was
grateful.

Candace stopped by the office every day to dispense
with urgent problems as best she could. She held several
production fittings with Luigi but she was too distracted.
Luigi didn't understand the changes she wanted to make.
After each fitting he reviewed his notes and tried to
figure out what they'd done, but by the time he looked
up to ask a few questions, Candace was already somewhere else.

Judy showed Candace her resort fabric and color presentation. Again, Candace didn't seem to react. She made
a few minor changes, then nodded her head for Judy to
proceed. But Judy couldn't really do that. She had no
idea how much of each fabric to order for their duplicate
yardage, and there was no one else she could ask. Maxie
had always handled that before, and Liz and Elliot were
in Hong Kong. So Judy did the best she could—she
guessed—and ordered what she hoped would be enough.

Liz and Elliot called from Hong Kong and asked
Candace if she wanted them to return early. No, she
said, carry on. When she gave no feedback about their
sketches, they decided to continue as they were. No news
was good news.

Three weeks passed this way, with no one actually
running the company. Maurice knew something about
numbers—but not production, operations, or sales. Larry

and Vince handled their departments as effectively as they could, and Luigi carried on with his work. Meanwhile, little cracks were widening into bigger and bigger holes in the foundation of the company.

The trade papers and magazines still needed interviews scheduled and questions answered. Sarah handled as many of these as she could, but it was more than a full-time job. Candace held quite a few in-depth interviews and the sales force pitched in and reviewed the lines with the fashion magazine editors yet again. Their selections for their editorial pages would be final very soon.

Finally, Jason corralled Candace late one night. She'd been running on nervous energy for so many days that he hadn't been able to get her to sit still for five minutes.

"Jesus, Candace, could you stop fussing around for a minute and talk to me!"

Jason refused to wear pajamas and a robe after that first week in the hospital and had either Candace or the housekeeper help him dress. "I'm going nuts here—I feel so out of touch. I want to know everything that's happening at the office."

"But haven't you been seeing Maurice every day?"

"Yeah, but no offense, he doesn't have a handle on anything yet. You go to the office. *You* tell me how things are doing."

"Well, everything seems to be moving along. Of course, nothing is moving at the pace we were at right before or right after the show, but that's to be expected."

"What about the sales force? Are they fucking off?"

Candace crossed her legs. "No, I wouldn't say that. I think everyone is just back to a more realistic pace, that's all."

"Then where the hell are the orders?"

"Every time I've spoken to Larry, he seems confident we'll get them. And the sales people are hustling. I think the stores are just a little slow to recover after such a shock. And the sales force couldn't push for orders right afterward—that would've been really tacky."

"Tacky? Who cares?"

"Really, Jason, relax. Our line is going to book just as we planned. Remember, magazines are all gung ho, and no one is backing away from us. Really!"

Jason rubbed his hands together. "I just feel so out of it, stuck up here. I need to get back."

Candace reached over and patted Jason's hand. "You will, you will. You just can't rush it. The doctors told you to take things slowly at first. A day at a time. You know how close you came to dying . . ."

"I know. But on top of everything else, Marcus's agent called again today. The deadline on the option is up next week and I can't do anything about it."

"Oh—"

Jason slammed his fist down on the arm of his chair. "Shit! I've wanted this for so long!"

"What exactly do they need?"

"They want a financial disclosure showing how I'll produce the play."

"How much do you think you'll need?"

"About a million—to do it right."

"Well, of course you'll do it right. You always do." Candace looked at Jason. "Do we have that million?"

"Yeah, we have it. I just didn't want us to risk it all on something like this."

Candace reached out and took Jason's hand. "You believe so strongly in this, how much of a risk could it be? *Use* the money. That's what it's for."

"Do you really think I should?"

"Absolutely."

Jason was more excited than Candace could remember seeing him in a long time. He leaped out of his chair and tried to kiss her, but the suddenness of his movement made him terribly dizzy. Candace caught him as he fell sideways, then led him back to his bed.

Twenty-Six

CANDACE BOOKED A flight to Hong Kong to check on Liz and Elliot before they came home. She'd been feeling secretly uneasy about their work for some time— she hadn't quite understood all of their sketches, but wouldn't admit that to anyone. Maybe if she actually saw some samples, she'd understand where they were going. And then, if she still didn't like what she saw, they could make the changes right there, instead of waiting until they got back to New York. Then it would be too late.

She arranged for a friend to stay with Jason and their housekeeper. He'd never again allow a nurse to walk through their door. And she extracted a promise from him that he wouldn't go back to the office yet. She'd be gone a week, maybe less. When she returned they'd go to Vail for a final rest together before he went back to work.

Candace arrived in Hong Kong on a hot, sticky May evening. It had been raining steadily for almost two weeks.

The Regent Hotel's driver met her at the hotel pick-up area outside customs and drove her in the Bentley she'd requested, directly to the hotel. Everything about the Regent spelled luxury, quite a contrast to the crowded, squalid conditions of greater Hong Kong. But now, at night, all that was hidden away, and the glamour of the city beckoned. The lights from the vast office sky-scrapers on both sides of the harbor twinkled. Throngs of people milled about on the streets, shopping, chatting and being entertained. The energy level in Hong Kong rose just after the heat of the day ended. And it continued late into the night.

Candace strode into the palatial lobby with its three-story-high windows overlooking the harbor. The view was breathtaking—ferry boats transporting their passengers from the island to the mainland and back again, as well as the ever-present junks gliding by. She walked to the concierge desk made of burl wood, leather, and gleaming brass. The concierges wore black morning coats and white gloves. They were well-trained in the British style of hoteliering.

They recognized and remembered Candace, of course, and they had managed to keep her favorite suite free for her, in spite of their full occupancy rate right now. Looking around the lobby lounge, Candace didn't spot anyone she knew, so the concierge escorted her to her room.

There were flower arrangements on the coffee table as well as by the bed. Wall-to-wall windows faced that glorious harbor. Champagne was brought in, compliments of the hotel, as was a fruit basket, a tray of cookies, and chocolates and jasmine tea.

The bathroom was all marble with a separate stall shower and a deep, soaking tub. The towels were of the thickest terry and the soaps were all imported from England. Everything was available here, merely by ringing a bell.

Candace loved Hong Kong.

Elliot and Liz worked late that night at their agent's office, readying everything for Candace. Liz grabbed one more sweater sample from the pile on the table and compared it to their detailed spec sheet.

"Oh, God, this one's screwed up, too," she said. "What are we going to do, Elliot?"

"See what I mean? You thought I was kidding when I said they can still mess it up, even though we went over every last detail. Hand it over, maybe it's not so bad." Elliot took the sample from Liz's outstretched hand. "Oh God, it *is* that bad!"

He remeasured the sweater, tried in vain to stretch it in some places and shrink it in others. "They really blew it," he said. "And this was one of our best styles, too! I'm going to get Daisy in here to find out what the hell is going on!"

They spoke in urgent tones to Daisy, their agent. After all, they said, how could they show something like this to Candace? Eventually, Daisy got the message.

She was tiny but tough, and determined to get action. She rang up the factory right away. Even though it was almost nine o'clock, the factory people were still working. It was common for Hong Kong workers to stay late. Now the factory promised to remake a few key samples for Candace by the next day.

"Well, now I feel a *little* better," Liz said.

She spotted the next group of samples still folded and bagged, and started taking them out. She looked at them closely.

"Look at these, Elliot! I think I'm actually going to like them. And Candace hasn't even seen sketches of this group. Think she'll want us to expand on this idea?"

Elliot nodded. "Let's hope so."

Liz held them up to herself and looked in the mirror. "God, this wrap skirt looks so new, so right. I feel so sexy yet free in it. I hope Candace can see where we want to go with all of this."

"Me, too. Let's hang them all up on that wall over there so she'll see them first thing. That ought to excite her."

"Great idea! And then let's get something to eat. I'm starving!" Liz yanked the last few samples out of their bags and danced around, hugging them. "At least *something* came out right."

They walked back to the Regent from their agent's office, which was housed in one of the many new buildings in the ever-expanding Tsimshatsui East area of Kowloon. It was not far from the hotel, but with the bridges and tunnels—called walkways and flyovers—built so pedestrians could safely cross the busy streets, it took a while to get back. And the humidity was so high, even at night, they were dripping from just this brief exposure to the outside.

"Which restaurant tonight?" Liz said.

Elliot let out a big sigh. "I don't care. You pick."

"How 'bout the Steak House? I'm truly sick of Chinese food and I can't stand all those fancy French restaurants here anymore. I could go for just a salad or something."

"Fine with me."

They walked down to the Regent's lower lobby and went into the Steak House. Even this late, the restaurant was packed. They waved to a lot of other garment people—designers, buyers, production heads—who were working there as well. For several weeks a year the Regent turned into a mini Seventh Avenue.

"I just love it here," Liz said after they were seated. "Don't you?"

"Not as much as in the old days."

"Old days? Give me a break, Elliot, you haven't been coming here that long."

"Oh, five years or so."

"What's so different?"

"Well, Hong Kong seemed a lot more gay then." Elliot saw Liz's puzzled expression. "What I mean is that people partied at discos and bars until dawn. Drugs were everywhere—Thailand is so close, you know. And definitely a lot of bed-hopping. You met someone and wham, bam, into bed. I mean the Oriental boys were positively sublime, so smooth and silky. It was a fantasy come true. And now . . ."

"Now, what?"

"I think AIDS has calmed the whole scene down. The decadent side of Hong Kong is a lot harder to find now."

"Well, I think that's good."

Elliot shrugged. "Maybe you're right. Anyway, it sure is different."

"Well, we haven't exactly been idle since we got here. I've never been to so many discos on so many consecutive nights before. I'm exhausted."

"We've been working our tails off during the day, too. Usually I work like crazy the first week, and then just hang out at the pool, waiting for the samples to come back."

"We couldn't exactly do that this time. There hasn't been one sunny day since we got here."

"That's why we've made so many visits to the factories while waiting for the samples. I thought it'd be a treat."

"Thanks a lot. Those places are absolute rat holes."

"I know. Quite a contrast to this neighborhood, isn't it?" Elliot waved his hand around indicating the hotel.

"I'll say. Hey, I wonder if Candace got in okay. Should we call her?"

Elliot shook his head. "We'll see enough of her starting tomorrow."

Liz laughed. "You're right. Did you check out our schedule for the next few days? Every single night Candace is here different factory owners are hosting dinners for us. Christ!"

"I know. They always do that when the honchos come to town. Bo-ring!" Elliot let out a mock yawn.

Liz laughed again, then stood up. "I'm going up to the salad bar. I can't wait another second."

The next morning—not *too* early—Liz called Candace in her suite to check in with her. Candace said she'd be at the office by eleven or so as she wanted to do a few things first.

Candace had even engaged a hotel car for her entire Hong Kong stay, despite the fact that their agent had several Mercedes sedans and drivers available to her. Candace just loved the feel of being in that Bentley.

Eventually she arrived at their agent's office and walked into the showroom to see the samples. Liz and Elliot had anxious looks on their faces.

"What's all this?" She pointed to the T-shirt group hanging on the wall. "I don't remember seeing sketches of these."

"It's a group we put in for fun," Liz said. "Do you like it?"

Candace slowly walked over and started fingering the samples. Finally, "I can't say I'm wild about the colors . . ."

Liz rolled her eyes at Elliot. "We had to use the only colors available for these first samples. They didn't have time to dye up any fabric yet. But they can for our salesmen samples. No problem. I think they did a beautiful job on the styles."

Candace looked at Liz. "You do?"

"Uh-huh. Here." Liz grabbed a sample off the hanger. "How about I try them on so you can see them better?"

"Good idea."

Liz, a perfect size eight, slipped out of her clothes and into the sample. Then she put on one sample after another, while Candace watched silently.

Liz twirled around in the final outfit. "So what do you think?"

"Hmmm . . . I'm not sure . . . What do you think, Elliot?"

"I absolutely love them. They'd add such fun to the resort line, especially compared to some of our more serious fabrications."

"True. But don't you think they're a bit youngish?"

Liz shook her head. "*I* don't. I mean, we don't have to run every style here. Maybe some *are* too young, but that's what vacations are all about!" Liz danced around, clutching the samples to her chest.

"I'll think about it—now show me what else you've done."

They showed Candace the other knit samples that had arrived, eliminating the obvious "dogs" and holding aside the few that looked promising. Finally Candace said she was exhausted and begged off.

Back in her hotel room, Candace reflected on the samples she'd just seen. Why were Liz and Elliot so hot on them? To her, they looked like cheap knockoffs, not like

Candace Evans material. It was at times like this that she knew she needed Maxie. Maxie knew how to harness that youthful enthusiasm and bring it up to a higher taste level. Candace didn't even know where to begin.

And *she* was supposed to merchandise all of this before they left? God help her.

Eventually Candace decided on a plan of action. She would put into work the few things she was confident about. The T-shirt group, she told Liz and Elliot, would have to be brought back to New York and shown to Jason if they felt so strongly about it. They would all decide together.

Candace spent every moment of her free time shopping. She had to get her mind off her problems, and Hong Kong was still fabulous for that.

But always hovering in the back of her mind was one inescapable fact: she alone had to shape the resort line. What if she couldn't guide the designers as she'd promised Jason she could? And *he* needed her help right now, too. What was she going to do?

Who would take care of Candace?

Twenty-Seven

STEVE TELEPHONED MAXIE late one afternoon. He sounded tremendously excited.

"What? What's happened?" she said.

"Tanaka himself just called, and he wants me to set up a meeting for you and him."

"What about? Did he say?"

"I asked him, but all he would say was he had a business opportunity he'd like to discuss with you."

"You're kidding!" Maxie twirled around the room, almost tripping on the phone cord. "When does he want to see me?"

"At your earliest convenience."

Maxie laughed. "I'll just look in my date book and see when I can squeeze him in. Let's see . . . what luck! I seem to be available anytime. Really, Steve, whatever's good for him would be fine."

"Okay, I'll set it up."

Maxie hung around the apartment for the remainder of the afternoon, keeping her phone line free for Steve's call. Finally, around six-thirty, Maxie's door buzzer sounded. It was Steve.

He leaned down to kiss her, but Maxie punched him good-naturedly on the arm.

"Ouch!" Steve rubbed his arm. "What's *that* for?"

"You never called me back! I've been going crazy!"

"I thought you wouldn't mind waiting a little while longer to hear it face to face. Guess I was wrong." Steve pretended to walk out the door.

Maxie grabbed him and kissed him. "Better?"

He just smiled.

"Now tell me!" Maxie hit her thighs in frustration. "When?"

"Tomorrow at nine."

"Nine? In the morning?"

Steve nodded. "I got it for as early as possible. The sooner the better—the suspense is killing me, too!"

"Oh, God, what'll I wear? Should I bring my portfolio?" Maxie ran to and fro.

Steve chuckled, then reached out to Maxie and held her to him. "Relax."

"But I'm so excited. This could be it!"

"Let's just sit down and discuss everything calmly." Steve led her over to the sofa and sat down next to her. "Now, shoot."

"Well, what do I say?"

"Don't you think first you'd better hear what he's proposing?" Maxie smiled. "Then, I'm sure, you'll know what to say."

"Hmmm . . ."

"Don't bring your portfolio. If he's proposing a new venture with you, then he's already comfortable about your talents. Besides, he already told us that he doesn't know anything about the garment business, so he doesn't know how to look through your portfolio. If he wasn't sure about your talents, then he wouldn't be proposing this kind of venture."

"You're right. I'm just so excited." Maxie kissed Steve full on the lips. "Thanks."

"For what?"

"For introducing me to Tanaka."

Maxie and Steve never got around to dinner that night. They celebrated their excitement the best way they knew.

The next morning, Maxie leaped out of bed, then ran around frantically trying to decide what to wear. Steve stayed in bed, chuckling.

Promptly at nine, Maxie was ushered into Tanaka's spacious office. Tanaka's antique desk was rosewood, elegantly detailed. The other furniture was all Western, but the lithographs on the walls were Japanese. It was a perfect blend of East and West, a feeling of both peace and power at the same time.

Tanaka shook Maxie's hand warmly, then indicated they should sit on the couch. He sat by a small table that held a tea set. He poured tea for them both, his motions gentle and graceful, a total contrast to the power of the man.

"I'm glad you could come this morning," he said. "Since our dinner together I've heard many wonderful things about you."

"Oh?"

"As I've said, I know nothing about textiles or clothing, but I have people here who do. They've been pushing me to expand our textile department. At first, I couldn't decide how to do it. Then we met. Many of the things you said that night about why you wanted to design made sense to me. Since then, I've learned a few things about the business."

"Really? And you're still interested?" Maxie smiled and sipped her tea. Tanaka looked confused. "Just kidding."

"Oh. Sometimes I miss your American brand of humor."

"Well, it wasn't important." Maxie realized she'd better cut out the smart-alecky remarks or she'd blow the whole deal. This was just too important. "What exactly do you have in mind?"

"How about starting a new division for us? A wholesale division. How does that sound?"

"Sounds interesting . . . What kind of clothes did you have in mind?"

"Ladies' sportswear."

No kidding—whoops, better not say that. "What I meant was, what price level?"

"We're thinking big. We see this in several stages, something that would probably take several years to come together completely." Tanaka took a sip of tea. "First, we'd start by launching a new designer house. Once we had that established, we'd open a bridge line, maybe a men's line and even a children's line. When we open the bridge line, that's when we anticipate the money really coming back to us. Before then we'll be spending a lot to market the name properly. But we feel we *need* the cachet of a designer name to make it all work."

Maxie kept nodding her head. "You *have* done your homework. And I completely agree with your strategy. Since I left Candace Evans I've been searching for something I could really believe in. This sounds like a real possibility. What role did you have in mind for me?"

"What role would you like?"

"Frankly, I want to be more than a designer. I know the business and I've dreamed of running my own company, with all that goes with it."

"Why not for us?"

"So that's what you see as my role? Not just the head designer?"

"Absolutely. As the president, you would run the company. I'm confident that you would surround yourself with really top-notch people."

Maxie kept nodding her head. She couldn't believe what was happening, but outwardly she managed to look professional. "When did you have in mind to get this all rolling?"

"Ideally, we'd like to open for spring, but only if you agree that would be realistic. I'd hate to rush it and ruin that first impact."

"If we get right to it, I don't see any problem with the timing."

"So I take it that you're interested?"

Maxie finally let her face light up with joy. "Interested? Tanaka-san, *nothing* could keep me from this!"

"Good. I couldn't be sure of your reaction."

They spent the next few hours hammering out specifics. By then, Maxie could tell that Tanaka would be open and honest with her, such a contrast to the people usually involved in the garment business. To have him as her partner was more than she had ever dreamed. They agreed to meet again on Monday to continue their discussions with more of his people.

Maxie practically danced down the street, barely containing her excitement. She spied a pay phone, ran toward it, and punched in the numbers for Steve's office. She tapped her foot impatiently, waiting for him to pick up.

"Steve, Steve, you were right!"

"What? I can hardly hear you." Maxie hadn't even noticed the jackhammers blasting not twenty feet away.

"I said, you were right! Tanaka *does* want me to start a clothing company. It's everything I've ever dreamed."

"That's terrific! Why don't you pop over now and tell me all about it?"

Maxie looked at her watch. "Oh, I'm sorry. I promised Susanna I'd have lunch with her and I'm late already. We'll talk about it later."

"I'm glad you let me know. I've been wondering all morning."

Maxie raced over to the restaurant. Susanna was already seated, sipping her Perrier.

"I can't stand how happy and relaxed you are these days," she said. "Look at the grin on your face right now. Whatever happened to the miserable, unhappy girl I used to know?"

Maxie laughed. "Was I really?"

"You bet. Just take a look at me—that's what *you* used to look like."

Maxie looked closely at Susanna. "Well, what horrendous things have happened to you today to make you look so . . . so harassed?"

"The usual melodramas at work, nothing more, nothing less. Certainly not man troubles, since there's no one."

"But didn't you go out with that guy you met at the health club?"

"Uh-huh. A total zero, nada, nothing. So how's Steve?"

"Wonderful. It's so great to know I've finally met the right person. He's terrific!"

"Well, does he have any friends? Or enemies? These days I'll consider anyone."

"I doubt it," Maxie said. "Somehow I don't think a scholarly lawyer-type would really make you happy."

Susanna smiled. "You're probably right. But maybe I could change?"

They ordered their salads.

"So what's doin' on the job front?" Susanna said.

"I've had tons of interviews—"

"Any worth mentioning?"

"Maybe . . ." Maxie broke off a piece of bread and ate it.

"What does that mean—maybe?"

"Well, you know how superstitious I am. I hate to jinx anything."

"Hey, this is me, Susanna." She tapped her finger on her chest. "Haven't we always shared everything?"

"Okay, but promise not to say anything." Susanna crossed her heart. "I met this morning with the president of Makiyama America."

"We buy their fabric!"

"Well, he wants me to open a designer house for them."

"How fabulous! How'd he find you?"

"I met him a while ago through Steve. He did a big acquisition deal for them, and I was invited to the dinner afterward."

"Gee, maybe I *do* need a lawyer boyfriend. Then this stuff could happen to me."

The following week Maxie met several more times with Tanaka and his people. She was especially pleased that they seemed to accept her in her role as president—not just as the designer. It seemed as if this venture really would get off the ground.

After each meeting, Maxie reviewed every detail with Steve, down to the tiniest nuance of body language. He would suggest what she should discuss at the following meeting. His advice was wonderful. After all, making mergers work was his business.

Finally, by week's end, the philosophical discussions were over. Tanaka was leaving for Japan for a week or so. When he returned, the negotiations would begin.

Jason had called Marcus Putnam to set up a meeting, circumventing his agent. Even though Candace had suggested using their own money to back the play, Jason wanted an extension on the option—if he could get it. He figured that if he could speak to Marcus directly, he'd extend the option. After all, they both wanted the same thing.

Marcus, a tall, thin young man, sat opposite Jason in the library. Marcus held a cup of coffee in his right hand, his left absentmindedly caressing the manuscript resting in his lap.

"I want to give you more time," he said, "but Shelly's telling me that the Friedman brothers want it now."

"You know they're only looking at this from a bottom line point of view. They won't necessarily hire the right director or actors. They'll sign the biggest names they can—whether or not that person's right for the job. It could be a complete flop."

"Look, Jason, I agree, you're the best to bring to life my vision—but they're ready to move on it now. Getting the play produced and seen is my most important priority."

"Give me time, Marcus. Just a couple more weeks, till I'm back on my feet again."

Marcus got up and threw his well-worn jean jacket over his shoulder. "Okay, Jason. Two more weeks, but that's all. No more."

Jason heaved himself out of his chair slowly. "Thanks, Marcus. You won't regret it."

Liz breezed into the office, cheerful and excited. The reverse jet lag hadn't caught up with her yet. The first thing she did was call Maxie.

"Hi there!" Liz said.

"Liz, is that you? Where are you?"

Liz laughed. "In the office, where'd you think I was?"

"So how was Hong Kong? Did you love it?"

"It was fabulous! The weather was lousy, which was a drag—I mean my clothes were never really dry—but other than that, it was all I ever dreamed it could be. The Regent's unbelievable!"

"I know! How'd it go with Elliot?"

"Real good. We put in some wonderful things." Liz spoke in between gulps of hot coffee. "It was like we were on the same wavelength, which really helped. Did you know Candace came over?"

"You're kidding? What for?"

"Guess she was feeling nervous about the line. After all, it's supposed to be her baby now."

"True . . ."

"But let's face it, she didn't exactly spend all that much time working. She spent a helluva lot more time shopping. Not to mention socializing."

"Yup, that's Candace. I'm just surprised she went at all—what with Jason still at home."

"Apparently they're going out to Vail this week, then Jason's coming back to the office next week. So he must be feeling better."

"That's good to hear."

"So what's up with you? Everyone in Hong Kong was dying to know why you quit. Any job possibilities?"

"Some . . . Nothing firm yet."

Liz twisted the phone cord in her hand. "Actually, that's sorta why I called. Do you have a few minutes?"

"Sure, what's up?"

"I need some advice on the job front. Do you know Joe Weinstein of LauraLyn?"

"I don't know him personally, but I'm familiar with the product. Small, upscale contemporary line. Nice."

"Yeah, that's what I think, too. I met him in Hong Kong, and we started talking. It's amazing who you meet in the Regent lobby."

Maxie laughed.

"Well, anyway, he's looking for a new designer and he actually offered me the job. It's a small company, so I'd be doing practically everything myself—knits, wovens, fabrications—the whole shebang. And I'd have to travel a lot. Can you believe they don't even have a pattern room in New York? They work directly with their factories overseas . . . What do you think?"

"I've heard a lot of positive things about that line. It's a small company, so I'm sure money is a lot tighter there. You wouldn't be as free with the expense account on trips as you've been used to, but it'd be a great opportunity."

"So what should I do?"

"Well, logically it's the next step up from assistant designer at a designer house. Contemporary lines do try to have a designer look, but of course a lot cheaper . . . What did you think of Joe, himself?"

"Intense, a workaholic. But we got along fine. And I really could relate to how he sees his line looking."

"That's important. You both have to have the same vision. Is the money good?"

"Good enough." Liz sat up and banged her palm on her desk. "You know, Elliot and I designed this really outrageous T-shirt group for resort, and it bombed with Candace. I mean, it was fabulous! You'd have loved it, but she's still hemming and hawing, and I betcha it'll get axed. The longer I stay here, the more frustrated I'm going to get. So what do you think? Should I take this job or not?"

"Take it! Why not?"

"When should I tell the wicked witch?"

"Well, when does Joe want you to start?"

"ASAP. He's already behind for spring—you know they open earlier than designer lines do."

"Then you've got to tell Candace as soon as she gets back from Vail. She's a big girl, she'll be able to handle it."

Twenty-Eight

CANDACE FLEW BACK from Hong Kong, unpacked, then repacked for Vail. They headed off the next day. Exhausted as she was, she knew this time together was too important to cancel. She wouldn't even talk about her Hong Kong trip just yet. Work could come later, first they had to restore themselves.

Jason still suffered from the occasional dizzy spell and throbbing headache. The doctors had done another battery of tests—EEG, CAT scan and MRI—but they saw nothing. They attributed his continued discomfort to a slight swelling in his brain. They weren't worried. It would go down, these things just took time.

Vail in the spring was completely different from the ski season. No crowds of skiers pushing in the lift lines, no need to make restaurant reservations weeks in advance, no need to be all bundled up against the cold.

The refreshing mountain air was just the change of pace Jason needed to feel revitalized. Candace could see the difference in him almost immediately. He wasn't pacing like a caged lion the way he had been in New York. They took long leisurely walks along the mountain trails and into town.

Candace had never felt so close to him as she did now. The wall she'd always kept up around her was gone. It was as though Jason's brush with death had jolted Candace from her own horrid memories, so she could now protect Jason with strength and love.

There was nothing she wouldn't do to make Jason totally happy. She would throw herself into her work— and if she needed help, she'd get it. She saw herself with a new honesty, and it felt good. They'd be a team like never before.

One evening, at dinner, Candace leaned across the table and took Jason's hand. Jason looked up, surprised.

"You know," she said, "this week has been so special for me. When I got back from Hong Kong, I was completely exhausted. The *last* thing I wanted to do was get on another plane, but I'm glad I did." She squeezed his hand a little.

"I'm glad, too. Vail's been terrific. Maybe we've been stupid all these years, coming out here in the winter instead of this time of year."

"And miss skiing? No way! But we'll come now as well."

"Absolutely."

"Jason . . ." Candace looked down at her plate, then around the restaurant. Finally, "Jason, you know I haven't been the best of wives . . ."

Jason was about to interrupt, but Candace held up her hand. "Let me finish." He sat back. "I know all I've put you through—the disappointments, never having a family." And, quietly, "Never really sharing a bed together."

"Look, what's done is done. I went into this marriage with my eyes open. I'd hoped for more—who wouldn't? But it just didn't happen."

"I know. And I'm really sorry." Tears started to well up in Candace's eyes. "Ever since your accident I've had a lot of time to think, and now I know the only thing that's important to me is you. I want to start all over again with you. Do you think it's possible? Could we try?"

Jason sighed. "Oh God, Candace. Do you know how long I've waited to hear these words from you? I'd do anything to start again. I love you, Candace Evans, your secrets, your fears, your problems, all of it."

"Then let's try."

Slowly they rose from their table and walked hand in hand up the mountain to their chalet.

Candace appeared in his room, wrapped only in her silk robe. She was nervous, but she knew she had to make the first move.

She walked over and stood above him, then reached out and caressed his cheek.

Jason let out a deep moan and enveloped Candace in his arms. He moved his lips over her face and neck. Just as suddenly, he stopped. "Are you sure?"

Candace nodded, and hugged him tightly. He untied her robe and pushed it away. Candace shuddered involuntarily, but she still reached out for Jason, embracing him again. She took some deep breaths, and began to relax.

Jason was gentle and considerate and Candace loved him even more for it. For a brief moment when he entered her, the memories from that horrible night in Budapest flooded her mind, but she put them to rest. She looked up at Jason, finally ready for his love.

The next morning, Candace turned to Jason and nuzzled him awake. How long had it been since they'd slept in the same bed?

Jason stirred and opened one eye. He saw Candace's smile and pulled her to him tightly. "It feels so good, you next to me and all."

"Me, too."

"You've made me very happy."

They spent the rest of the week together, playing golf, tennis, and even riding horses. Their last night in Vail they chose to stay home. Candace made a simple dinner and Jason lit a fire, trying to warm up their cavernous living room. He mixed a couple of drinks and pulled a rug up in front of the fire. They leaned back against one of the sofas, their bodies comfortably close.

Jason raised his glass. "To us, Candace. To the best damn vacation we've ever had."

"Yes, it really has been."

"And now I'm ready to get back and slay a few of those dragons."

"Great!"

"I really need to light a fire under that sales force. Those orders still aren't in yet. Thank God I passed on the consignment deal the stores wanted. We haven't even booked the base amount, let alone chased any extra business."

"We'll get it. The stores are really slow this year when it comes to actually writing the paper. Everyone was talking about that in Hong Kong. The factories are suffering, too. A lot of them aren't even working overtime—"

"You're kidding? That bad there, too?"

Candace nodded.

"Wow, that's unbelievable. And how was the stuff Elliot and Liz put in? You seemed so worried about it before you left. Is resort as fabulous as fall?"

"Well . . . I just don't know." Candace sipped her drink. "There were some nice sweaters but the two of them were all excited over a T-shirt group they'd put in without my knowledge. Frankly, I don't like it at all."

"Oh?"

"Maybe it's just me—maybe I just can't cut it anymore. Maybe we really need to get someone to replace Maxie."

Jason patted Candace's arm. "Relax. Maybe their idea was lousy. Couldn't that be it? For years I've trusted your instincts and we've gotten by just fine. I'd bet on you anytime against those two kids."

"Thanks, honey." Candace smiled at Jason. "Well, I told them we'd all take a look—"

Suddenly Jason grabbed his head with both hands.

"Jason? Jason, what is it?"

"God, these damn headaches just won't go away! It's excruciating! I'm so dizzy."

"Come on, I'll help you up. You'll lie down a while, then you'll feel better."

Candace struggled to help Jason to the sofa, but halfway there, he slumped against her. She almost lost her balance, but somehow she managed to hoist him onto the sofa.

She looked down at him. Something was wrong.

"Jason? Jason?" She shook him, at first gently, then more roughly. No response. "Jason, what's wrong?"

She couldn't think straight. "Oh, my God, I've got to call for help!"

Ten minutes later, the emergency medical team was racing an unconscious Jason to the medical center in Vail. Candace sat by his side the whole way. The doctors ordered tests and discovered that Jason had suffered a stroke. They still weren't sure how extensive the damage was, but the longer he remained unconscious, the worse the damage would be. His condition was so critical, in fact, that they cautioned against moving him to Denver where the facilities were much better.

Apparently Jason had developed a blood clot from the internal bleeding he'd suffered during Pamela's attack. It must have been too small to show up on any of the previous tests. And it explained his recurring dizzy spells and headaches. All they could do now was wait and see if he would recover.

The doctors didn't actually expect Jason to make a full recovery—he'd been unconscious for so long that there had to be some damage. Most likely he'd be partially paralyzed.

Candace couldn't think about the alternatives. She stayed by Jason's side all that night and into the next day. But there was no change. Finally, the staff ordered her to go home and rest.

Monday morning, when Candace and Jason didn't show up at the office, Sarah and Charles grew concerned. Charles had gone to pick them up at the airport, but they hadn't been on their flight from Denver. When he called their Vail telephone number, there'd been no answer, and there'd been no answer at their Fifth Avenue apartment either.

Finally, Charles burst into the showroom to find Sarah. Maybe she knew about a change of plans and forgot to tell him. But she didn't, and now they were both worried.

Sarah tried the Vail number again. This time Candace answered the phone.

"Yes?"

"Candace? Is that you?"

"Who's this?"

"It's Sarah. Are you all right? We expected you yesterday."

Candace started to cry. "Oh, Sarah . . . It's horrible. Jason's had a stroke!"

A few minutes later, Sarah hung up the phone; her face was pale. "Jason's suffered a stroke. Can you believe it?"

"My God, what's gonna happen next?"

"You should have heard Candace—she sounds really out of it. I've got to go tell Maurice. She hasn't called a soul and she's out there all alone."

Candace dragged herself out of bed and on automatic pilot got dressed to go back to the hospital.

She glanced in the mirror and almost didn't recognize herself: she looked old and tired. The last few weeks had finally caught up with her.

She spent another day by his side. All day she just held his hand, hoping her strength would travel through his veins. Occasionally she walked out of the room for a cup of coffee, but that was it.

There was no change. Jason remained in a coma.

That night, she was getting ready for bed when she heard a loud knock at her front door. Maurice was standing there.

"Thank God you're here!"

She fell against him, crying.

"Shh, shh. It's all right. I'm here now."

Candace wiped her eyes. "It seems I've done nothing but cry since it happened."

"That's perfectly understandable. You cry if you want to."

Candace tried to put on a good face and put her hands up to her head. "Oh, I must look a fright!"

"No, you don't. You look like someone who's concerned about her husband." He led her into the living room. "What we need are a couple of good stiff drinks."

"Okay." But Candace just stood next to him, not thinking, not acting. Just waiting.

Maurice handed her a Scotch. She stared at it. Finally he led her over to the sofa and gently pushed her down into it. "Now, drink it."

Candace took a gulp. It stung on the way down and she coughed. But it did warm her up; she could feel her blood begin to circulate again.

After a time, she said, "Jason and I were having the best week of our lives." She beat her fist against the arm of the sofa. "It's just not fair! We were getting so close again. Why, Maurice? Why now?"

Maurice got out of his armchair and went over to comfort Candace. They hugged, and she began to sob again.

He gripped her shoulders and shook her. "That's enough, Candace. You've got to pull yourself together. You're not helping Jason any by falling apart. What we need is some action!"

Candace stared at him.

"I mean, what kind of place is he in? Is it the best?"

"I don't know . . . But they won't let him go to Denver, they say his condition is too critical to move him."

"Okay, then we'll have other experts fly in. Couldn't we do that?"

She nodded.

"Good. I'll call some people I know in New York tomorrow and see what they say. I'll take care of it all. And now, my little sister, why don't you go to bed?"

But they didn't make any phone calls the next day. Jason died during the night.

Twenty-Nine

MAURICE TOOK CHARGE. He took care of all the arrangements—flying Jason's body back to New York, closing up the chalet. He handled the press release and informed the office of the news.

Candace functioned, but through a haze of drugs. She insisted on seeing Jason one last time, so Maurice reluctantly took her to the hospital late that morning. She stood over Jason, then pulled back the sheet and stared down at him. During those long moments, their entire life together—the good and the bad—flashed before her. She took hold of Jason's cold, stiff hand, and instead of shrinking away from the feel, she clutched it even tighter.

"I'm not going to disappoint you ever again, Jason Gold. You'll be so proud of me. Just you watch."

Then she covered him with the sheet again and turned away. There were no more tears. She was ready for action.

She returned to the car where Maurice was waiting and slid into the front seat. Her face still looked haggard, but already color was returning to her cheeks.

She smiled weakly—but it *was* a smile. "Okay, big brother. Onward to Denver. We've got a flight to catch."

The news of Jason's death, coming so soon after the news of his attack, stunned the entire garment community. The Candace Evans employees were in an uproar—naturally, since their futures were at stake. Would the company keep going? Who would run it?

Candace arrived back from Denver Tuesday night. At ten o'clock Wednesday morning she arrived at the

office. Dressed in black, she looked pale, but calm. She
stood alone in the center of the showroom, the entire
staff assembled around her, waiting for her to speak.
She paused for a moment and surveyed them.

"I'm sure you are all shocked by Jason's death," she
said. "Believe me, no one more than I." She dabbed her
eyes with a handkerchief. "I will miss him—his counsel
most of all. He had many great plans for this company,
and I, for one, am going to work to see them happen."

The staff looked at each other with a mixture of hope
and doubt.

"I promise this company will carry on in Jason's
memory. He worked too hard for it." Candace clenched
her fists tightly at her sides and urged herself to maintain
control. "I'm not going to disappoint him. This company
is here today. And it will be here tomorrow. I will
see to it.

"That's all for now. We've all got a lot to do."

Candace walked into her office. The employees looked
to each other in silence for a moment, and then everyone
started to talk at once.

Maurice handled the funeral arrangements for Candace.
Even though Jason wasn't a practicing Jew, Candace
wanted a rabbi present and a burial at the Jewish cemetery where his parents were. She knew that underneath it
all, his religion was part of what made him who he was.

The funeral was held at Riverside Memorial on the
Upper West Side that Friday morning. The place was
jammed—even the standing area was packed—with
everyone from society customers to garment center
hustlers.

Candace held herself with controlled dignity the entire
time. Dressed entirely in black, including gloves and
veil, she looked every bit the grande dame. Not once
did she break down. Her grieving would be done in
private.

Michael Lipmann and Jason's brother gave the eulo-
gies. Both were very eloquent in capturing the essence

of the man. There were few dry eyes that morning at Riverside Memorial.

Candace went to the cemetery with only a few close friends and relatives, and there they paid their final respects. The polished mahogany and brass box was lowered into the open pit after a few short prayers were spoken. Candace threw the first shovelful of dirt on the casket, then grabbed another handful and wrapped it in her handkerchief to hold onto Jason for a little longer.

Jason's brother came back to the apartment, but he didn't stay long. He was heading back to Chicago and his medical practice. Maurice left by early evening as well, and finally Candace was all alone. She allowed herself this one night to grieve, but one night only. Tomorrow she would have to get out there and work. She'd have to make her own decisions and fight her own battles again.

But tonight she savored all of her memories: how they had been a team together in the beginning, and again at the end. How Jason had wanted only to make Candace's dreams come true, and he had. Who would have thought that anyone could do all that for her? But he had. And now Candace would try to give the same back to him.

Maxie heard the news of Jason's death, too. She couldn't envision the garment center without him. Her mother—at daytime rates—called from Columbus when she'd heard the news there.

Susanna went with Maxie to the funeral, and they stood together in the back, safely away from Candace. She knew Candace wouldn't want to see her. That hurt after the three of them had spent ten long years getting out line after line, with all the pressures and joys that went with it.

Maxie saw Candace approaching, and tried to shrink back into the crowd as Candace made her way up the aisle. But Maxie was too slow. For one split second their eyes locked. Maxie wanted to hug her to show how much

she cared. But she couldn't. She saw a tremendous anger
in Candace's eyes—as though Candace blamed her for
Jason's death. Maxie turned away quickly.

After the funeral, she bumped into many of her former
colleagues out on the sidewalk. She spied Sarah and
Luigi standing off to one side, and went over to them.
Their eyes were as red from crying as her own.

"Who think something like this happen to our Jason?"
Luigi shook his head. "My God, what next, eh?"

"I know," Maxie said. "We'll all miss him." She
turned to Sarah, who was blowing her nose. "And how're
you doing? Hanging in?"

Sarah could only nod her head. Maxie hugged her
tightly, offering what little comfort she could.

Sarah took a few deep gulps of air. "What am I going
to do now?"

"What do you mean?"

"I mean, I don't have a job anymore."

"Candace fired you?"

Sarah shook her head. "No, but now what?"

"Yeah, I see what you mean." Maxie patted Sarah's
back gently. "Try not to worry. I'm sure you'll be taken
care of just fine."

Sarah just nodded and began crying again.

Maxie turned to Susanna. "Let's get outa here. I can't
handle this."

Susanna nodded and led Maxie away from the crowd
still gathered on Amsterdam Avenue. "Let's head over
to Broadway and grab a cab from there. Do you want
to have some lunch?"

"Uh, I don't feel very hungry. Sorry."

Susanna patted her arm. "I understand, kid. We'll just
share a cab—you drop me off at my office, then get
yourself home."

Maxie spent the rest of the day holed up in her apartment. Even Buddy didn't cheer her up. Mostly she stared
blankly at the television screen. All she could see were
Candace's angry eyes.

When Steve showed up later that evening he found her still in front of the TV. She'd changed from funeral clothes to sweats. Her red and swollen eyes were ringed with smeared mascara, and her hair was a tangled mess.

"Quite a picture you make!" Steve said.

Maxie looked up at him, then down at herself. "Oh, God, I'm sorry, I look terrible. You go sit down. I'll only be a sec."

Maxie splashed cold water on her face, then scrubbed it clean. Now at least she had a rosy glow. She grabbed as much of her hair as she could and harnessed it into a stretchy terry cloth band.

"Much better," Steve said when she reappeared. "Now at least you don't look like you should've been the one they buried."

Maxie dropped herself down next to him and sighed. "It was so sad today. Seeing everyone was more difficult than I thought it would be. I really miss them, you know, even though I don't work there anymore. We were a family for a long time. And now to see them because Jason died . . ."

Steve took her into his arms. "I know it was hard." He held her that way, patting her back and rocking her a little.

Finally she raised her head and looked at him. "Thanks. I really need you here right now." She got up and went out to the kitchen. "What do you want for dinner?"

Steve was still dressed in his suit and tie; he'd come directly from work. He took off his jacket and loosened his tie. "Anything that's easy. Do you feel like going out to eat?"

Maxie poked her head out the kitchen door. "Not really."

"Okay, maybe you will later."

"Maybe." She sat back down on the couch. "So what happened to you today? Anything special?"

"Actually, yes. Makiyama sent over their first draft on your contract."

"How was it?"

"Pretty good. I've got to clean it up a lot, though. Some of your interests, like rights to your name and licensing and royalty fees, weren't clear."

"I'm so glad I've got you on my side. I know you'll get me exactly what I should have."

"Frankly, it's turning into a real headache."

"Really?"

"Yeah. Tanaka called to discuss my relationship here. It's a terrible conflict of interest for me. Theoretically, I should be handling *their* side of this contract."

"Oh, I never thought—"

Steve waved her off. "Tanaka has been fantastic. He agreed to let me handle this one contract—and so I'm dealing with one of their in-house lawyers."

"Do you think it's all going to work out?"

"Oh, sure. I've no doubts about it, you've got yourself a deal."

"You mean I can forget about these damn job interviews?"

"Absolutely."

Maxie bounced up and down. "Oh, my God! I don't believe it!"

She grabbed Steve's arm and pulled him up. She twirled him around the floor and shrieked at the top of her lungs. Steve started to laugh.

Suddenly she stopped. Tears welled up again and she shook her head. "It just doesn't seem right to have good news like this. Not when Jason was buried today."

"Oh, don't be ridiculous! You quit there over a month ago—and long before then in your head. You're moving on with your life now. You've just been presented the answer to your dreams! Go for it!"

"And by the man of my dreams!" Maxie hugged and kissed Steve until there were no more tears to shed. "You're right!" She smiled. "You know, suddenly I'm starving. Let's go get something to eat."

Monday morning Candace arrived at the office early. She was ready for action. She had back-to-back meetings scheduled with Larry, Vince, and Maurice, together and separately. If she was going to run this operation, she'd better find out where they stood.

They assembled in Candace's office—she wasn't ready to use Jason's office yet. So they all sat in the uncomfortable, but beautiful chairs in her office.

"Right now we've got about seventeen million in for fall," Larry said. "We've bought for twenty, right Vince?"

Vince nodded.

"Well, I'm hoping we'll have the balance shortly. I'm not exactly sure how to read the buyers right now."

Candace looked at him questioningly. "What do you mean? You've told me all along—and I've told Jason—"

Then she stopped. Jason wasn't here anymore. This was *her* regime. "You've told me you'd have no problem meeting the projection."

"Look, Candace, a lot of buyers have already called us wondering if we're really going to produce fall, or even if we do, will we be going forward with the line after that. If we're closing up shop, they don't want to sink any of their money into a dead line—if you'll excuse the expression."

"You better believe we're going forward. I'm not going to throw away all of Jason's hard work! You get the word out that Candace Evans is here to stay. There'll be a resort line, a spring line and so on, as long as I have any say in it!"

Larry held up his hands. "Okay, Candace, okay. Calm down. They just wanted a little reassurance. You can't blame them. This is business and if they're committing mega bucks, they have every right to know what our future plans are. Count on me—I'll have that last three million in right away."

"See that you do."

"Since we're going forward," Vince said, "we've got another big problem. I need to open a lot of L/Cs immediately—"

"What?"

"L/Cs? Letters of Credit?"

Candace asked Maurice, "What are they?"

"The money the banks will loan us to buy the fabric and make the garments."

"Oh, that. Well, Vince, why don't you?"

Vince tried to conceal his impatience. "Jason was supposed to talk to the banks about a month ago to get an increase on our line of credit, but that was when the attack happened, and he never got to meet with them. We're okay on our initial orders—we had enough credit for them—but we need the money for the reorders. And it's getting late."

Candace put her hand to her right temple. The vein there was pulsing painfully. "I *do* remember something about that." She turned to Maurice. "And you didn't meet with them?"

Maurice opened his hands apologetically.

"Well, call them up and we'll all go meet with them— you, Vince and me. Let's get this straightened out."

"Will do," Maurice said. "You also have to discuss the store with them. Jason signed the lease for it, and I believe Jose has started working on it, but we don't have the money."

"Hmmm . . . Jason left all of these things open?" Candace continued to rub her temples. "What else?"

Vince said, "You still need to finish approving the balance of fall patterns, and we've really got to get rolling on resort."

"I know. I'm going to meet with Liz about that. Don't you worry about design. *I'll* keep us on schedule."

"Good." Vince looked at Larry and rolled his eyes upward.

Candace saw him. "Look, gentlemen," she said, "I'm doing whatever I can to keep this company rolling. But I need your support. And if you're not going to give it, then I suggest you leave right now. Anyone here who doesn't want to be on the team?"

No one said a word.

Candace stood up and crossed her arms. "Good. Then I take that to mean you're all going forward with me."

They all got up and turned to leave.

"Maurice, just a minute."

When the others left, Candace said, "Look, I'm going to need your help most of all. I'm counting on you. I know you and Jason weren't the closest—"

"That's for sure. He never let me do anything!"

"Well, that's going to change. I can't believe that just two weeks ago I was telling Jason that everything was running fine. How could I have been so wrong! There's so much to do, I don't know where to start . . ."

Candace sank back in her chair.

"Relax. We'll get it all back together. I'll call the banks to schedule a meeting as soon as possible." Maurice went and put his hand on Candace's shoulder. "Don't worry about a thing. Your big brother is here. I'll take care of it all."

Candace smiled up at him weakly.

That afternoon Liz met with Candace. Liz had been agonizing since she'd heard about Jason's death. How could she desert Candace now? But Joe wouldn't hold her job open—he needed someone now. And it was such a great opportunity.

When Candace called her into the office, Liz felt both anxious and relieved at the same time. Candace, on the telephone, signaled her to sit down. She hung up and said, "We really have to discuss resort soon. Luigi needs to get moving on it if we're going to be on time."

Liz looked down at her hands, then up at Candace. And then down again.

Candace waited. Then, "What is it? What's wrong with you?"

Liz took a deep breath. "I really hate to say this . . ."

"Well . . . go on. Say it."

"I've accepted another design position and it starts right away. I've been wanting to tell you for a few days, but it hasn't exactly been the best time." Liz opened her hands, then let them drop.

Candace sat back. "Anybody I know?"

Liz shook her head. "I doubt it."

"And there's nothing I can say? Offer?"

Again, Liz shook her head. "No, it's a wonderful opportunity. Look, I know I'm leaving you in a lurch and I feel really bad about it. Believe me!"

"Not bad enough to stay—"

"I'm sorry." And she really was. "But I have tons of sketches I've already done for resort. I'll get them. I think you'll find quite a few nice ideas."

Candace's reply was icy. "I certainly hope so."

Liz returned quickly, a large stack of papers under her arm. "Here they are."

Candace skimmed through them, then looked up. "Well . . . anything else?"

"No, not really. I just want to thank you for the opportunities you've given me here. Really. And I'm so sorry about Jason." She turned and fled.

Candace sat and stared out at the open door for some time. Now what was she to do? Everyone was deserting her. First Maxie, then Jason, now Liz. She glanced again at Liz's sketches. Some were actually quite attractive, and she decided to give those to Luigi.

But she had no ideas of her own for the line. She'd just have to recycle some of the best styles from fall, that's all. And she could certainly let Judy and Elliot try their hands at designing some woven garments, too.

Candace called the two designers into her office. "As you're probably aware, Liz has resigned. While this news doesn't come at a great time, we can overcome it—if we pull together." She looked at each of them. "We need to be a team right now. That means I need help completing the woven end of resort. I'd like each of you to sketch at least five ideas—and I need them immediately."

"But I'm not sure I can do wovens," Elliot said.

Candace smiled. "Sure you can. You, too, Judy. You're both very talented. *Try.* Now we're all going to do this together, aren't we?"

They both nodded their heads, somewhat half-heartedly, then left.

Candace watched them go. Maybe something good would come out of their sketches, you never knew. And spring was just around the corner.

Candace rubbed her temples again and again.

Thirty

FOR THE NEXT few weeks Maxie was on the go non-stop.

She called Michael Lipmann and told him she wasn't interested in the job they'd been discussing. She suggested a few others he might wish to contact, including Susanna. Maybe she and Michael would hit if off. Then Maxie called all her other job prospects with the news.

Now only one thing spoiled her total feeling of joy.

She'd put off going home to Columbus as long as she possibly could, but she knew she had to. She was concerned about her father. And after these next few weeks, who knew when she'd have the time to get away again. So she flew to be with them.

When she got her first glimpse of her father, she was shocked. No longer was he the strong, trim man with the perpetual tan. His face had softened, his frame seemed slighter now, and the first traces of white flecked his hair. By the end of her stay, at least she'd gotten him to agree to go back onto the golf course, if nothing else. He had to get active again.

Back in New York, Maxie had little time to brood. The agreement was ready for her signature. Maxie Siegel was about to go into her own business.

Steve had reserved a small conference room for the signing. Maxie was the first to arrive, and she sat anxiously, tapping her toe repeatedly on the richly carpeted floor. She wore a severely cut suit of lightweight fuchsia wool, another of her own designs.

She jumped up when she saw Steve. "Are they here yet?"

Steve shook his head. "Relax. They'll be here any time now."

Just then Tanaka and the head of his textile division and their lawyers were making their way from the reception area to the conference room. Tanaka's face lit up when he saw Maxie.

"Are you ready for our big day?" He took her hand in both of his. "We're very pleased with everything."

"I'm glad. Me, too."

Tanaka walked toward Steve, extended his hand in greeting. He looked around the room and said, "Quite different from the last time we were here. Remember?"

Steve eyed him quizzically.

"The electronics takeover? That room was so smoke-filled and crowded. This time, the room is fresh-smelling and there's so few of us."

"Well, let's hope all goes well."

Steve had worked out quite a good deal for Maxie. She drew a reasonable salary starting the beginning of July, and then shared fifty-fifty with Makiyama on all profits. But most importantly, she controlled her name. If the deal went sour—for any reason—she could walk out and still use her name in the future. Not every deal in the garment center had been carved out so carefully.

They all sat down on opposite sides of the table and signed the papers. After the last page had been signed, Steve got up, acting the host at this auspicious event, and said, "I've got a bottle of champagne chilling outside. I'll get it."

After he had handed everyone a glass, he raised his hand in a toast. "To the easiest deal—and the most pleasurable—I've ever put together for Makiyama America."

Maxie smiled broadly and raised her hand in another toast. "To the Maxie Siegel Company! Long may it prosper!"

Hoots erupted around the small room.

Then Tanaka raised his hand for the final toast. "To Maxie Siegel. Long may she be inspired and inspire us."

Maxie bowed her head slightly at this compliment.

Soon the bottle was empty and everyone rose to leave. Maxie stayed behind and pulled Steve aside.

"Thanks for making all this possible for me. I'll never forget all you've done."

Candace met with the lawyers and accountants on Wednesday. Jason had left everything to her—his assets as well as his debts. Some of these items surprised her greatly.

Candace had left all the financial management of their marriage to Jason. Now she discovered that the business had used all of their homes as collateral for its loans. Although this was not an uncommon arrangement, it was a surprise to her.

Jason had a portfolio of stocks, bonds, and CDs totalling several million dollars. That, along with their real estate assets, gave her a total equity close to ten million dollars. Plus Jason had made her the beneficiary to his life insurance policy and she would collect insurance from the business as well because of his death.

On the other hand, she was also responsible for the ten-million-dollar bank loan that the company was paying off, as well as the new commitment for the Madison Avenue store. Candace would still have to pay Andrew the two-and-a-half million dollars owed him over the next two years in lump sum payments every quarter.

All of the numbers were making Candace's head swim. All she knew was that they had a lot of debts. It was too much to absorb. Everyone left the room, and Candace sat there for a few minutes in stunned silence.

Finally she stood up, smoothed down the black suit she'd worn that day, and walked around the room, trying to think. But she had been bombarded by too many things, and she couldn't absorb it all.

When her lawyer returned, she sat back down and removed her black gloves. "I'm not all that clear what my situation is yet, but I do understand that Candace

Evans has got to survive or I'm wiped out. Is that a
reasonable interpretation?"

Her lawyer just opened his hands in a gesture of
concurrence.

"Well, I've worked hard before, and I'll just have to
do it again. I'm not going to lose all of this—that's for
damn sure."

For the next few weeks, Candace worked harder than
she had in years. She tried to familiarize herself with the
entire Candace Evans operation.

She made Sarah her assistant, and gave her the job
of handling their PR for now. Sarah didn't seem wild
about working for her, but she wanted a job. Maybe
if she really developed a flair for PR, Candace would
move her over to that full time.

Candace decided to hire an outside PR firm to help
organize the fashion shows. This way, Sarah could grow
into the job—for now handling only direct contact with
the media. This setup relieved Candace from having to
look for a new person right away, and it just might
work.

Candace also got the resort line into the works. She
didn't add Liz and Eilliot's T-shirt group because she
just hated it. And she wasn't about to ask for anyone
else's opinions either. This was her line.

She *did* use a lot of Liz's sketches and a few from
Judy and Elliot. It would get them by, but that's all. No
excitement there. Thank God Jason had insisted on the
more innovative color story Maxie had come up with—
that was the only really new aspect of the collection.

Candace decided she had to find someone to replace
Maxie, a strong assistant head designer. She had put
the word out she was looking but hadn't found anyone yet.

Judy was showing her lots of ideas, but her inexperience was obvious. She needed guidance, and Candace
just didn't have the time or the energy.

And spring was looming over her.

*   *   *

Sheldon Feinstein, Marcus Putnam's agent, called
Candace at home just as she finished her workout with
her personal trainer. She picked up the phone with one
hand while using her other to towel her sweaty neck
and face.

Shelly explained why he was calling.

"But I thought Jason already paid the million for the
option."

"He got Marcus to agree to an extension—one I didn't
agree to, I'd like to add. But even that was up last
week."

"So you mean Jason never did go ahead with it?"

"That's right."

Candace sat down and fingered the damp towel she
had folded neatly.

"Ms. Evans?"

"Oh, I'm sorry, I was just thinking."

"Well, I assume you want to release the play, right?"

"Give me your number and I'll call you right back—"

"I have to have the answer today. You're already over
a week late."

"I promise."

Candace hung up the phone and sat staring at it a
long time. What should she do? Should she pick up the
option and pay the million dollars and try to produce the
play? But she had so many other things fighting for her
attention—and those things couldn't be dismissed. She
had the business and now the store to keep running—or
she'd have nothing. As much as she wanted to produce
this play as a final gift to Jason, she knew she just
couldn't.

Candace looked up at the ceiling and whispered, "For-
give me, Jason, I can't."

She called Shelly back and released Jason's option.

The next day, Candace met with Jose at the Madison
Avenue space. Final decisions had to be made—and
made now—if they were going to open on time.

It had been completely gutted to the bare concrete walls. Candace and Jose walked around, carefully stepping over pipes and open electrical wires.

"Are you sure you feel up to this?" Jose said. "We could do it some other time, you know."

Candace shook her head. "We don't have any other time. We've got to get moving on this right away. I've got too much at stake . . ."

"Really, Candace—people would understand. You did just bury your husband."

"The banks don't care about my problems, my dear. They just want the numbers to work."

"I've never seen you like this. Try to relax."

Candace's shoulders began to shake and she turned away from Jose.

"Candace, darling, what's wrong?" Jose held her awkwardly in his arms until she got control of herself.

Candace ran her hands through her hair. "I'm sorry. I don't know what came over me."

"Well, *I* do. You're doing too much, you need a break."

"Right now what I need is to work. Believe me, it gives me less time to think about Jason. It's better this way." She straightened up and checked her face in the compact she pulled from her purse. "Now let's get on with it. Show me exactly where you propose to do what."

Jose took her through everything. She and Jose used to mull over the smallest of minutia for hours, but not today. Candace made selections right there on the spot, no considering and reconsidering of anything. Once a decision was made, she moved on to the next one.

"God, Candace," Jose said. "We got everything done. I'll have all the prices for you by the end of the week."

"Make it by Thursday afternoon, dear. I've got my meeting with the bankers on Friday and I need the exact budget for the store to go over with them."

"Consider it done. My gift to you. I want to help make this transition as easy for you as I can."

Candace kissed his cheek. "You've been a dear, believe me."

Jose gathered his swatches and sketches into his portfolio. "You know you're positively turning into a hermit, you've really got to get out more. When can we get together for a real lunch? It's been ages!"

"I just don't have the time right now. Maybe in a few weeks things'll settle down."

"I hope so. Working this hard, people are bound to talk." Jose smiled at his own joke.

Candace wasn't amused. "Let them!"

Charles was waiting for Candace outside the door.

"Where to, Miss Candace?"

"The office."

Charles helped her into the car, then slid into his seat up front. "You know, Miss Candace, I've never seen you work so hard. You've gotta take care of yourself, too."

Candace smiled half-heartedly. "Don't you worry about me, Charles."

Candace sank back into the plush leather seat. Everyone was so concerned about her these days. But she really felt fine. She had a purpose in life again and was working toward that end. Maybe she couldn't keep up this pace forever, but she'd survived much worse than this before. And this time, at least she could surround herself with wonderful memories.

Thirty-One

CANDACE, VINCE, AND Maurice met with the bank that Friday. Only two weeks had passed since Jason's death, but many more had elapsed since Andrew's departure.

The bankers were cordial, certainly, but Candace could see they were wary. She wore another severely cut black suit to this meeting, and with her hair pulled back into a chignon she looked every inch the grande dame when she walked into the conference room. She shook each man's hand firmly and then sat at the mahogany conference table, flanked by Vince and Maurice.

Maurice began with a review of his computer runoffs, showing their sales projections and orders to date, the summer cash flow status. Then he speculated on their anticipated resort budget and went through the company's overhead, showing wherever he'd trimmed costs. The bankers could just as easily have read his analysis as heard it.

Vince talked about the production flow and when he'd require additional cash outlays and how much. The bankers asked a lot of questions, but Vince and Maurice managed to field them all.

Then it was Candace's turn. According to plan, she brought up the new store proposal and handed over the designated budget for it. But she was astounded at their reaction. The store was a total surprise to them! Apparently Jason had never even mentioned it to them. Naturally, their response was cool. They promised to consider the proposal and advise her of their decision later.

"And just what are your plans for the company, Ms. Evans?" James Wouten, the head banker, said.

"My plans? What do you mean exactly?"

"Are you planning on keeping this company going or are you going to sell?"

Candace leaned forward slightly. "Gentlemen, let's get something straight right now. Candace Evans is mine, and it's going to remain mine."

"You do know that until this current season the business was facing a steady decline in revenue. What steps are you taking to ensure that it won't fall back again?"

"Well, let's see . . ." She tried to think. "I'm planning on adding an assistant head designer again. I had one until last month, but she left the company. This time I want a real heavy hitter who'll be able to design the collection practically without me. I'll supervise, of course, but won't be involved in the day-to-day aspects of it, so I can oversee the whole operation more effectively—"

"You plan to oversee the company yourself? You're not going to hire someone for that position?"

Candace shook her head. "Too much is riding on this for me not to be directly supervising everything."

Mr. Wouten lit a fat, foul-smelling cigar and stared at its lit end for a while. "Hmmm . . . Didn't I read somewhere that you felt you needed to design full-time in order that the line look right? Isn't that what you said?"

Candace waved off his remark. "A lot of what I said in the papers was just hype. That happens all the time in this business. Maybe I exaggerated. I'm not saying I wasn't involved with the line, or that it doesn't need me, but I know if I get the right senior designer and I remain involved, the look of the line won't suffer in the slightest."

"But now you want to open a store. Don't you think you might be spreading yourself a little thin so soon?"

Candace splayed her hands on the table. "I give you my word that Candace Evans will turn out a beautiful spring line. Nothing will jeopardize that."

The bankers stood up. "We'll consider all that you've shown us," Wouten said, "and we'll get back to you early next week about the additional line of credit and the store proposal."

In the elevator to the street, Candace, Vince, and Maurice were alone.

"Well, what do you think?" Candace said to no one in particular.

"Oh, we'll get the money for the line of credit," Vince said. "They saw we've got the orders in hand already, so that's pretty much a gimme. But money for the store?" He shrugged.

"How about you, Maurice? What do you think?"

"I don't know how to read them. I wish Jason or Andrew were here. They knew how to smooth talk these bankers into just about anything. Andrew especially. And frankly, I don't know how good a job you did selling them on the store idea—"

"It's not *my* fault," Candace said. "I thought Jason had already talked to them about it. If I knew I'd have to sell them on the idea, I'd have made a much more dynamic pitch. Damn it!"

The doors opened at street level and Candace stalked off to her waiting car.

Candace spent the weekend by herself in the Hamptons. She walked along the beach and just sat outside on the verandah gazing out at the sea. She had declined several invitations from friends, because she wasn't ready to be in anyone's company just yet. She was still nursing the hole that Jason's death had left in her. And now she had to focus her energy back on herself and her future. How was she going to make Candace Evans work?

She thought about each of her managers. After all, it was now up to her to keep them or not. Larry Taylor, as weak as he was, had great relationships with the stores. Jason had known that, too. That must have been why he'd never fired Larry—he was too good at his job. And Vince, he was a top quality man. She had no problems with him.

Maurice, though, was another story. He was an accountant, plain and simple. Jason was right about that, too. Finessing numbers to tell a different story was not Maurice's bailiwick. She had seen that clearly enough at yesterday's meeting with the bank. He could read a report, but anyone could do that. He'd even worn his best suit, but it didn't help. There was simply no way he could fit into the old boy network. And that was part of the job, too. He was good for pencil-pushing only, just as Jason had said. She needed someone strong dealing with the bank, that was apparent.

But he was her brother. She loved him. She knew he only wanted to help, and that made things more difficult. Also, he'd always been there for her. *Always.*

For now, she'd postpone any decision. Maybe he'd grow into the role.

Makiyama America issued an announcement to the press at the end of June. They were launching a new designer house—the name, Maxie Siegel.

By now Maxie was caught up in a whirlwind of activities. Actually, the only thing she didn't need to involve herself with was the finance department. Makiyama was setting one up for her. She had set up shop at their New York office until she could move into a space of her own. She spent her days trudging around to countless office buildings, and finally found a great loft space around the corner from 550 Seventh Avenue. It was near the hub of the designer market, yet apart. The Makiyama people were still negotiating with the landlord.

Maxie couldn't begin thinking about the actual construction of the showroom until the lease was finalized. In the meantime, she interviewed interior designers to find one who'd be able to interpret her visions— and the Jose Alvarez look was not one she was even considering. Maxie saw the American woman looking fresh and comfortable and she wanted her showroom to reflect that. Jose's cold, stark interiors wouldn't work at all.

Finally she chose Bryan Reed. Bryan had built an excellent reputation for himself in a few years, having designed several of the most exciting new shops in the Flatiron district. And he was young, so his work had the freshness Maxie so desired.

Makiyama had budgeted a rather generous amount for the construction and decorating of the showroom, but Maxie tried her hardest to keep costs below budget.

At the same time she was interviewing people for the top jobs—head of sales, head of production and head pattern maker. Maxie needed to be able to relate to her staff, and especially to respect them. She wanted people who were not only tops in their own field, but who could pinch-hit with other things as well.

This was a new company, and she wanted to keep it as lean as possible.

Maxie sat in the dining room of the Algonquin Hotel waiting for Diona Stevens to arrive for their breakfast meeting. Maxie had heard a lot of wonderful things about Diona even though they'd never actually met. She sounded so different from the half dozen other "Mr. Smooths" the headhunter had recommended.

Just then a tall, very striking woman with flaming red hair strode up to the maitre d'. And then he was leading her over to Maxie's table.

"Maxie?" Diona extended her hand with a firm handshake.

Maxie liked her immediately. Diona had a strong sense of style and probably a personality to match.

"I feel as though I already know you," Diona said, and slid into a spot on the banquette next to Maxie. "I've heard so much about you over the years. I just loved the Candace Evans line this fall. It was so right. At the store we've been praying for someone to come up with something like that."

"Thanks, I'm glad you liked it."

"Look, we both know that was *your* line."

Maxie smiled and sipped her steaming coffee. "How come you want to switch to the wholesale side of the business?" she said. "Marty said you could explain it better than he could."

"I just feel that I could really make a contribution to a line, help make it show better at the retail level. Let's face it, I know what your customer wants, and I think wholesalers these days need to learn that all over again."

Maxie nodded. She let Diona talk for a while without interrupting her. And the more Maxie heard, the more she knew Diona was the right person to be her vice-president of sales. Her background was ideal. She'd been a buyer and then fashion director for several of the most prestigious stores in the country. And she had contacts in her own stores as well as the competition. She'd get them all in to see Maxie Siegel's new look for the American woman.

Then they tossed marketing and merchandising ideas back and forth. It was hard to remember whose idea was whose.

"God, Maxie, it's terrific to meet someone who really understands what I'm saying. For years I've been bumping my head against a stone wall, trying to get those gothic monoliths that think they know fashion to make any changes. We could really go somewhere together."

Maxie smiled. "I think so, too."

Diona would drive a hard bargain but ultimately she'd sign aboard.

To find a head pattern maker, Maxie contacted Luigi discreetly. He would have been perfect for the job, but she understood his loyalty to Candace Evans. After all, he had worked there for almost fifteen years. But he suggested a few people, and Maxie hired his old friend Sergio. With pattern makers, it's hit or miss. Until you develop a rapport with each other, not every garment is a winner. Maxie just hoped Sergio would understand her ideas quickly.

Finally, Maxie hired Tommy Faherty as her vice-president of production. He'd been abroad for several years, working for various factories in Italy and Hong Kong, and he brought a lot of enthusiasm with him. Maxie liked that. What he lacked in years of experience, he more than made up for with his energy.

Finally, after a month of searching and negotiating, Maxie had hired all of her key people. The team was ready to roll.

Maxie was also trying to design the spring line. She'd be doing it all by herself—no assistants—much like Liz over at LauraLyn. The only difference between them was that Maxie had no price ceilings. She could use anything she wanted, from anywhere. Anything at all! Her only requirement was that it be exciting.

She shopped the fabric markets exhaustively, seeing everything from Europe, Asia, and the States. Unlike the other designers, she also had the entire Makiyama textile archives at her disposal. They brought her countless swatches of fabrics before anyone else ever saw them.

But Maxie was looking for a real inspiration—something that would set her apart from everyone else, something that no one else had—to make her mark, as Norma Kamali had done with rayon matte jersey and gray sweats her first season, or Donna Karan with the bodysuit.

Maxie was stuck. So Mr. Matsuda, the head of Makiyama's textile division, suggested she take a trip to Japan. Maybe she'd find what she was looking for there.

That night when she got home, Steve wasn't there. They'd basically decided to move in together, although they'd never formally acknowledged their status. It just sort of happened. Steve kept his apartment, but more and more of his clothes and personal effects wound up at Maxie's.

It was late. What could possibly be keeping him?

The phone rang. Steve.

"Steve, where are you? I thought you'd be here—"

"Better question is where the hell have you been! I waited over an hour at the restaurant but you never showed."

"Restaurant?"

"Yeah, I said I'd meet you at eight over at Settanta. Didn't you get my message?"

"No—when did you call?"

"Late afternoon sometime. I spoke with your receptionist—oh, what's her name?"

"Carol?"

"Uh-huh."

"But I never went back to the office," Maxie said. "I rushed from one fabric place to the next all afternoon, then I was holed up over at the fabric library for half the night. I'm sorry."

"Carol said you were coming back."

"I thought so, too, but the time just slipped away. I'm really sorry. Am I forgiven?"

"Well—"

"I apologize. Really. Why don't you come down anyway?"

"Oh . . . all right. See you in half an hour."

Steve arrived and Maxie hugged him, but he backed away. He was still hurt by Maxie's no-show even though intellectually he understood how the mix-up happened. This was the third time this week—although the first two times she'd cancelled at the last minute.

Steve tuned the radio dial to WNCN, a classical music station, then sat in the oversized armchair across from Maxie. He hunched over the drink he was holding with both his hands.

"You know, Maxie, I really think you're losing your perspective."

Maxie looked up at him. "What do you mean?"

"Nothing is so important that you forget about everything else in your life. Even during my big Makiyama deal, I got away to see you. And how did I manage that? I just did it, that's all, because it was important to me."

"But, Steve, I'm starting a whole new company from scratch. I'm being pulled in a hundred different directions at once, and decisions are constantly being thrown at me. Surely you can understand."

Steve crossed the room to sit beside her. "Of course I do. I know the pressure you're under, the deadlines . . . I've been there, too. But you're working nonstop!"

"You're right. I promise, tomorrow the night'll be ours."

"I've got a better idea. How 'bout we go away for the whole weekend? It'd do both of us some good."

Maxie just shook her head. "That would've been so perfect, but I've got to fly to Japan on Saturday."

"Give it a rest!" Steve stood up and began to pace. "What's so urgent that you're suddenly running off to Japan?"

"I haven't found my base fabric yet, and it's the key for the entire line. Matsuda-san felt I might do better going over to Japan to look for it myself. Time is running out."

"Jesus, Maxie—"

"I promise, when I get back from Japan, we'll spend more time together."

This was not what Steve had wanted for their relationship. He wanted to share in the excitement of Maxie's new challenges, not feel excluded. Now they seemed to be moving apart as quickly as they'd come together. And what hurt even more was that he didn't think she was noticing it.

That night Steve felt more alone in bed with Maxie than when he was in his own bed, alone.

Thirty-Two

CANDACE STARED AT Makiyama's announcement in *Women's Wear*. For a minute, she didn't quite believe what she was reading. Betrayed! Yes, that's how she felt. How could Maxie do this to her? And after all Candace had done for her. Just when Candace was trying to get her feet back on the ground, Maxie comes along to compete for the tight dollars the stores had to spend. It wasn't fair!

Candace closed the paper. Well, she wouldn't succeed. Maxie's talent wasn't all that great. No matter how much money she had backing her, she'd never be a designer house with the prestige of Candace Evans. Never!

Candace finally hired an assistant head designer—her old friend and former colleague Pauline Jarvick. Jarvick had been in the business for years. For the last decade or so, she had jumped from one company to another, never able to hold onto any job for long. She and Candace had always stayed in touch and now Pauline—in between jobs again—was available.

When Judy found out, she was so upset she called Liz at LauraLyn immediately.

"Oh, I'm glad you called. You wouldn't believe all the paperwork here. Everything's done by fax, since we have no workroom. It's so exhausting!" Liz was knee-deep in faxes, answering questions from her agents overseas about the sketches she had faxed them the night before.

"At least you're working for someone who loves fashion."

"Uh-oh. Sounds like something is rotten in Denmark."

"Well, you'll never guess who Candace hired to replace Maxie."

"Frankly, I didn't even know she was looking. Last I heard, she was telling us how *she'd* be directly involved with designing the line, right?"

"Yup, that's what she said then. But now's a different story—of course."

"So who'd she hire?"

"Pauline Jarvick."

"You've got to be kidding! That old fart hasn't designed anything decent in years!"

"Tell me about it."

"So much for keeping the line looking new and different."

"I know. Elliot and I are both freaking out."

"I don't blame you. You'd better get those resumes out fast. That line is not long for this world."

"Guess you're right. What a drag."

"Keep your chin up, and in the meantime, start looking!"

"I will."

Liz hung up, and immediately dialed Maxie—but Maxie was in Japan.

After ten days, Maxie found what she'd been searching for. It was a brand-new fabric that Makiyama, in partnership with a local textile mill, was developing for the Japanese market. It wasn't for export—at least not yet—and no one had worked with it yet.

The fabric was a silk and rayon blend that draped better than either fabric alone. It had a heavy, gutsy weight to it, yet felt light and silky to the touch. Perfect for spring and fall. Best of all, it didn't wrinkle! The American market would love it, and Maxie would be the first to have it.

She'd use it as her base fabric. And it took to color just like silk! It was more than she'd ever hoped to find in one fabric. She'd get unbelievable runway impact out of it.

Makiyama offered her an exclusive for the first year. They'd wait another year before they'd offer it to the rest of the States market. This way she'd have time to build her reputation with it and have everyone clamoring to get their hands on it. A wonderful marketing strategy for both Maxie Siegel and Makiyama.

She put in all the colors she wanted for dyeing and had some available fabric sent to Sergio so they could work with it as soon as she got back.

Maxie was so thrilled that she couldn't wait to share her news. She called Diona who was positively ecstatic. Then she called Steve.

"Maxie? Is that you?" Steve had a wide smile across his face. "How are you?"

"Great! Positively fabulous!"

"You sound it. The trip must be going well." Steve sat on the couch, settling in for a long conversation.

"It is. I found the perfect base fabric—and no one in the States has even seen it yet!"

"That's terrific!"

"Yeah, Diona thinks it'll add to the panache we're trying to develop."

"Oh? Diona knows about this already?"

"Sure. I called her the minute I got back to the room."

"I see . . . Look, Maxie, I've got to run. I was on my way out the door when you caught me."

"Oh . . . Steve?"

"Yeah?"

"I miss you."

"Me, too. And I'm real happy for you."

Steve hung up the phone and stared at it. Maxie had called Diona first. She could just as easily shared her discovery with him first, but she hadn't. And it wasn't that he was feeling jealous of Diona, not at all. There'd been a time when Maxie would've shared her news— good or bad—with him first. But not anymore. And that hurt. They'd had such a good thing going.

Well, now he knew where he stood. He'd never had to fight for anything in his life before. Everything had

always come easy—women, money, jobs—and he wasn't
about to start now. Not even to keep Maxie.

Steve resolved to do the only thing he thought he
could—back off.

Candace, her pince-nez glasses perched on the tip
of her nose, looked up from the stack of sketches on
her desk.

"What is it, Vince?" She removed the glasses quickly
and hid them in a drawer.

Vince sat down with a sigh. "We've got a problem."

"What?"

"Luigi says we've run out of some of the resort dupe
yardage. I can't cut every style in every color the way
you want."

"Oh, no. That'll kill the show!"

Vince threw up his hands. "I know, but what can I
do? We've only got three days left to finish everything."

"How come I'm just hearing about this now?"

"Look, Candace, you and I both know how late you
were in doing resort—understandably, of course, what
with Jason and all. It's been a real push on all of us.
Everyone's doing their best, believe me."

"Well, just what *can* we do?"

They began to review what styles and colors had
already been cut, and which they wouldn't have enough
fabric to show.

"A couple of the new styles that I really think are good
won't get shown at all," Candace said. "It's ridiculous
to find ourselves in this situation. This'll hurt us badly.
You're absolutely sure there's no way to get any more
fabric?"

Vince shook his head. "I've had Judy try."

"What about faking it with some other fabric in the
right color?"

"We've already checked. Nada."

Vince left and Candace stared blankly at the sketches
on her desk.

How many more crises before she'd throw in the towel altogether? The bank had made it very clear that the company's projections couldn't slip in the slightest or they'd bring in a hired gun and salvage what they could. If they did that, what would she be left with? Would they force her to close her store?

This news of the resort screw-up couldn't have come at a worse time.

Resort collections opened everywhere on Seventh Avenue the first week in August. While the season was small compared to fall and spring, it was still newsworthy for the fashion press. The fashion shows were more low-keyed than other seasons as well. Candace Evans held theirs in their showroom.

Sarah handled much of the preparations—except for organizing the accessories, music and lighting—and did quite well. Luigi came through with as many of the samples as he could scrape together. (Judy had ordered the duplicate yardage, and since Maxie hadn't been around to guide her, Judy could only guess how much of each fabric to order. Some she ordered too much, some not enough.) The impact on the runway was definitely diminished, and it was felt by all who attended.

Candace wasn't pleased with their weak presentation, but the show had to go on. Cancelling the show would have been worse.

The press and the buyers were kind and understanding. After all, this was the first collection since Jason's death. The reviews in *Women's Wear* were certainly not as brutal as they would have been if they were truly honest. The line lacked any sizzle whatsoever, but the paper never said it in so many words. They accentuated the positive instead—the brilliant and very different color story.

Candace Evans would get by for the season, but just barely. There was no celebration held as there had been after the fall opening.

Two days later, Candace held a strategy meeting with Vince and Larry.

"It ain't easy out there," Larry said.

"What do you mean?" Candace said.

Larry looked over at Vince before he continued. "I mean no one is going to write any big orders for *that* line."

Candace shuffled some papers around. "Well, we weren't anticipating any big orders. After all, this is only resort."

"I know that," Larry said, "but I think we've got to revise our buy downward."

"Absolutely not. I need those figures met. What's the bank going to say if we start changing numbers on them already?"

"Better to alert them now than have them find out later."

"They might pull the plug on the store, and I won't have that." Candace slammed her hand on the table. "It's scheduled to open the end of this month. Nothing's going to stop that."

Larry shook his head. "Sorry, Candace. I'm paid to tell you how I see it. The line is not that strong."

"It would've been fine if we'd been able to make all the styles." Candace looked pointedly at Vince, but he sat unperturbed. She still hadn't realized that the mess up had been her responsibility. And the line would still have been weak regardless of how many samples they could've shown. "Just how much *do* you think you can do?"

"Probably three, three and a half million—tops!"

"How much did we buy for, Vince?"

"Four million."

"Well that's only half a million off." Candace tapped her pen repeatedly. "Let me think a minute."

Larry got up and walked over to the windows and looked out at the New York skyline shimmering under the oppressive August heat. The tension in the room made it seem just as stifling.

He turned as Candace spoke again. "How about dumping the rest? I'm sure we could get some off-price people to take it."

Larry shook his head. "Even they're inundated with inventory at this point. Besides, if we did get them to take it, the price would be so low, we'd be losing money. No, not that way."

Candace tapped her pen again. "Jason once mentioned 'consignment'—I believe that was the term he used. Could we do that to move the other half mil? That way we'll be able to meet the figures we've submitted to the banks, and half a million isn't that big a risk."

Larry considered the option. "It's possible, but let me run it by a few stores before I commit to it." He nodded. "But I think that just might work."

"Good." Candace started to push her chair out.

"We need to talk about something else, Candace," Vince said.

"Oh?" She sat back down again.

"The gab arrived late—because of the delay in approving the final colors—and we're going to be in a real squeeze to get it all produced before August thirtieth."

"Shit, Vince," Larry said. "That's *big* trouble."

"Oh, God, now what do we do?" Candace rubbed her left temple, trying to control the pulsing vein. "Can't you push it through any faster?"

Vince shook his head. "Not unless you want it looking like shit. You know how impossible gab is to sew. I was afraid of something like this."

"So how late will you be?" Larry said.

"A couple of weeks, anyway."

"I'll call the stores and see if we can get extensions."

"Oh, that's a *great* idea—" Candace said.

Larry looked over at her. "It doesn't come free, you know. We'll have to offer them some sort of discount, but at least we won't be stuck holding it all."

Candace waved her hand in the air. "Do whatever you have to. We can't lose fall, too."

*   *   *

The pressures were taking their toll on Candace. Every day brought another crisis. And how could she possibly solve them all? Candace just shook her head in frustration. Was this what being in business was all about?

Fall was behind in production. Resort was in trouble booking. The store was set to open in three weeks, but it was behind schedule, too. There were so many things yet to do, and the cost of everything was going up. And spring was around the corner.

Pauline had been working on spring with Judy and Elliot. They'd made their presentation to Candace last night and she thought the boards looked nice. Actually, she thought they'd make a beautiful spring collection. But could she really tell anymore?

She got up and collected her things. It'd been ages since she'd taken even a week off—not since that week in Vail—and usually she spent the whole month of August in the Hamptons. She just had to get away from all of this.

It was becoming an impossible situation.

Thirty-Three

MAXIE STRUGGLED THE last few steps to her apartment, her sample case and heavy suitcase in tow. She had just arrived back from Japan. She opened her front door, but only Buddy came bounding up to greet her. No Steve. And she had told him what time she was due in.

She knelt down and rubbed Buddy's belly. Then she dragged her luggage inside, flopped down on her couch, and picked up the phone to call Steve.

She got the machine.

She unpacked, showered after the long plane ride, then tried Steve once more.

The machine again. He wasn't out of town on business—at least, he'd never mentioned a trip.

By now Maxie was feeling very strange, and very alone. She wanted to share all her excitement of her trip with Steve, and she missed him.

She tried once every half hour until she collapsed from jet lag, but never reached anything except that damned machine.

The next day, Maxie finally got around to her back copies of *Women's Wear*. It'd been weeks since she'd last sat down to read the paper. She saw the review of the Candace Evans resort collection and smiled as she read between the lines. The reporter was being kind, at best. But Maxie didn't have time for gloating, she had a line to get out. So she pushed back her chair and got to work.

The Maxie Siegel company had finally moved into the back room area of their new loft. Their desks and sewing machines were surrounded by tools and lumber, but the staff was too enthusiastic to care. They had a line to get ready and that's all that mattered.

Maxie walked over to Sergio's work table and saw her favorite design coming to life. Sergio had interpreted her sketch beautifully, and the new fabric was a dream to work with.

Diona joined her and together they reviewed the styles that had already come out of the machines. There was a jacket that could be worn alone as a sexy top for night or with a blouse underneath for the office. It accentuated a woman's curves, yet didn't flaunt them—the perfect balance for the 90s woman. Pants, skirts, and dresses made up in this new material were dynamite as well. They had both hanger appeal and beautiful style when worn.

"Who would've thought a woman could look sexy and be properly dressed for the office at the same time!" Diona said. "This is revolutionary! I'd love to call a couple of fashion directors and get them up here for a sneak peek. They'll positively die when they see this!"

Maxie looked up from the dress she'd been checking out. "I'd rather you didn't. I want to announce the collection at our show, not before."

"I thought it'd be good to have a couple of the heavy hitters in our back pocket. They could spread the word around a bit. Let excitement build from the gossip and rumors. And then explode with the show." Diona swung her hand above her for emphasis. Everything about Diona was larger than life—from her hair to her energy.

Maxie shook her head. "I'm not convinced. I'll think about it and let you know."

Maxie discussed a few more sketches with Sergio. She was quite pleased with how he was working out, especially his enthusiasm for her designs. He wasn't Luigi, but their rapport was developing nicely.

Back in her makeshift office—an old desk and chair surrounded by temporary cinder-block walls on two sides—she was still thinking about Diona's idea. The way they handled this did make a difference: it would help shape the buyers' response to the line.

Maxie needed to talk it out. Tanaka wasn't the one to

call for advice, she knew that. He didn't know a retail
buyer from a ball bearing. But Steve would have an opinion, and it'd be a helpful one. Yes, she'd call Steve.

She tried his number, but he was out of the office.
So she left word for him to call back, then turned to the
thousand other things requiring her attention.

Moments later a thunderous crash reverberated through
the showroom. Maxie dashed to it, skirting the construction obstacles in her path.

She found Bryan with Bob, the construction foreman,
beginning to pick up steel rods and clear aside fallen
pieces of Sheetrock.

"What happened?" Maxie said.

Bryan stood up, dusting some plaster dust from his
linen jacket. "Christ, we've got a problem."

"What's wrong?"

Bryan walked over to a table and unrolled the blueprints, already rather tattered. Bob and Maxie stood on
either side, peering over his shoulder.

"We've got problems here, and here." Bryan pointed
to the showroom booth sections. "Bob says they can't
build the display racks we've designed with the material
we picked. It won't hold up."

"But you said they'd be fine," Maxie said to Bob.

"Hold it—I didn't know how heavy those racks were
gonna be. We made a set and *boom!*—those suckers just
won't hold 'em."

The display racks were the backbone of Maxie's marketing concept. If the buyer saw the line properly, she'd
buy it properly and then the customer would understand
Maxie's concepts easily. Without the racks, she felt
vulnerable to a buyer's whimsy, and she didn't like
that one bit. She didn't want the fate of her company
left in the hands of a buyer. No way!

"What can we do? This is something I can't budge
on."

"Let Bob and me try to work out some way of getting
them up. We might have to switch to a different material

or something, but we should be able to come up with something."

Bob nodded.

"I'll leave it to you guys, then. But please, please try to find something acceptable. Okay?"

"We'll try."

Maxie was learning from the daily bombardment of so many decisions that compromise was acceptable—in everything but design, that is.

Back in her "office," both of her phone lines lit up at once. One was Matsuda-san.

"I'm afraid I have some bad news," he said.

"Oh, God. I can't handle too much more bad news today."

"Osaka called this morning. The mill is having a little trouble with our new cloth. There'll be a slight delay with your duplicate yardage."

"How long is a slight delay?"

"About a month."

"A *month?* Are you crazy? Matsuda-san, you've got to do something."

"We're working on it, believe me. But better we get the problems ironed out now then have trouble later."

"Well . . . if it's only a month, I suppose we could live with it. I still have some yardage left to design in . . . But not one day later."

"I'm handling this situation personally, Maxie. Believe me, it's as important to us as it is to you."

Maxie groaned as she punched her other phone line, but no one was on the other end.

Maxie buzzed Carol. "Who called me?"

"When?"

"Just now. I had two calls at the same time—why did you put them both through anyway?"

"Oh, sorry, Maxie, I really didn't mean to. I guess I just wasn't thinking."

"Well, who was it?"

"I don't know."

Maxie decided Carol had to go. She was a space cadet.

And if she couldn't keep the phones straight now, what would happen as the company grew? Why was it so hard to find a decent receptionist?

Well, whoever called would probably call back if it was really important.

On Saturday morning Maxie drove down to Bucks County to visit Susanna. Susanna had always taken a share in the house that Maxie usually rented. This summer, with all that'd been going on, Maxie didn't have any weekends free to relax. Every day was a work day.

But today was going to be hot and humid in the city— a typical August day. And she'd had enough. Buddy would enjoy the trip, too. Besides, Maxie needed some good advice.

Steve had never returned her call, and she hadn't seen him at all that week.

What was going on? They hadn't had a fight, at least not one that they hadn't resolved. She really was confused, and hoped that talking to Susanna would help.

Maxie and Buddy drove down in just under an hour and a half, crossing New Jersey and the fast-moving Delaware River into Pennsylvania. The hills were covered with dense woodlands and on the farmlands the corn was already six feet high.

She pulled up in front of the old stone farmhouse that she'd lived in for so many summers, and Buddy leaped out of the car. He knew where he was. His tail wagging, he barked to announce their arrival.

Susanna, in T-shirt and cut offs, came out of the house. They hugged and then laughed as they watched Buddy.

"It's nice to have him around again," Susanna said. "We were going nuts from the peace and quiet." She led Maxie inside.

The house was relatively cool from the thick stone walls, and the ceiling fan on the screened-in porch offered a welcome breeze.

Maxie sighed. "God, I've missed this place."

"Well, you *have* been quite the workaholic this summer. I haven't seen you even once."

"I know, I know. But there's so much to do."

Susanna sat down next to her on the chaise. "We all have busy schedules, but that doesn't mean we forget our friends."

"I hope you don't think I ever could—"

"I don't, I know you too well. But someone else might."

"Steve?"

Susanna nodded. "He called me this week and we had lunch—"

"And you didn't tell me?"

"He was the one seeking advice, not you."

"Advice? About what?"

"Before we get into that, I need some sustenance." Susanna got up. "Let's have lunch."

In the country kitchen, Maxie leaned over the counter and watched as Susanna prepared a huge salad full of fresh vegetables from their garden.

"Tell me—"

Susanna shook her head. "Not yet." And she continued to chop up the vegetables.

"Come on, I can't stand this."

"Uh-uh."

"Christ, Susanna! You're being unreasonable!" Maxie slapped her thigh in frustration. "All right—so tell me how it's going over at Clothco."

"Actually, it's great. I really have to thank you again for recommending me to Michael. I'm having a fabulous time!"

"I'm glad someone's job is going so smoothly. Whenever I talk to anyone else, all I hear about are disasters. How've you avoided that?"

"Don't forget, I walked into an already established organization. It makes it a lot easier. In fact, right now I'm working up a plan to streamline my department. Believe it or not, I've got too many people working for me. We're all tripping over each other."

"That's nice—someone who's actually got too much help."

"Let's not sound like the evil green-eyed monster here. You're working your butt off, but it's for yourself. I wouldn't be complaining too loudly if I were you."

"You're right. So how do you like being the manager?"

"It's a challenge—"

"*Tell* me about it—"

"But I'm glad for the opportunity. This takes me to a whole new level in my career. I don't plan to wind up a has-been like Candace or what's-her-name?" Susanna snapped her fingers in the air, searching for the name. "Pauline, right?"

Maxie nodded.

"Violà! Our meal is ready!" Susanna carried the huge bowl over to the table.

After a few mouthfuls, Maxie put down her fork. "Okay, now tell me exactly what you and Steve talked about. I've a right to know."

"I don't know about a 'right,' but I'll tell you anyway. He's hurt."

"Hurt? What'd I do?"

"He feels you've pretty much shut him out of your life—you come home late and exhausted, and you hardly have the energy to talk."

"That's all true, but I haven't shut him out—"

"Well, *he* thinks you have. And I'll tell you, if I didn't know you as well as I do, I'd feel the same way. People who aren't in our business don't understand how consumed with it we can get."

"Oh, God," Maxie said. "What should I do?"

"If you want him"— Susanna looked up at Maxie— "and I take it by your expression that you do . . ."

"You're damn right!"

"Then you're going to have to seek *him* out and fix it. He's a proud man and ain't gonna go too much further out on that limb just to have it knocked out from under him."

Thirty-Four

AS SOON AS Maxie got back to the city, she called Steve's apartment. No answer. So she called his office. It was late Saturday afternoon and someone told her he was there.

Half an hour later she stormed through his office doorway. "Just what the hell is going on here?"

Steve looked up from the pile of papers on his desk. "What do you mean?"

Maxie walked in and glared down at him. "I mean it's time we stopped playing silly games with each other."

Steve tossed his pen onto his desk and leaned back. "Games?"

"Yes. Don't act innocent with me! Look, maybe I started to believe some of my own PR and got a swelled head. But mostly I'm sorry if I hurt you."

"And I'm sorry, too."

"But I never wanted to do that. I don't know how this ever happened." Maxie slumped into the chair opposite Steve, her eyes welling up with tears.

Steve sat back upright. "I wanted a partnership with the woman I love—and I thought I'd finally found that with you. We seemed able to talk about anything. But then all of that started to disappear. You didn't want to talk about anything with me anymore."

Maxie nodded her head and sniffed loudly. "Actually that's not true, but I can see how you might think so. I'm sorry, really." She leaned toward the desk. "In fact, just this week I wanted to talk to you about something important. I could've called someone else, but I didn't. I called *you*. And you weren't there. You never even called me back."

"I did call you back," Steve said in a quiet voice.

"You did?" Steve nodded. "I never got a message. It must have been Carol—she's only the worst reception-ist on the planet. Look, I know I've made a mess of things, but couldn't we try again? What we had was too wonderful."

Steve got up and came around his desk, then held out his arms to her. Maxie rose to meet him. He enveloped her in his arms, and held her tight.

It was the last night of August, the heat heavy in the air. The last nails had been hammered just a few hours before on the Candace Evans store on Madison. Vince had pushed through the store's order of gabardine so it'd be there, the last rack of clothes had just been hung. Everything was in place.

Candace, dressed in her favorite new fall style in white wool, looked cool and composed. She walked around the still empty store with Jose at her arm, fingering everything.

"It looks fabulous, darling," Jose said. "You should be ecstatic."

"Oh, I am. And I couldn't have done it without you." She kissed his cheek.

Then they were interrupted by the caterer with last-minute questions. Candace had arranged a champagne and caviar party for the press, key buyers, and friends.

By the time she turned back to Jose, the room was beginning to fill. Everyone who was anyone showed up.

"You've done an amazing job, Candace. It's a truly novel approach to merchandising—"

"You look wonderful, my dear. It's been ages since we've seen you. Surely you can find time for a girlie lunch one of these days real soon—"

"The line looks even better than it did on the run-way—"

"Where have you been hiding yourself, you naughty girl? You can't just work all the time. A girl's got to have some fun—"

And on and on it went. Candace's head was full of the praise and attention she was getting. This was the first real event she'd attended since Jason's death.

The store had opened late and way over budget, but the results justified it. She'd deal with the bank later. Nothing was going to ruin this moment for her.

The first week after the store opened, the daily numbers were almost double the projections. The press had been enthusiastic about the store as well. They were touting it as *the* retail concept for the next decade. Candace was elated.

Vince had promised her the gab would be ready to ship to the majors within the next two weeks. Of course, they had to give the stores sizeable discounts to accept it this late, but with the positive reaction at the store, she wasn't worried. There'd be no markdowns. America was going to love her fall line.

Now all she had to do was get spring out.

Maxie and Steve seemed to have smoothed their relationship out. Steve stopped by her office almost every night, checking the progress of the line as well as the construction of the showroom. Then they'd leave together, hand-in-hand, for dinner and bed. Weekends, Maxie made a concerted effort to stay home from the office so she and Steve could have some time together, too. She was learning about balance.

For a lark, one Saturday they spent hours bowling at the University lanes. They saw a lot of movies that September as well, all the ones they'd missed that summer. But mostly, it didn't matter what they did, as long as they were together.

The clock raced forward to October. Ready or not, Maxie Siegel would open.

It was just after everyone had returned from Premier-Vision in Paris, the ultimate in fabric shows that was held twice a year.

Judy had found Paris to be inspirational, and she hoped Pauline and Candace would agree.

Now Judy was preparing her fall presentation boards to show them. Even though the spring line had not actually opened, designers already had to think about next fall.

They all met in the conference room. Jason's seat was empty now and Pauline had taken the spot next to Candace, making Judy and Elliot shift seats.

When Judy's presentation was complete, she looked from person to person, seeking a reaction. She caught Pauline stealing a glance at Candace before she dared give her reaction.

"Is that all there was in Paris?" Pauline said. "Hardly anything in all of this will be suitable for our customer."

Candace paused before responding. "I agree. I'm afraid this just isn't appropriate for us."

"Exactly what isn't appropriate?" Judy said. "I thought Paris was terrific this season—a lot of new ideas and colors and pattern mixing. It's all here on these boards. How can you say this wouldn't be appropriate for Candace Evans? Aren't we trying to be young and fresh-looking?"

"Absolutely," Candace said. "And it's not that we couldn't use *some* things on these boards—this one, for instance, and those two—I just think they need some refinements." Candace looked to Pauline. "You agree, don't you?"

Pauline nodded.

Candace looked back to Judy. "Pauline can help you expand on your concepts and I'm sure we'll be able to pull a fall line together."

Candace rose, nodded to everyone and left. Judy sat back in silence, stunned. Her boards *had* been good. Finally she got up, gathered them up, and left. She even avoided Elliot when he tried to console her.

She spent the rest of the day thinking about what had happened, trying to decide what to do. It seemed inevitable, and at four o'clock she met with Candace and resigned. Judy didn't have a new job waiting for her, but she was just too frustrated to stay. She loved fashion, and Candace Evans didn't seem to have it at all anymore.

The next morning she called Maxie for advice. And Maxie immediately offered Judy a position as assistant designer. Maxie told her she desperately needed some help—she couldn't keep doing everything herself—and she knew Judy would be the perfect choice. Judy was thrilled.

Candace wasn't upset by Judy's departure. Actually, she was relieved. If Judy thought Candace Evans would ever run some of those sheer fabrics and flashy colors, then it was just as well she quit. Pauline would get the next line out with the refined look Candace stood for. Pauline was a professional, something these youngsters just were not. Pauline knew what the Candace Evans customer had come to expect. But giving her client what she expected, was that fashion?

Candace had no time for philosophy. She had to meet with Vince, Larry, and Maurice in just a few minutes. Candace had heard from the bank just that morning, requesting a meeting as soon as possible. What could they want now?

In the conference room five minutes later, Candace relayed the bank's request for a meeting.

"I just sent them our quarterly report," Maurice said. "Maybe it has something to do with that."

"Why?"

"Well, we went a quarter-million over budget on the start-up costs for the store, and resort dollars are still only trickling in."

"I thought we'd agreed to do the balance on consignment so that we'd meet their numbers." Candace looked at Larry.

"I'm still working on it, but no one wants to take anything extra. The stores are piled to the rafters with inventory. Nothing's moving anywhere."

"How much do you think you can do?"

"At the most, three point six million. That's the absolute top."

"And we've produced how much?" Candace turned to Vince.

"Four million. We should be ready to start shipping the end of the month."

"Then let's hope for good retail to help move out the balance."

They all stood to leave.

"Maurice, stay a minute."

Maurice sat down.

"How come I didn't see this report before the bank did?"

"But I sent you a copy two days ago!"

"Damn. I guess it's somewhere in my office. Look, I made an appointment for us to meet with them at ten tomorrow. You'll be prepared by then, won't you?"

"No problem. I figured this would happen."

At precisely ten o'clock, Candace and Maurice were ushered into the bank's private conference room. Maurice's briefcase bulged with all the reports he'd lugged along. Candace again looked professional, but the vein at her temple pulsed every so often, belying her outward composure.

The bankers all rose to greet them, but the meeting quickly turned to the matter at hand.

"Your August shipping was way off—"

"Yes, we had some unexpected production problems," Maurice said, "but we shipped fall out complete by September fifteenth."

"We saw that, but at prices significantly lower than you'd led us to believe you would get."

Maurice searched through his briefcase for a report. "I have the initial sell-throughs of fall so far and I think you'll find them better than anticipated." He passed the reports across the table to the three bankers seated opposite. "As you can see, the sell-throughs we're already getting ensure we won't have to pay any markdown money for fall. So while our shipping prices might be lower, our bottom-line prices have not eroded too much from our projections." Again Maurice sent copies of the actual cost sheets across the table.

Candace sat back and smiled.

The bankers perused them quickly.

"We'll review them in more detail later," James Wouten said. "We also wanted to discuss the overrun on the store."

"I'm sure you've all read what a success our store is already," Candace said.

"Yes, Ms. Evans, and we're pleased. But that doesn't explain the overruns."

"Again, we ran into construction overtime due to unforeseen building problems," Maurice said. "It happens with most total renovations, and we had anticipated some delays and cost overruns, just not quite this many. But as you can see in our most recent cash flow report, we've just about completely recouped that overrage in additional revenues. The store's numbers are well above our previous estimates. If this continues, we'll be right back on target by the beginning of the year."

Mr. Wouten closed his folder. "We plan to keep a close eye on your monthly outlays. The Candace Evans operation has yet to prove itself to us."

Candace pushed back her chair and stood up. "Well, we shall, gentlemen."

When they were settled back in the car heading across town, Candace said, "At first I couldn't understand why in God's name you brought that bulging briefcase. But I was really impressed with how you handled those guys. And they were, too."

"Thanks. I tried."

Candace patted his hand. "Remind me to get you a new briefcase. This one is shot."

"You don't have to."

"I *want* to. In fact, we should buy you some suits, too. You could use a few new ones and it'd be fun for me."

Maurice smiled. "I'm so pleased with how it went today. You weren't hesitant at all. What came over you?"

"Oh, I don't know . . . I just remembered how I used to meet with Andrew before every one of his meetings with the bank and what I'd do to prepare him for them, and I decided to do the same thing for myself. So I was ready for them this time."

Candace smiled. Some things were looking up. Maurice just might grow into this job.

"And they didn't even ask about resort, thank God. Maybe we can pull that one off, too."

Thirty-Five

IT WAS TWO weeks to show time for Maxie. Today she arrived at the office by seven, before anyone else, and surveyed the scene around her.

The showroom wasn't quite finished yet. Tools and workbenches were strewn around, and sawdust covered the floor as though the cleaning service could never quite get everything swept up. Footprints could still be seen. Only a couple of the modified display racks were put up. Would it ever be finished in time?

She walked toward the darkened back rooms, turning lights on as she went. She reached Sergio's workroom and turned the lights on there, too. Sawdust had even made it back here.

She looked around, something didn't seem quite right. "Oh, my God!" Maxie said. "All the samples—they're gone!" She ran over to the clothes racks along the inner wall. Empty! Just last night they'd been full of her show samples.

Maxie stood for a moment, staring in disbelief at the emptiness. "Oh, my God!" she kept muttering. "What am I going to do?"

Just then Sergio walked in. He also came in early every day to get the workroom organized before his sewers arrived.

Maxie jumped when she heard his footsteps.

"Maxie, whatsa matter wit you?"

"Sergio, look—the samples are all gone." Maxie tried to control her crying.

Sergio surveyed the scene. "Oh, my God! I no believe this. What happen?"

"I don't know. I've been trying to figure it out myself. The cleaning service hadn't gotten here when I left late last night, but I know I locked up when I left. I'll call them. Maybe they know something."

Maxie ran to her makeshift office and grabbed the phone. Her hands trembled as she searched her Rolodex for the number. Finally she found it.

She tapped the floor with her toe as she waited for them to pick up. "Come on, come on . . . Someone answer the goddamn phone—"

Someone did finally, and Maxie had them check who'd cleaned her office last night.

While waiting for them to call back, Maxie returned to the workroom.

"It not so bad, Maxie," Sergio said. "I make list all we do, and not so many. We just make again, simple. Thank God we just get in the fabric so that's fine."

"But do we have enough sample yardage left and the time to get them all made again?" Maxie was clutching her head with her hands.

"We gonna have to, yes?"

"Yes."

Sergio patted her arm awkwardly. "Don't worry, I take care."

Maxie had calmed down and went to call Steve. She turned down his offer to come over and didn't want to call the police yet. First she wanted to hear what the cleaning service had to say.

The less publicity, the better. She didn't want the opening of her line turning into a sideshow.

Sergio got the sewers going on new samples as soon as they arrived. He extracted promises from each to work whatever hours were necessary to get the line made in time.

Maxie heard back from the cleaning service. Yes, there had been a relatively new employee working at her place last night and no, he couldn't be reached at this time.

Maxie had no choice but to call the police. They came over quietly—only one squad car parked in front of the building, and no sirens.

A detective stood in the pattern room with Maxie, going over the area. She told him what little she knew.

"Look, Ms. Siegel, we'll get on it right away. I'll give the cleaning service a call—that's Kleen-Up, Inc., in Bayside, right?" She nodded. "But between you and me, don't count on getting your stuff back. It's usually some junkie trying to score as much cash as he can to support his habit. And that's all they can think about."

"How much could someone really hope to get from all this?" Maxie spread her arms out wide.

"A few hundred bucks."

"Unbelievable! A few lousy bucks and my future could be ruined. It just isn't fair—"

"No one said anything about fair. This has been happening for years in the garment center, and it'll keep on happening."

Maxie stood with Diona, who was there for moral support, while the detective finished his search.

He flipped his note pad closed. I'll be in touch."

Maxie had known all along the uselessness of calling the police. They had bigger problems than her small robbery. Her samples were probably long gone anyway.

Well, she wasn't going to wait for them to decide that they couldn't find the samples, no way! She called Tanaka, and he offered to dig up additional sewers and cutters—whatever she needed. But she declined for now, and assured him that things were under control. She'd get this line out, one way or another.

After all, it could've been worse. The samples could've been stolen the night before the show and then Maxie Siegel would really be dead in the water.

That night Steve wanted Maxie to go to a horror movie revival with him. She was still unnerved and shaken by the robbery.

"Come on, Maxie, it'll do you good." Steve tried to pull her off his couch, but she was a dead weight.

"I couldn't possibly sit still for the whole two hours—"

"It's only an hour and a half and it'll get your mind off things. There's nothing you can do right now anyway. Sergio promised to recut all the samples that were stolen, so you've got nothing to worry about."

"But can he do it in time?"

"Worrying today over something that will or won't happen two weeks from now is ridiculous, and you know it." He dragged her off the couch and finally got her to the movie.

It was the best thing she could have done. The finale was so frightening she found herself screaming—and getting rid of her pent up frustration at the same time.

Once again, Steve had found the perfect solution.

Just three days before the line was due to open, Tommy Faherty arrived back from his whirlwind trip to Italy. He looked exhausted as he dragged his garment bag through the doors of Maxie's showroom.

Maxie jumped up and ran around her desk to hug Tommy. "You're back! We've missed you."

"I almost didn't recognize the place. The showroom looks fabulous—and clean, too."

Maxie laughed and leaned back against her desk. "Clean is the most important thing. To not have sawdust in my underwear when I get home is a welcome relief!"

Tommy plopped into one of Maxie's roomy chairs. "Well, I'm glad to be home."

"How was the trip?"

"Fabulous! The two factories I felt strongest about using are dying to get involved with us, and they're willing to be as flexible as we need. They'll give us the quality, too."

"Terrific! And their prices?"

"Workable—not great, but we'll get the right product from them."

"Good. So when can we cost the line?"

"I started it on the plane coming back."

"Oh, Tommy, you're a saint. I was already panicking we'd be opening without a price list—it *is* only three days till D-day."

The next morning she, Diona, and Tommy costed the line together. These styles were so different from anything else in the market, Maxie wasn't frightened by any of the prices she'd have to charge. There could be no comparison.

They all grabbed a quick bite together that night, something they'd done often enough over these last few weeks. Tonight was a little different. The opening was only two days away, and each tried to hide his fear and excitement. They all hoped they were a part of something that would be important.

Afterward, Maxie rushed home to Steve, who gave her the strength to face the next few days.

It was the night before the Maxie Siegel line was to open. Hers would be one of the first shows of the spring season. Before she turned out the lights and locked the doors to the showroom, Maxie took one last look at all of the clothes—some just finished. They were all steamed up, ready to be moved the next morning to the Soho loft where the show would be held. She looked at them with mixed emotions. Yes, these were clothes that would be comfortable and elegant for the woman of today—everything Maxie wished to represent. Yet would the fashion press agree?

The stolen samples had never been recovered, no surprise to anyone. But Sergio had come through for her as promised. He'd had his sewers working grueling hours, but they all seemed happy to do it. Even Judy had pitched in, searching frantically for Sergio's last-minute trim. Maxie was proud of the camaraderie that was shared by everyone in her little company.

She had hired a PR firm to handle the show. They'd met for countless hours over the past month, reviewing every minute detail of the show. She'd wanted a spare

ambience, so the clothes could speak for themselves.
And they would, she was sure of that. Still, she wanted
to stop by and make sure there were no problems.

When she got to the loft, Steve was inside holding
some electrical cords for the lighting guys.

Maxie walked over to him, a tired smile on her face.
"What? Are you the new electrician?"

"Hi there!" Steve kissed her. "I got here early, so I
decided to help out."

"I didn't expect you to be here at all. I thought we
were meeting at the apartment—"

"I knew you wouldn't be able to stay away from here,
so I stopped by. Looks like I was right."

They both chuckled.

"How's everything going?" she asked.

"Take a look for yourself."

Maxie meandered around, stopping to talk to the PR
person handling the show as well as the lighting and
sound crews.

And then she found Steve again. "Just being here
now," she said, "makes me realize more than anything
that tomorrow's really going to happen. I'm so *nervous*."

Steve grabbed Maxie to him. "Don't be, it's going to
be great! Take it from someone who knows absolutely nothing about clothes—even I can appreciate what
you're about to give the women of the world, so it's
got to work!"

Maxie laughed. "Oh, Steve!"

"Look, you're exhausted and they've got everything
under control. We might as well get the hell out of here.
We're just in the way."

Maxie and Steve went to her apartment which wasn't
too far away. They ordered in Chinese—they'd been
doing that a lot lately—and cozied up together into the
corner of the couch.

Steve had his arm around Maxie and was twirling a
stray strand of her curly hair through his fingers. She
felt lulled into a moment of quietude.

"Maxie?"

"Hmm?"

"Nervous?"

Maxie turned to Steve. "How can you think that?" she said. "I've only got my whole future riding on tomorrow."

"Your whole future?"

"Be real. If the show flops, there'll be no second chances."

"It won't flop and you know it! Your stuff is terrific!"

"Well, there is one thing that I really am sure of."

"What?"

"Nothing can top how I feel right now—us together and my first line opening tomorrow."

Maxie reached over and sealed her reply with a kiss.

Epilogue

MAXIE SIEGEL WAS heralded by every fashion magazine and paper as the new designer of the year. Her new fabric and clothes were talked about for weeks. Pictures of her and her clothes were splashed across every major daily, and she was welcomed into every designer organization.

Candace's spring line in no way equaled fall. Bookings were down, way below projections. She held countless meetings with Larry Taylor, but he couldn't alter the inevitable.

"Look, Candace, every manufacturer is out there fighting for what little money the stores have to spend. This line is just not cutting it."

"But we own real estate in these stores—"

"It's a whole new ball game out there these days. If the buyer doesn't believe in us, she ain't going to buy the line, or, at best, she'll cut us way back. She's gotta worry about *her* bottom line—and her job now, too. The good old days are gone."

Candace massaged the vein in her temple yet again. "But we've only got half of what I promised the bank."

"When I gave you those figures, I assumed we'd keep the momentum from fall going. But now, there's none left."

Candace strode through the double-glass doors to the bank's offices, putting on a good face. They had called that morning and requested a meeting immediately. Maurice had already shown her the figures he had sent them, and the numbers weren't good.

She hoped the meeting wouldn't last too long. She had

the Council of Fashion Designers of America Awards dinner tonight, and she had to get ready.

James Wouten ushered Candace and Maurice into his oak-paneled office. Candace looked around surprised— the meeting wasn't being held in the conference room.

"I wanted us to meet privately." Wouten gestured to the upholstered chairs facing his big oak desk. "We've been going over the numbers you sent us, Maurice, and what we've concluded is not a pretty picture."

Candace's stomach suddenly started to churn. "What do you mean?" she said.

"I mean that your company is going to have to take some very serious steps very quickly if you plan to stay in business."

"Aren't you being a touch dramatic? It can't be that bad—"

"It *is* that bad," Wouten said. "You said that the store would be generating cash by January. It's now February, and we're still in the red. In fact, the store is losing more and more money each month. What began as a resounding success has slipped appreciably. Why?"

Candace shrugged.

"I presume the fall line is finished and you've got resort and spring merchandise in there now?"

Maurice nodded. "We held a couple of private sales to move the goods, but with only minimal results."

"I see . . ." Wouten hunched over his desk. "I'll be blunt. You've got to close the store."

"Oh, no, I couldn't do that," Candace said.

"I'm afraid you have to, Ms. Evans. That store is losing almost a hundred thousand dollars a month. It's bad business to keep it open."

"But it's my dream—"

"Look, we're in business to make money, not to throw it away on dreams. We are no longer willing to back this project. It's as simple as that." Wouten paused. "You could sell the fixtures and at least recover some of your costs."

Candace walked over to the windows, pushing aside

the drapes to look out. How could this be happening to her?

With a sigh, she turned and sat down again. "What else?"

"From what I gather, it appears your recent lines are nothing like last fall. I trust you're taking appropriate action."

"Such as?" Candace said.

"Such as reviewing your design and merchandising staffs for a start. In fact, until we see a dramatic improvement, I'm afraid you're going to have to cut your entire staff back to the bare bones—and I mean bare bones."

"We'll work on a proposal and get it to you by early next week," Maurice said.

Candace looked at him, stunned, then stood and walked out.

Maurice held back and shook Wouten's hand. "I knew this was coming. We'll work something out."

Candace was angrily punching the elevator button when Maurice reached her.

"How could you agree to their demands?" she said. "The nerve of him telling me how to run my business! To say I should review my design and merchandising staff. What the hell does he know?"

"Maybe he's right."

"Oh, now you're deserting me, too, and after all I've done for you!"

"Come on, Candace. What choice do we have? You don't want to sink any more of your personal money into this, do you? Without the bank, there's no Candace Evans. We've got to address the problems they're raising."

"What problems?"

"Like our enormous overhead, for one thing. We're going to have to trim in every department."

By now they'd reached the limo.

"I have to go get my hair done for tonight," Candace said.

Maurice shook his head. "Not now, you don't. What

we've got to discuss is a helluva lot more important than any beauty parlor appointment."

Maurice was right, but she just couldn't accept it. Candace sighed and slid into the car. She told Charles to take them back to the office.

Maurice brought his spread sheets into the conference room and he and Candace reviewed them endlessly all afternoon.

Candace was finally beginning to accept reality. In the design room, she'd be able to keep only Pauline. Elliot and all the assistants would have to go. Luigi would have to cut his staff by two-thirds. Larry would have to fire his national sales manager and the other big-salaried sales people, and work that much harder to train his younger staff. If need be, he'd just have to work the line himself. Vince would have to fire one assistant and several of the warehouse employees. And accounting would have to be cut in half as well.

By doing all of this, Candace Evans would save almost a million dollars a year, which would make a big dent in their overhead. But with this reduced staff, she couldn't run a big operation—well, they weren't that anymore, anyhow. Maurice had helped Candace finally realize she'd have to do whatever was necessary if she wanted to keep the company afloat. And she would. She would survive. Candace Evans might become a small company, but at least she'd have something.

Candace barely had time to run home and change for the Council of Fashion Designers of America Awards presentation dinner that night. Several hundred of the most powerful people in the industry attended, seated at round tables around the room. Candace Evans had bought a whole table—a huge extravagance in light of today's events. But most major designer houses did that, and Candace would accept nothing less.

People came up to her all evening long, and even though her head still pounded from that afternoon's stress, she was radiant from all the attention. She looked as elegant as any doyenne of fashion should. She'd had no time to do anything with her hair so she wore it in her customary page boy rather than up. She wore a long black wool dress—an understated look while others wore yards of satin, tulle, and lace. This was one of the biggest events of the year, and fashion people always thought that more is better.

Seated at the Candace Evans table were Larry Taylor, Vince, Luigi, Pauline, Sarah, Maurice, and Jose Alvarez as Candace's escort. They were a subdued bunch, so different from the year before when they were about to launch that fall season. A lot had happened since then.

Maxie was there as well. She, Steve, Diona, and Tommy shared a table with Dick Montgomery, another new name on the fashion scene. Their table was not as prominently situated as Candace's, certainly, but that was okay. They were young. Their time would come.

Now a hush fell over the crowd—the moment that everyone there had been waiting for. The announcement for Designer of the Year. And it went to . . . Candace Evans.

Candace made her way slowly to the dais to accept the award for her fall collection. She looked out over the room, revelling in the standing ovation she was receiving. Then she spotted Maxie, standing and clapping along with everyone else. Their eyes locked for a split second.

In that moment, Candace accepted what she'd been denying for months, even years. It was Maxie who had the talent now, not herself. In the future it would be Maxie who would be receiving these honors. And in fact, Maxie should be the one receiving this one—after all, fall was her design.

But Candace wasn't going to give this up—or share it—for anything. She hugged the statue when it was presented to her. Her last moment in the spotlight.

Then she took a deep breath and began her acceptance speech.